MEET
ME AT
MIDNIGHT

HOLLY MARTIN

CHAPTER 1

Iris McKenzie walked around the darkened room, mingling with the tourists who had all come to see the jewellery exhibition. People oohed and ahhed over the beauty of the pieces, some of which were the rarest jewels in the world; stunning necklaces, rings, brooches, bracelets and earrings dazzled them all.

But it was the Ocean Flower locket in the middle of the room that held her attention. It was a large oval gold locket, embellished with precious jewels in the shape of a flower. A blue-green pearl sat in the middle of the flower with petals made from rare blue jadeite surrounded by blue diamonds, blue topaz and tanzanite gems. It was stunning. Everyone had been obsessed with it since Christopher had announced it as part of his collection. It was hundreds of years old with gems that had been rare and unheard of fifty years before, so how it had been made before the discovery of these gems was a complete mystery.

It was so rare it was considered priceless, whatever that meant, but it was set to sell for millions in a private auction the following month.

There had been no record of this locket even existing, something that her nan had hoped to maintain. It had never left her neck since she'd got married sixty years before, but she'd always enchanted it to look like something ordinary so it wouldn't draw unwanted attention – until one day she'd forgotten and Christopher had seen it. He had charmed his way into her nan's life, visited her regularly, chatted to her over tea and cake, and then drugged her tea and stole it.

Iris was so angry, she'd spent weeks thinking of all the despicable things she could do to Christopher once she got hold of him. But she was more angry with herself, because Christopher was her ex-boyfriend. She had been charmed by him too and she was the one who'd introduced the slimy little worm to her nan in the first place.

Iris had wanted to go to the police as soon as it happened but her nan had refused and Iris didn't know why. So the arsehole had got away with it and her nan had been left heartbroken.

But Iris was going to make it right, firstly by stealing the locket back and then she would exact her revenge on the piece of turd she wished she'd never met.

The room was filled with easily a hundred people drifting in and out of the shadows but that didn't matter.

It was showtime.

She felt her magic fill her but then she stopped as a man entered the room. He was tall, dark-haired and ridiculously sexy, as if he'd just walked straight off the pages of a fashion magazine, but he was large too, broad and muscular as if he worked out every day. He was actually too big to be a model, but certainly big enough to play a sexy action hero in some Hollywood blockbuster. As he walked past people, women turned to stare at him. He was undeniably beautiful but that wasn't what held Iris's attention. It was the magic that flowed through him – she could see it, feel it, she felt like she could reach out and touch it. He glowed like the sun.

Having a witch here could be an interesting obstacle to her plans. But would he be friend or foe?

Lynx Oakwood walked through the room, watching everyone looking at all the jewels. Everyone was very excited about the Ocean Flower locket and it was the reason he was here, too. His job, retrieving lost and stolen magical artefacts, was an interesting and exciting one, not least because most of the time he had to use every magical tool in his arsenal to retrieve them. It always gave him a little thrill when he pulled off stealing the artefact back for the owners, or if there were no owners and the artefact was considered dangerous, he would store it in the vaults under Midnight Village, never to be seen again.

That was the case for the Ocean Flower locket. Despite its beauty, it came with stories and legends of a great power strong enough to control the seas and oceans. The locket had featured several times in their magical history books, but no one had known where it was until now. Idly flicking through a catalogue for a big jewellery exhibition one day, he'd suddenly come face to face with it and known instantly what it was. He didn't know how or where the owner of the exhibition had come across it, but there was no way he could let it fall into the wrong hands. Mundanes handling it with no knowledge of what it could do was bad enough, but if it fell into the hands of a dark witch who knew exactly what it was, there was no telling the devastation they could wreak. And if he recognised it, what if other witches recognised it too and sought it for their own gains?

He had to steal it and lock it away in Midnight Village forever. He would wait until things were a little quieter, later on in the day, before he made his move. For now he was just here to observe. He would watch the security guards, the cameras, the exits as he concocted his plan.

But then he felt it. The tell-tale prickle that told him magic was in the room and it wasn't coming from the locket. As he opened himself up to it, he could feel it was a living, breathing, force of nature. He quickly scanned the room and saw the woman standing at the back of the room opposite him, watching him. It was her aura that made her stand out amongst the crowds. He'd always been able to see another witch's aura, their magic glowing from them like some kind of internal light, but this was different. Her aura shimmered as if she was made from water, or maybe the aura was. She sparkled as if he was viewing her through crystal-clear water on a sunny day.

Lynx had missed her sparkling aura when he'd walked in because the whole room had been in darkness, apart from the spotlights over and under each item of jewellery, and he'd assumed the bright glow from the other side of the room had been coming from another podium. But there was nothing artificial about her light.

She was a witch, there was no doubt about that. Only witches glittered like that, their magic a visible thing, at least to other witches, but he had never seen anything like this before.

Of course the mundanes, the non-magical people who filled the room, couldn't see it. They would probably freak out if they could, but no one in the room had noticed her at all.

The woman moved round the other exhibits and, as she did so, the watery sparkle around her seemed to ripple. It was extraordinary.

She walked straight up to him as if they were old friends and he couldn't help smiling when he saw her eyes were filled with mischief.

'What are you doing here, witch?' she said.

She said the word 'witch' almost as if it was an insult, which was odd considering she was one too.

'Just... admiring the exhibits.'

She moved to his side as she looked out on the room. 'Oh sure,' she said, not sounding like she believed him.

She took his hand as if it was the most natural thing in the world and he looked down at her in surprise, even as he found himself entwining his fingers with her own.

'You're a fire witch. Powerful too. Although you've never used that power in anger.'

He stared at her in shock. It was true he also could sense whether most witches were fire, air, water or earth witches, but that last statement was uttered so casually, it was almost as if she was reading him like a book.

'Lynx Oakwood,' she said confidently. And then her eyes widened in surprise. 'You're an Oakwood witch, now that's a powerful line of witches. I don't know many witch families but the Oakwood name extends back hundreds of years.'

'Wow, that's an impressive skill.'

'Just one of my many talents.'

He smirked and, while their hands were still linked, tried to get some kind of reading from her, although he was nowhere near capable of getting the same level of information. And her magic felt so different to what he'd been used to living in a village of witches, it was something special and unique. He felt a pull he'd never felt before, as if she was a magnet drawing him in. He studied her. She was pretty with her blonde hair and blue eyes but it wasn't her looks that he was attracted to. There was something about her that drew him in.

'Trying to get a read from me?' she said, knowingly.

'Yeah.'

She smiled. 'How's that going?'

'Frustratingly so.'

She laughed. 'Sorry about that. You're like an open book though. You have a brother called Wolf, a sister-in-law called Star and a niece and nephew.'

He felt a small burst of triumph that she had that wrong.

'Just a niece, no nephew.'

'Ah yes, you'll meet him in seven or eight months.'

He stared at her. 'Star's pregnant?'

'They haven't told you? Some women like to wait until they're three months gone before they announce it.'

He frowned. His niece, Blaze, was only seven months old; he'd figured his brother and Star would wait a while before trying for another baby, but maybe fate had other ideas.

'Hang on, if you are reading me, how can you know something that I don't?'

She shrugged. 'That's just how my magic works. I can see glimpses of people's futures, although not everyone's. Witches are easier to read, mundanes tend to be a lot harder. I think it helps when I can feel someone's magic, there's that connection that I don't get from mundanes.'

He sighed with frustration. 'My grandmother, Zofia, gets premonitions too. It's always bothered me that she knows more about my life than I do.'

'Are you bothered by powerful women?'

'I'm in awe of powerful women,' he said, looking her straight in the eyes.

She stared at him and her eyes widened in shock. 'You're attracted to me. Oh my god,' she laughed.

'I'm not attracted to you.' Lynx frowned. Surely she couldn't see that before he'd even realised it himself. He didn't mind her knowing about his brother and sister-in-law or their kids but surely he should be the first one to recognise an attraction. He didn't even know her to be attracted to her. But there was something between them, some kind of pull. Maybe it was that she could feel. But that was just their magic connecting surely, nothing more than that.

'You're going to be so disappointed when you get to know me.' She touched her hair. 'This isn't even real. None of it is.'

He looked at her in confusion. What did she mean by that? 'I'm not attracted by your blonde hair. I feel a pull to you like a moth is attracted to a flame. A moth doesn't love the flame, but it wants to get closer to look at it, feel its warmth.'

'A moth is disorientated by artificial light. Flying near it makes it feel like it doesn't know which way is up and which way is down.'

'That feels like a pretty accurate analogy,' Lynx admitted.

She smiled and shook her head.

'So you already know so much about me, do you know why I'm here?' Lynx said.

She studied him. 'You're a good witch, I can feel that, yet you're here to steal the locket.' She tutted playfully.

'Why do I feel like you're only here for the locket too?' Lynx said.

'I am. I planned to walk in, grab it and walk straight back out again. I hadn't counted on meeting you.'

'It seems we have a stalemate on our hands.'

'Oh no, this game is wide open. We should have a wager. Whoever walks out of here with the locket wins.'

He grinned. He loved a challenge. 'What do I win?'

'Whatever you want.'

He was surprised by that. 'You'll let me take you out for dinner and you answer all my questions.'

She laughed and shook her head. 'Such a gentleman. If I win, one night, no strings, *no questions*, just one incredible night of sex and then I walk away and you never see me again.'

He felt his eyebrows shoot up into his hair. He didn't even know what to say to that. He couldn't deny the connection between them, but he found her fascinating, he wanted time to get to know her, to talk to her properly.

'Have I embarrassed you?'

'It takes a lot more than that to embarrass me.'

'So we have a deal?'

He narrowed his eyes. He had no intention of letting her walk out of here with that locket so he nodded. He didn't think she wanted it for nefarious means, but he couldn't get a read of her like she could of him, though he sensed she wasn't a dark witch. It was more likely the huge price tag that attracted her, but letting her sell it on to the highest bidder was too dangerous. He had to stop her.

She stepped up to him and ran a finger down his

neck at the opening to his shirt, her lips mere millimetres from his. 'I'm going to give you the best night of your life, Lynx Oakwood.'

He swallowed a lump in his throat.

She stepped away with a look of triumph in her eyes.

Suddenly, she waved her hand in an upward gesture and a mist rose from the floor, the kind that hung heavily over lakes and ponds. It filled the room in seconds until he couldn't even see his hand in front of his face. Everyone started panicking, screaming, running, falling over one another.

But he had tricks of his own. With a wave of his hand he summoned the wind and it tore through the room, driving the mist and fog into the corners. It cleared just in time for Lynx to see her melting the glass case with one hand and grabbing the locket with the other.

She looked straight at him and laughed before she turned and ran, the locket in her hand. Lynx couldn't help smiling at her brazen audacity.

'Stop her!' screamed a man in a suit.

Several security guards charged after her but before she had even got halfway to the door she seemingly vanished into the panicking crowds.

'Seal every exit to the building, no one leaves until they've been searched,' the man screamed after the guards and then picked up his walkie-talkie and started barking similar orders to whoever was on the other end. And then, to Lynx's surprise, the man pulled a gun from underneath his jacket. 'I knew she'd try something like this. She's hired some kind of magician to get the locket back. Well, she's getting that locket over my dead body.'

'Oh hell no,' Lynx muttered. There was no way he was going to let this asshole shoot a witch, even if she was a thief. Besides, there were too many mundanes around who might get hurt too. He flicked his hand and the gun suddenly glowed red with heat. The man yelped and dropped it. Lynx twisted his hand and the weapon flew across the floor towards him. The man was too busy nursing his hand to notice and Lynx grabbed the now cool gun, shoving it in his pocket before joining the crowds charging out of the room.

He had to find this woman and thanks to her unique aura, she shouldn't be hard to find. Lynx could see people at the far end of the corridor hanging around the exit, shouting at the security guards to let them go. There was no sign of her shimmery blue aura in the crowds by the door but the corridor had lots of rooms leading off it with other artefacts inside. A thought occurred to him: while there was such a big distraction with everyone trying to leave, was the witch systematically going through each room and stripping them of all the other priceless jewels? He had no interest in any of those, just the locket, but the other rooms might be a good place to start.

'Search the other rooms.' The man in the suit had appeared in the corridor and it seemed he had the same idea. 'We're looking for a blonde woman, in a blue dress.'

Lynx went into the first room on the left but it was completely empty; everyone in here had clearly heard the panic and screams and made a run for it too. The room was in darkness, the only light coming from underneath each piece of jewellery. As far as he could see, every plinth still had a piece of jewellery on it so stealing the other exhibits couldn't be high on her list of priorities. He was just about to go back outside when he noticed a blue shimmer from a darkened corner of the room. He wandered over and, sure enough, found her standing in the corner, a big grin on her face, not remotely bothered at being caught.

'I knew you'd find me. Bloody witches,' she laughed.

'I could see your magic, shining from you like a beacon,' Lynx said. 'You shimmer like an ocean basking in the gold of a midday sun.'

She smiled at that. 'You glow like the sun, I saw you as soon as you entered the room in there. But if you're here to claim your night of passion, you're going to be very disappointed. I only offered that so you'd let me win.'

He laughed. 'I should have known.'

'I'm not in the habit of jumping into bed with strange men, no matter how hot they are.'

He smiled at that. 'Well, I'm not that strange, you already know my name. Although you have me at a disadvantage as I don't know yours.'

She studied him thoughtfully, looking at him as if she didn't trust him. But eventually she stuck out a hand. 'Iris McKenzie.'

He stepped closer and took it. Her hand against his sent a spark of energy shooting through him.

He cleared his throat. 'Good to meet you Iris, but I'm afraid I need that locket.'

She shook her head. 'Not going to happen.'

'It wasn't a request. I can't let you leave here with that locket.'

'And I can't go home without it. So what was it you said, we find ourselves at a bit of a stalemate.'

He frowned. She looked so sweet and innocent, she definitely didn't look like someone who was used to a life of crime. It wouldn't be the first time a witch had been enslaved to use their magic for nefarious means. History was littered with such stories. It didn't really happen so much in this day and age, but nothing would surprise him anymore.

'Is someone forcing you to do this? If they are, I can protect you. I live in a private village of witches called Midnight. It has high fences around the perimeter and security guards on the gates. No mundanes are allowed to enter, even witches can't visit unless they're related to a witch that lives there. You would be very safe.'

She smiled. 'You're a bit of hero, aren't you.'

'I don't know about that but I don't like to see people taken advantage of, especially not witches.'

'No one is forcing me to do this. I'm here to right a wrong.'

He didn't know what she meant by that but he knew he couldn't let her walk out of here with that locket.

'Why do you want it?' Iris said. 'Is your plan to sell to the highest bidder?'

'My job is to retrieve lost and stolen magical arte-facts. This locket, if the legends are true, is used to control the seas and oceans. That's not the kind of thing we want to fall into the wrong hands.'

She laughed. 'Do you always believe in fairytales? That locket is a wedding gift, there's nothing more to it than that.'

'I believe that locket has a magical energy, I can feel it now.'

'That's just me, darling. What was it you said, I shimmer like the ocean?'

'Your energy is something else entirely.'

Something magnificent but he wasn't going to say that.

'Are you really expecting me to believe that you just

want the locket for the greater good, not for its billion-pound price tag?' Iris asked.

'I'm not expecting you to believe it, but it is the truth.'

She frowned as she realised he was serious.

Just then he heard someone run into the room behind him, and he moved right up to her so he was protecting her from view with his body, although he was pretty sure no one could see them in the darkened corner. But Iris suddenly leaned up and kissed him. He froze for a split second before he realised what she was doing. A couple kissing was not likely to arouse suspicions. Hell, he'd seen Tom Cruise pull the same move in one of the *Mission Impossible* films. He gathered her in his arms, shuffled her back against the wall and kissed her back.

But this kiss was not like any other kiss he'd ever experienced. Energy surged through him, her magic and his. What started off as a quick, simple kiss quickly developed into something more. How could a kiss be so potent, so powerful? Lynx felt like he was drowning and Iris was the air he needed to breathe. He was vaguely aware that the security guards had left but the kiss was still continuing. He needed to stop but he couldn't let her go. She let out a soft moan against his lips and he felt his stomach clench with need and desire. He lifted her and she wrapped her arms and legs around him, but with his hands at her hips, he suddenly felt something sharp against his palm. He realised his hand was resting against her dress pocket. Was it the locket? He slipped his hand inside and realised it was. He quickly and carefully pulled it out and shoved it in his own pocket, just as she moved her mouth to his neck. The noise he made was nothing short of a growl. He needed to stop this, but he also needed so much more.

'Iris,' he gasped.

She looked up at him with clouded eyes, her breath heavy on his lips. Her cheeks suddenly flushed, her face clearing. 'Sorry, might have got a bit carried away with that cover.'

'I'm definitely not complaining. This is fast becoming one of my favourite jobs.'

She lowered her legs to the floor and he held her steady for a moment because he could feel she was trembling. He was desperate to kiss her again and the way she was looking up at him told him she was thinking the same.

'I never came here expecting that,' she said. 'I just needed to get the locket. And then there you are.'

She stroked his face and he instantly felt guilty for stealing the locket from her. He had resorted to some underhand tactics in this job to retrieve lost magical artefacts, but stealing the locket while enjoying the best damn kiss of his life felt like a low bar.

He took the locket from his pocket. 'I took this while we were kissing.'

She stared at it and hurt washed over her face. 'Oh, so that's why you were pretending to enjoy the kiss so much, just so you could get the locket?' she shook her head. 'I'm such an idiot.'

'There was no pretence in how much I was enjoying that kiss, but I did use it to my advantage.'

'So you got the locket and a cheap thrill, you must be feeling pretty good about yourself.'

If he was honest, he felt really crappy. He had hurt her and he definitely didn't feel good about that. But then she was unlikely to just hand the locket over to him so he'd had to do something.

'Why do you want the locket?' he asked.

She sighed. 'I'm not sure I have enough time to tell you the sorry tale of the last time I trusted someone. You'd think I'd have learned my lesson when it comes to matters of the heart. But here we are again.'

'You can trust me, Iris.'

She laughed. 'You just kissed me and stole my locket.'

'You kissed me,' Lynx clarified. 'Look, there's no way you're getting out of here with that locket. They're searching for you everywhere and if they find that thing on you, it's not going to end well for you. I'll look after it for you. Come and find me when all this is over, tell me your story. If I feel you have some kind of claim to the locket, I'll give it back to you.'

There was the noise of shouting and running outside the room again.

She sighed. 'You're right, I'm never getting out of here looking like this.'

She waved her hand and suddenly transformed to an older woman with black hair. Even her clothes changed to something completely different.

He took a step back in surprise. 'You're a metamorph?'

She did a little curtsey as if accepting applause.

'Is this the real you?'

'No.'

'Was the blonde?'

She laughed. 'Do you think I'd come here to steal a locket as myself?'

'So who the hell did I just kiss?'

She smirked. 'I like that you're worried. That feels like a small amount of revenge for you stealing the locket from me.'

He grinned. He liked this woman.

'I will be back to get that locket,' Iris said.

'I'd be disappointed if you didn't try.'

'Can I have your assurance that you won't give this locket to anyone until you hear my side of the story?'

'You have my word. The locket will be safe with me.'

She shook her head. 'I have no choice but to trust you.'

She turned to go and he snagged her hand, feeling

that energy pulse through him again. 'Iris, you need to take care of yourself. That man in there, the one in charge, he was furious. He said he knew you would try to take the locket, so I'm guessing he knows who you are. He's going to come after you.'

She paled slightly and then her face became determined. 'I can take care of him.'

'He had a gun.'

Her face fell and for the first time he saw real fear. 'You're joking.'

He pulled it from his pocket to show her. 'That billion-pound price tag is going to make people do desperate things. But if you come to Midnight, we can keep you safe.'

Iris chewed her lip. 'I better go.'

She started to walk out of the room and he watched her go. She turned back to look at him and as she gave him a wave, she changed again from the woman with dark hair to a six-foot, large, bald-headed man, dressed in the security guard uniform. Lynx laughed and waved goodbye, crossing everything he would see her again soon. He only hoped he would recognise her when he did.

CHAPTER 2

L ynx walked through the village of Midnight and looked around. Growing up, he'd been desperate to get out as soon as he could. He wanted to experience the world, not closet himself away. But since his brother Wolf, who lived here, had got married and had a daughter, Lynx had spent more and more time back here and now he lived in Midnight permanently. He adored his niece Blaze and loved spending time with her. He realised he'd reached a stage in his life where he wanted to be close to his family, not run from them.

He knocked on Wolf's door and his sister-in-law, Star, answered with Blaze on her hip and a smile on her face.

'You're back, we weren't expecting you here so soon.'

'Hey Star.'

He leaned down to kiss her on the cheek. Blaze was already reaching out towards him and Star handed her to him. Blaze had a big smile on her face as she grabbed hold of Lynx's curly hair, babbling away to him as if having a proper conversation.

'I missed you too,' Lynx said, giving his niece a hug.

He followed Star down to the kitchen and sat down with Blaze in his lap as Star added some chopped apple to the cake mix she was making. Blaze reached out for a spoon on the other side of the table and it floated across the table to her outstretched hand before she started banging it on the wooden surface.

'She's getting so much better at controlling her magic, isn't she,' Lynx said, grabbing a spoon himself and joining in with her music-making. Blaze giggled loudly.

'She really is. She can't tell us what she wants yet but if there's something she wants on the table or somewhere in her sight, she can certainly help herself using her magic. I have to watch her like a hawk because everything goes in her mouth, whether it's food or not.'

'Children's magic is erratic, things just happen around them with very little control. The fact that she can summon this spoon with so much accuracy is pretty impressive.'

'Wolf said the same. And she made it snow the other day.'

'Did she?'

'Yes, while she was in the bath. One minute she's playing with her rubber toys, the next it starts snowing from a little cloud that appeared above the bath. I know my magic can be a bit unpredictable at times, but I know it wasn't me.'

'Your magic is fine, you've learned to control it very quickly. Even the most experienced witches make mistakes sometimes.'

'Thankfully my magical mishaps are very few and far between these days.'

It had been eighteen months since Star had arrived in Midnight with no idea she had any magical abilities or about the world of magic and witchcraft. It had caused quite the stir in a village full of witches, but she had adapted very quickly.

Viktor the cat jumped up on the table and Blaze reached out to stroke him. Viktor wasn't remotely affectionate, he was sarcastic, grumpy and demanding. So Lynx was surprised when Viktor allowed Blaze to stroke his head, just once before he casually moved away.

'Did you bring me a present back from London?' Viktor said, avoiding Blaze's grabby hands.

Knowing that Viktor would never let him forget it if he hadn't, Lynx rooted around in his bag and pulled out a packet of shortbread biscuits.

'Biscuits?' Viktor looked at the pack disdainfully.

'They're from Harrods,' Lynx said.

'Very well.' Viktor flicked out his claws and sliced open the box as if using a knife. He stuck his face inside the hole and started munching away at the biscuits inside, the noise of his eating punctuated with the odd appreciative grunt.

'I got you and Wolf some chocolate-covered strawberries.' Lynx slid the box across the table to Star. 'I'll leave it up to you whether you want to share them with Blaze.'

Star laughed and quickly put them in a cupboard before Blaze set her eyes on them.

Lynx fished a small cuddly lion from his bag and gave it to Blaze before his niece noticed the chocolates.

Wolf walked into the room. 'Hey, wasn't expecting to see you today.'

Wolf kissed Star on the cheek and Blaze on the top of her head.

Lynx offered his own cheek up for a kiss but Wolf rolled his eyes.

Lynx laughed. 'Oh, I hear congratulations are in order.'

They both stared at him in confusion. 'For what?' Wolf said.

'You're expecting again.'

They stared at him blankly. 'Expecting what?' Star said.

'A baby.'

Star's mouth fell open in surprise.

Viktor whipped his head out of the packet of biscuits. 'Another baby?' he said, in horror.

'News to me,' Wolf said.

'And me.' Star stroked her flat belly gently, staring at it as if it would give her the answers.

Lynx wondered if Iris had got it wrong, but she had been so confident and accurate about everything else.

'Who told you that? Was it Zofia?' Wolf asked.

'No, it doesn't matter. I was clearly mistaken.'

'I think it does matter if someone gave you a premonition about us.'

'They were clearly wrong, I wouldn't worry.'

Viktor went back to eating the biscuits.

'I'm a little worried,' Star gave a nervous laugh. 'Two baby witches under the age of two. That's a lot to handle.'

Wolf took her in his arms. 'And if it's true, we'll face it together.'

She smiled and nodded.

Wolf let her go and turned back to Lynx. 'Sounds like you met someone interesting,'

'Iris McKenzie, she's a witch.'

'And she gave you that premonition about our baby?'

'Yes, she knew my name, yours, and glimpses of my future.'

'Like Zofia does?'

'Yes, kind of.'

'I guess we'll have to find out if what she saw is right,' Star said.

Wolf nodded. 'So, premonitions aside, did your trip go smoothly?'

Lynx frowned as he thought about how to answer his brother's question. 'I wouldn't say smoothly.'

'Did you get the locket?'

'Yes.' It still didn't sit well with him how the locket had come into his possession.

'Then what's the problem?'

'Iris McKenzie is a metamorph.'

Wolf sat down. 'You're kidding?'

'No, I saw it with my own eyes.'

'What's a metamorph?' Star asked.

'For want of a better word, a shapeshifter,' Wolf said.

'Like a werewolf?'

Wolf shook his head. 'Werewolves change physically, they grow fur, claws sprout from their fingernails, their bones break to encompass their new size and shape. Metamorphs change magically. I don't fully understand the magic behind it. I've never seen one before.'

'Me neither,' Lynx said. 'Metamorphs are incredibly rare. In fact they've become more of a myth than a reality. There were stories about them hundreds of years ago but they're not something we see nowadays.'

'What did she change into?' Star said, her cake completely forgotten.

'She was a young blonde woman when I first met her, then she changed into an older dark-haired woman and then a six-foot bald man.'

'How did she change?' Wolf asked.

'It's hard to explain, she just kind of melted into a completely different shape. And her clothes changed too. Not even just the colour of them – she was wearing a blue dress and then she changed into a black jacket and white shirt, and when she became a man she was wearing the security guard's uniform.'

'Maybe some kind of illusion,' Wolf said.

'Maybe. Her aura wasn't like anything I've ever seen before either.'

'Aren't everyone's auras completely different?' Star asked.

'All auras are different but essentially they are all a glow of light. Her aura shimmered as if it was made of water. It sort of rippled around her.'

'That's odd,' Wolf said.

'I know, she was... mesmerising.'

Wolf and Star exchanged glances, Star's face lighting up in delight. 'I've never heard you use that word about a woman before.'

'I don't mean I was attracted to her,' he said, knowing that was a lie. 'I don't even know what she really looks like so it's not a physical attraction. There was just something so captivating about her. As soon as I saw her I was entranced by her aura. I couldn't take my eyes off her.'

'Yeah, that doesn't sound like you were attracted to her at all,' Wolf said.

Lynx sighed. His brother was probably right.

'How does she fit in with the locket?' Wolf asked.

Blaze lifted her favourite toy owl from the far side of the room. It floated into her hands and she babbled excitedly.

Lynx explained how he had found Iris because of her aura, and how she had stolen the locket by raising a mist from the floor. He then told them about the man with the gun. He paused when he got to the part about the kiss, he really didn't want to tell them that but it was sort of key to how he pickpocketed the locket from her. So he briefly mentioned it too, eliciting another smirk of delight from Star.

Wolf thankfully bypassed that part.

'And the man definitely said, "I knew she'd try to take the locket back"?'

'Yes.'

'So it seems Iris had the locket before he stole it from her.'

'Looking back, yes, I think so. She said she didn't

want the locket for its price tag. She also said the locket doesn't have any power, it was just a wedding gift, but I could feel the energy coming from it.'

Wolf shook his head. 'We knew the locket existed but no one knew where it was until we heard it was in this collection in London. I presumed the seller had found it in some lost archives in some remote museum in Scotland, I never realised it had been owned by someone.'

'What's so special about this locket?' Star asked.

'It's been talked about in stories handed down over hundreds of years,' Wolf said. 'And of course these stories have been embellished and exaggerated and in many cases completely made up, but many of them involve using it to control the oceans and rivers. I'm not sure how true that part is but there were too many stories for the locket not to exist at all.'

'There are many stories about dragons and unicorns too, which to the best of my knowledge don't exist either, but one story fuels another,' Star said.

'That's true, but there have been many accounts of people seeing it too, and they all describe it the same way. It could of course be a cheap imitation but the fact that Lynx can feel its magical energy suggests this could be it.'

'What will you do with it now you have it, if it is the locket?' Star asked.

'The original plan was to lock it away in the vault

below the village. If the stories are true we don't want it to fall into the wrong hands. However, if Lynx's girlfriend has a legitimate claim, it will be returned to her,' Wolf said.

Lynx frowned. 'She's not my girlfriend. But I said the same. I told her to come here and I would listen to how she's connected to the locket and make a decision from there.'

Wolf nodded. 'We can chat with her together.'

'I'm also concerned that she might have got herself caught up in something dangerous. If this man stole the locket from her and now knows how valuable it is, I worry how far he will go to get it back.'

'We can protect her,' Wolf said. 'There is a house here in the village that's free. Mrs Baxter decided to move up to York to be closer to her children and grand-children. I was going to sort out advertising it today. I can hold off until Iris comes back for the locket.'

'No, do it now. My bet is she'll be looking this place up so she can get the locket back and then she'll see the vacancy.'

'She can stay as long as she needs to,' Wolf said. 'As long as she's a witch.'

Lynx frowned in confusion. 'She's a witch.'

'Are you sure?'

'Where are you going with this?'

'It's just that in the stories surrounding the locket, a lot of them involve kelpies.'

Lynx felt his eyes widen. 'I hadn't realised that.'

'Kelpies?' Star said. 'Aren't they some kind of malevolent and cruel water spirit or fairy? They take the form of horses and if people try to ride or touch them, the kelpies drag them back to the river, drown them and eat them.'

'That's right. They're shapeshifting water fairies, they live near the edges of the rivers and lochs. And yes, there are lots of stories about kelpies that involve eating children, or disguising themselves as beautiful men or women to attract the hikers that walk nearby. In fact, none of the stories I've heard about kelpies are good,' Wolf said.

'But that's myths and legends surely? They don't actually exist?' Star said.

Wolf nodded. 'They do, or did. Witches have had lots of dealings with kelpies over the years. They're quite insular, they like to be left alone, which is probably where the horror stories come from – to discourage mundanes and witches from coming near them. But most of our meetings have been fairly normal. They're notoriously grumpy but no witches have ever been dragged to their watery deaths after meeting a kelpie. No mundanes have either, as far as I can tell. The stories are a nice cover.'

'I met some kelpies once,' Viktor said, cleaning his face of biscuit crumbs.

'In this life?' Lynx asked. Viktor had lived hundreds of lives and he remembered every single one of them.

'Oh no, several lives ago. I think it was in the Victorian times. I was a young man, travelling around Scotland, and I saw them sitting by the lake. One of them threatened to eat me. I showed them my magic and they laughed and invited me to join them for dinner. It was a good night, they had the most amazing mead. And I was pleasantly surprised to find out I wasn't going to be the main course. I feel like they've been misunderstood over the years.'

'But they aren't around any more?' Star asked.

'There weren't many of them,' Wolf said. 'They lived in small groups and were quite spread out. I think they just slowly died out. As far as I know, there haven't been any dealings with kelpies for the last hundred years. I've not heard of their existence at all in my lifetime.'

'But you think Lynx's girlfriend is one?' Star asked, with wide eyes.

'I don't know but the shapeshifting ability is an interesting one, as is her watery aura and her ability to raise a mist similar to the kind you might find over the lochs.'

'Dear Gods,' Lynx muttered. 'I guess we'll see when she comes here.'

'Will you be able to tell?' Star asked.

'As you know, we ask for a drop of blood from

anyone that applies to live in the village, to make sure all residents are witches and no mundanes slip through the cracks. We should be able to tell from Iris's blood if she's a kelpie.'

Lynx rubbed his hand across his face and shook his head. What had he got himself involved with?

CHAPTER 3

Iris flicked her hands and clothes flew into her suitcase.

'I'm not living with a bunch of witches,' Ness said, grumpily.

'Nan! Don't be like that. Lynx is a good man and from what I know of Midnight, the people there are just normal, good witches too, just trying to live private, decent lives. You don't need to be all anti-witch just because...'

She trailed off, not wanting to bring that up again.

'Just because my great-great-grandmother was enslaved by one.'

Iris sighed. She'd heard the stories of course. How a handsome witch had tricked Marisa, how he'd charmed his way into her heart and, after they had slept together, while she was fast asleep, he'd slipped some kind of magical collar around her neck and enslaved her for the rest of his life, which thankfully had been rather short. After six months of being her keeper, he had met a very nasty death which had freed her from her bonds to him. The story had been passed down through the generations, told as a stark reminder never to trust witches. Although a lot of their family had ignored that sage advice.

'You're half-witch yourself,' Iris reminded her nan.

'Not the good half,' Ness said, folding her arms across her chest.

'You can't deny who you are. Your son-in-law, my father, was a witch too.'

'I never liked him.'

Iris shook her head, knowing that wasn't true. Ness had adored her son-in-law, but she'd often said, he was the exception to the rule. Iris had been raised with her grandmother constantly reminding her that she could never trust a witch and for the most part Iris had avoided them like the plague. But Lynx Oakwood had got under her skin, she couldn't stop thinking about him and that incredible kiss. Although he had rather proven the point when he'd betrayed her by stealing the locket.

'And what about Morag? You can't leave her.'

'I was going to bring her with us.'

'I don't think she'll like that. This is her home.'

'Morag is very good at making new friends,' Iris said. Unlike some people, although she kept that thought to herself.

She understood why her nan was dragging her feet. This had been the only home Ness had ever known. This house had been in their family for hundreds of years. Memories were etched into every corner, every crevice. There were marks on the furniture and scratches in the floors that held memories, too. The place had seen births, deaths and marriages and all the highs and lows of several generations. It had weathered harsh storms and basked in fierce sunshine. Children had grown up here, their laughter filling every room. It had seen pet dogs, cats, guinea pigs, rabbits come and go, and most recently a pet fox – although Iris could never call Morag a pet, she'd never talk to her again if she did. And Scotland was in their blood, the lochs, the rivers, the hills and mountains. That wonderful smell of the moors and lochs was something she loved when she stepped outside the house every morning. She and Ness would swim in the lochs and rivers every day. There was nothing that could replace that feeling. This was home.

'Is this all because you think this *witch* who's caught your eye is some part of your future?' Ness asked.

Iris waved her hand and more clothes flew into the

case. She wished she'd never told her nan that. Her gift, if that was what you could call it – to see things, to know things, to see people's future – had never extended to herself. She couldn't see what was going to happen to her in an hour's time, let alone ten years from now. But when she'd kissed Lynx, she'd seen flashes of his future and, inexplicably, she'd been a part of it. She wasn't sure if it was romantically but she'd seen them laughing and talking together. She'd seen him holding her hand. Maybe they would just be friends but she knew that her future was tied to him somehow.

She pushed that thought away.

'I'm doing this because Christopher is a dangerous man, because I think he will stop at nothing to get that locket back. I did this. I brought him into your life and you lost your locket because of it. Now this threat is hanging over us and I'm not going to let him hurt you again, emotionally or physically.'

'Why has he got you so rattled? The Iris I know is brave and fiery and powerful, you're not afraid of anything.'

'I'm afraid of losing you. If he came here I could raise a tsunami to take him out, I could fill a room with water in minutes and drown him. But that kind of magic takes time and what if I'm not here?'

'Let him come, I'm not scared of him,' Ness said,

waggling her fingers and making a blue shimmer sparkle in the air.

Iris knelt down in front of her nan. 'He had a gun. He knew I'd come for the locket and he'd brought a gun to stop me. You'd have to be pretty fast with your magic to stop a speeding bullet. I need to know you're safe, so we're going to Midnight just for a few months until all this blows over. And if I have to magically enslave you to drag you there, then I'll do it.'

'OK, OK, no need to be quite so dramatic. You don't even know if they'll let us in. Don't they have strict rules about only allowing witches in there?'

'They'll let us in.'

Iris had seen that too – in the flashes of her life with Lynx, she'd known they were in Midnight, despite never having been there herself. She'd got back from London the night before and had phoned Wolf, the mayor of the village, first thing that morning to tell him she'd take the house he was just about to place the advert for. If he'd been surprised that she'd known about the advert, he hadn't shown it. She was sure, with a village full of witches, he was used to magical irregularities. He'd insisted that she and her nan each provide a drop of blood to prove their witchiness. Iris had already done that and it was on its way to deepest Cornwall at this very moment via a magical courier company – or 'more bloody witches' as her nan had called them. But with their own abilities, she and Ness would probably arrive around the same time. Wolf could test their blood while he made them a welcome-to-the-village cup of tea.

'We need to go and get your locket back anyway,' Iris said.

'I need that locket. It's a part of me and I need it back.'

'I know, I'm sorry.'

'It's not your fault. I was the one that let Christopher see it for what it really was. I was the one that forgot to charm it so he didn't see it. It's my fault. But I really have to get that locket back. How do we know they'll give it to us?'

'Because we have proof it belongs to us. The list of Great-Great-Aunty Edith's possessions. The vintage book of pressed flowers with the diagram of it on one of the pages. Plus the photo of you and Pops inside the locket. Once we show them those things, they'll have to hand it back.'

Ness looked at her sceptically but Iris knew they would; she trusted Lynx, at least in that regard. They just had to get there. She certainly didn't want to wait around for Christopher to catch up with them. Another hour packing up their home and they'd be gone and it couldn't come soon enough. And that urgency had nothing to do with seeing Lynx Oakwood again, absolutely nothing at all.

Lynx, Wolf and Star stared at the two drops of blood on the piece of paper, one of them Iris's, one of them her grandmother's. This was the only entry requirement for anyone who wanted to live in the private village of Midnight: a drop of blood to see if they were a witch or not.

'Well?' Lynx said, as they sat around Wolf's dining table.

Wolf shook his head. 'Honestly, I have no idea. There's magic there, I can feel that, both of them have a lot of magic running through their veins. And like you said, the magic feels different to any other magic I've felt before. But I can't say whether they're kelpies. I've never met one. I thought it would be obvious when I touched their blood but it's not. If I had to guess, I'd say they're both part witch, part... something else.'

'Does it matter?' Star said. 'This rule was put in place to stop non-magical people from coming to the village and exposing our secret way of life. Iris and her grandmother are magical, they know about witches and how important it is to keep that way of life a secret. Isn't that enough?'

'From a personal point of view, I'm fascinated with all kinds of magic and if they are kelpies, or part kelpies,

I'd love to know more about them and what they can do,' Wolf said. 'But, from a professional perspective, I'm not sure bringing kelpies into the village is the right thing to do.'

'Why not?' Star said.

'I don't know if we can trust them.'

'My gut says we can,' Lynx said.

'I'm not sure that's your gut talking.' Wolf pointedly looked at Lynx's crotch.

Lynx rolled his eyes, although his brother had a point. He really wanted to see Iris again and he knew it wasn't anything to do with a professional fascination. From the moment she had held his hand, he had felt a connection to her he'd never had to anyone else before. He wasn't sure what that connection was but he wanted to know more about her.

'We have a lot of families and children arriving in the next few days for the summer solstice celebrations next week. I have a responsibility to them too,' Wolf said.

'You said the horror stories surrounding the kelpies were just that, stories to keep the mundanes away,' Star said. 'They are hardly likely to come here for our help and then systematically start picking us off one by one.'

Wolf looked at his wife, a smile spreading on his face. 'Why are you fighting their corner? You don't even know them.'

'When I first came here there was a lot of concern because I'm a weather witch, and history has shown weather witches in a very negative light. There were those in the village that were concerned I might kill them all with a tornado or a massive lightning strike that would wipe out the entire place. But in the end the villagers supported me, voted for me to stay. This village has always been about giving a home to someone who needs it, no matter what their background is. Iris and her grandmother need our help and I don't want to turn our backs on them just because they aren't strictly witchkind.'

Lynx grinned. He loved Star's passion to help those in need. 'I agree.'

Viktor jumped up on the table and sniffed the drops of blood. 'I have concerns.'

'You have concerns because you know they're bringing a talking fox with them and you like being the only talking animal in the village,' Star said.

'A fox has no business in this village. And where is the fox's blood in all of this? Shouldn't we be testing that for witchiness too?'

'It's not a condition of entry that our pets are witches, most of the pets here aren't,' Wolf said. 'You're the only witch cat in the village, is that not unique enough for you?'

'Half those pets could end up dead with a dangerous fox walking the streets.'

'I'm not turning them away because of a pet fox. Don't forget we have pet snakes here too.'

Viktor mumbled something under his breath and jumped down from the table, clearly in a strop.

Wolf sighed. 'Well apparently they're here, outside the gates.'

'Iris is here,' Lynx said, standing up.

'Stay here. I want to talk to them without you getting in the way or influencing my decision. I need to make a decision that's best for the village, not for you or for them.'

Lynx wasn't happy about that. His brother was known for being very straightlaced and by the book. He took his responsibilities as mayor very seriously.

But Lynx knew he couldn't exactly be impartial when it came to Iris. He hadn't been able to stop thinking about that kiss.

'I'll come with you too,' Star said. 'As mayoress of the village, I should have some say as well.'

Wolf smirked and shook his head. 'Come on then. Lynx can you stay here in case Blaze wakes up?'

Lynx nodded and watched them walk out, hoping that Star could work her magic, maybe literally, to help Wolf reach the right decision.

Iris sat in the car chewing her lip as she stared at the armed guards manning the gate into Midnight Village. Morag had barely said a word during their journey down – she wasn't happy about their new living arrangements and Iris didn't blame her. Her nan had been a lot more vocal about it all, grumbling in the seat next to her about the journey, about leaving her home, about the over-the-top security, but at least they would be safe in there. If they let them in. She wasn't quite sure where she would go if they didn't.

She understood this was a wrench for her nan. Ness had never left Scotland before, let alone the tiny village she had called home for her entire life. Even Iris had spent most of her life in that farmhouse. Her parents had raised her in that farmhouse with her nan and it had been the four of them until she was twenty-two. She'd moved into her own tiny cottage just a mile away, but when her parents were killed in a car accident, Iris hadn't wanted her nan to be alone so she'd moved back in with her. It had been the two of them ever since. And now they were here and everything was so new and different, it was understandably daunting.

She saw a man and a woman approaching the gates and knew, from having seen inside Lynx's head, that this was his brother Wolf and his sister-in-law Star, the mayor and mayoress of the tiny village.

The gates opened but only enough to let them out, certainly not enough to let a car in.

Iris sighed. The blood clearly had not been enough to convince them.

'Stay here, let me go and talk to them for a moment,' she said, getting out of the car.

Ness grumbled under her breath that she didn't want to talk to witches anyway.

Iris walked up to Wolf and Star.

Wolf held his hand out. 'You must be Iris, Lynx has told us a lot about you. I'm Wolf and this is my wife Star.'

Iris shook both their hands. 'Good to meet you.'

'Have we met before?' Star asked, gazing at her curiously.

Iris looked at her in confusion. 'I don't think so.'

'You look really familiar. Especially the red hair. Maybe I'm confusing you with someone else,' Star shrugged. 'Although Lynx did say you have the ability to shapeshift so I don't even know if this is the real you.'

Iris smiled. 'This is the real me. You all have been so kind to let us stay, I couldn't then lie to you about who we are and what we look like. And I just want to thank you so much for letting us stay. I was an idiot and brought this man into both our lives and not only did he turn out to be the biggest shitbag I've ever met, but a very dangerous one too. Lynx said if we came here, you'd protect us and I'm so grateful. Finding people we can trust is a lot harder than it should be.'

She hoped she'd laid it on thick enough.

'It's not a done deal, I'm afraid, not yet,' Wolf said, seriously. 'And trust works both ways. Your blood shows a kind of magic I've never seen before and, based on what Lynx told us about what happened in London and your extraordinary metamorphic abilities, I'm wondering if you're a kelpie.'

Iris's mouth went dry. She'd had no intention of sharing that information. There were many dark, horrifying stories that preceded the kelpies and because of that she'd never told anyone what she truly was before. But if Wolf suspected she was lying, there was no way he would let her in.

She swallowed the lump in her throat. 'My nan is half-kelpie and so am I. Although if you want to be truly accurate, I'm probably around thirty-seven-and-a-half-percent kelpie.'

Wolf's eyes lit up in a way she hadn't expected. No one who knew anything about the kelpies was happy to meet one. Witches tended to be the exception, but it was more a wary acceptance than excitement.

'I have to say, I've never met a kelpie before,' he said. 'And as someone who is fascinated with all kinds of magic, I would love to have you here so I can talk to you about your heritage. But kelpies are not known for their... positivity.'

She laughed. 'That's a nice way of saying, "I've heard about the child-eating rumours and I'm a tad concerned."'

'I don't believe those rumours. There is nothing in our history books that shows any kind of malevolence from kelpies, just a general grumpiness and a desire to be left alone.'

Iris nodded. That kind of summed her and her nan up perfectly.

'The rumours aren't true, and if it helps, I'm a vegetarian so children tend to be off the menu. Kelpies are a private people, just like you are. You must understand that need for privacy, your kind built a whole village so you'd be left alone and no one would ever be able to bother you again. The rumours about dragging children to their watery graves were kind of the same thing – they meant we'd be left alone.'

'I understand but what we've built here is a community and I worry about how your isolated way of life will fit in.'

Iris was wondering that herself, especially her nan, who wasn't the most... sociable person, especially when it came to witches.

'My dad was a witch, so I do understand that way of life too. And we don't need to be the life and soul of the party, this arrangement will only be for a few months and then we'll be out of your hair. If any of the residents are wary of us because of our heritage, I'm sure they'll appreciate that we keep to ourselves.'

Wolf rubbed his hand across his jaw as he seemed

to consider the matter. He glanced at his wife and Star gave him a little nod. He smirked.

'Welcome to Midnight Village.'

Iris practically sagged in relief. 'Thank you so much. Listen, my nan has had a rough day. She's left the only home she's ever had, to live with witches who she doesn't particularly like, so please be kind.'

'Oh, Wolf can be very charming if he wants to be,' Star said.

'Why doesn't she like witches?' Wolf said.

'Because her great-great-grandmother was enslaved by one, she's never forgiven them.'

Wolf's mouth pulled into a thin line. 'Sadly there are bad people in all walks of life, witches, mundanes, and I'm sure kelpies also have bad apples. But I can assure you that nothing like that has ever happened here.'

'I believe you.'

'I'll go and introduce myself,' Wolf said.

Wolf walked off to the car and Iris willed her nan to be polite, even if she couldn't be friendly.

'I think Lynx is looking forward to seeing you again,' Star said, with a smirk.

'Oh, he told you how he cheated me out of the locket?' Iris said. It still didn't sit well with her but then the kiss had just been a cover, a distraction if the guards caught them, and he'd known that. If the kiss hadn't been real for him, then she could hardly blame him for taking advantage of it to win the locket. It was something she probably would have done herself. But the kiss had been real for her, which was silly – she didn't know Lynx, so how could a kiss from a complete stranger mean something? But she couldn't deny that there had been a connection she had never felt before.

'I know he feels bad about that,' Star said.

'Hmm, it might just be best if we stay away from each other,' Iris said.

She really didn't need any complications. She intended to keep to herself, do her time and get out as soon as it was safe to do so. Obviously she wanted to explore her new home but she wasn't going to get roped in to doing flower-arranging at the village fete or making cakes for her neighbours or whatever else a village of witches got up to. She'd always been better off on her own. Her classmates growing up, even her boyfriends when she'd been older, had all been mundanes and she had never been able to truly be herself with them. She'd met a few witches in her time but, as her nan had always told her witches couldn't be trusted, she'd kept her distance from them, despite being half-witch herself.

'I can't see Lynx agreeing to that. He wanted to come down here to meet you but Wolf talked him out of it.'

Iris wondered what would have happened if he had come down to see her. Would he have kissed her again?

No of course not, so why was her stupid heart racing at the idea? He might not even find the real her attractive. She needed to get Lynx out of her head, though that was going to be hard, living in the same place as him.

Suddenly she heard her nan laugh and Iris couldn't help smiling. That was something she very rarely heard. Wolf really did have the charm and unfortunately so did his brother.

Wolf came back to her. 'Well I'll let you two get settled in. Your road is second on the left, Hazel Lane, number sixteen. When you're ready, and that doesn't have to be today, we'll have a chat about the locket. If we feel you have a legitimate claim to it, of course it will be returned to you.'

'Just like that?'

Wolf shrugged. 'We have no reason to keep the locket, the only reason we wanted it was to stop it falling into mundane hands or anyone that might use it for nefarious means. But let's have a chat about it tomorrow.'

He waved his hand and the gate opened wide enough to let the car through.

She nodded. 'Thank you. Honestly, this means so much.'

Wolf smiled and she got back in her car and drove through, feeling a huge sense of relief as the gates closed behind her.

She glanced over at her nan who had a smile on her face.

'Your attitude has changed.'

'That Wolf seems like a nice man.'

Iris smiled and shook her head as she drove towards the centre of the village. It was time to get a look at her new home.

CHAPTER 4

As they rounded a corner the village came into view, all quaint little cottages painted in bright colours. But the houses were so close to each other; there definitely would be no solitude here.

Iris drove past a large fountain in the middle of the village green where kids were running around in the sunshine, and turned up Hazel Lane, looking at all the house numbers until she found number sixteen, and what was going to be her new home for the next few months. It was a pale blue house with roses climbing up the walls and looked very cute, if you liked that sort of thing.

She got out and looked around. It was nice and quiet here, peaceful. She opened the door for Morag and the fox slid out from the back seat and blinked her large golden eyes as she looked around.

'We're definitely not in Scotland anymore,' Morag said.

'Sadly not. But it's just for a few months.'

Morag sniffed the air and then skulked off, disappearing behind one of the houses.

Iris sighed and turned back to the car to see her grandmother getting out. She gave her home the once-over.

'It's a bit small,' Ness said.

Their farmhouse in Scotland had been small and she'd never complained about that.

'Come on, let's have a look inside,' Iris said.

They walked up to the door and Iris was surprised to find it unlocked. She pushed it open to find a cosy little lounge on the other side with a turquoise sofa and chairs clustered around a log burner. Leaving Ness downstairs, she went upstairs and saw there were two large double bedrooms, with the beds already made for them, and a large bathroom with a walk-in shower. She went back down to find Ness looking around her despondently. The place was immaculately clean so Iris knew her nan couldn't find fault in that.

Iris went into the kitchen to see a welcome hamper filled with bread, butter, coffee, tea, milk, biscuits and two fresh-looking scones. They smelled amazing and there was cream and jam too.

'Hey, we have fresh scones in here, we can have them for lunch in a bit.'

She heard Ness make a noise that was nothing short of a harrumph. Iris raised her eyes to the heavens. She knew this was her fault, none of this would have happened if she hadn't trusted Christopher enough to bring him into her home. She had made her bed and now she had to lie in it, but the next few months were going to be unbearable if her nan was going to be like this.

She peered out of the window into the little garden and saw flowers spilling over from the borders. It was very pretty and Ness had loved sitting in the garden at home, enjoying the flowers and the wildlife. Surely she could grow to love this garden too.

Just as she was turning away from the window she saw something at the back of the garden that made her heart soar.

'Nan, quick, look at this,' Iris said excitedly, taking off her shoes and socks and running outside. The grass felt warm under her feet as she picked her way to the very back of the garden. And there hidden amongst the trees was a little stream that tumbled over rocks as it wound its way through their plot of land and back out again.

'What's all the fuss about?' Ness said as she came outside.

'Look,' Iris pointed at the stream.

The scowl on Ness's face deepened as she made her way across the lawn. Iris waited for her nan to see it and when she did her whole face lit up as if she'd won millions of pounds in the lottery. She quickly kicked off her sandals and stepped into the water and Iris joined her, smiling to see her glowing with happiness. The water bubbled and danced as it ran past them and Iris closed her eyes, feeling the restorative powers of the water filling her, like a dried plant grateful for the long-awaited rain. She took several long deep breaths and felt herself relax, all the stresses ebbing away.

Everything would be OK, she could feel that.

She opened her eyes and Ness was still smiling.

'We never had this at home,' Iris said. 'We had to walk across two fields when we wanted to do water bathing.'

Ness nodded. 'I think I could be very happy here.'

Iris smiled and gave her nan a hug. 'Right, you stay here, I'll get unpacked.'

Her nan didn't argue, she just closed her eyes again as she relished in the water.

Iris went back inside, slipped on her shoes and went out to the car. She opened the boot with a wave of her hand and as she waved the other hand, all their possessions lifted out of the car and floated into the house. Iris followed them in, directing them to their places with a few more waves. The suitcases floated upstairs and started unpacking themselves, pictures hung themselves on the walls, her nan's knitting and embroidery stuff went into the ottoman next to the sofa and all of their herbs and spices flew into the kitchen cupboards. The plants took themselves to optimum positions around the house, some in shade, others in bright sunshine, whatever they needed. Within five minutes, everything was where it should be.

She went to the back door to find Ness still standing in the stream, which made her smile. 'I'm heading out to explore.'

Her nan gave her a wave of her hand which said, off you go, but other than that she didn't move at all from her position, looking blissfully happy.

Iris walked back out the front and looked around. A lawnmower was mowing the lawn by itself at the house opposite and a car was cleaning itself two doors down. There was definitely something to be said about living in a private village. Despite her home being out in the middle of nowhere there'd always been a risk of being seen, so previously she'd always kept her magic hidden, only doing it behind closed doors where no one could see. It would be nice to relax and truly be herself here.

She moved off down the road a little way but she'd only got a couple of houses down before she felt something from the other side of the street. She couldn't really describe it, a nudge maybe, no it was a pull. She walked towards one of the other houses and felt that pull get stronger. As she approached the door, she could see it was open a crack. She looked around and then peered through the gap.

'Hello!' she called out but there was no reply.

That pull was still there so she pushed the door open a bit more and knew straightaway this was Lynx's house. She could feel it. From what she'd seen when they'd driven in, the village was quite sizeable, maybe three or four hundred houses in total, so it didn't seem particularly fair that she would end up living two doors away from the man who had constantly occupied her thoughts ever since she'd met him.

Still, she was here now so she might as well face the reunion. She'd tell him that just because she had grabbed him and kissed him like her life depended on it, didn't mean that she wanted to revisit the moment. Even though, if she was honest, she desperately did. She'd tell him they were both adults and they could obviously behave sensibly around each other without the need to kiss each other. Although Lynx might not have any intention of kissing her again so that would be an awkward conversation. No, she'd tell him they could move past the kiss, and there was no reason for it to be weird between them, but that she still hadn't totally forgiven him for the way he'd stolen the locket.

The locket. Was that here, was that the pull she'd felt? She refused to think it was Lynx's presence that had drawn her to the house. It would make a lot more sense for it to be the locket.

She pushed the door fully open and stepped inside. 'Hello?'

There was no answer, no sound, no sign at all that anyone was there. And while stealing back the locket was tempting, partly because she'd love to wipe the smile off Lynx's face, Wolf had trusted her enough to let her into his village and she had to prove she was worthy of that trust. She decided to go. She was sure she'd bump into Lynx again soon enough and Wolf had promised her he would return the locket to her if he believed she and her nan had a claim over it, which they did and had proof of.

She was about to turn around when she suddenly got an overwhelming sense that she belonged there, which was the weirdest feeling to get from somewhere she'd never been before. She moved further into the room and looked around. It was a cosy-looking lounge, with a large grey corner sofa facing the TV, a simple grey rug in front of the fire. It was smart, masculine and really not to her taste, so why did it feel like she'd just come home?

She touched the sofa and suddenly got flashes of Lynx's future, just a few seconds of each image, like a photo slideshow played on fast forward. Lynx kissing her on the sofa, Lynx making love to her there, her lying on the sofa with her head in his lap, heavily pregnant, the two of them cuddled up on the sofa with their baby between them.

She gasped. 'No, no, no, no.'

She quickly turned and ran from the house and banged straight into Lynx. She bounced off his hard chest and would have hit the floor if he hadn't reached out and steadied her with his hands at her waist.

He blinked in surprise. 'Iris?'

She realised that this was the first time he had seen her as her real self and not the pretty blonde he'd kissed in London. She guessed he recognised her from her aura.

She huffed out a breath. 'Yeah, hi.'

He reached out a finger and touched one of her red curls. 'Is this the real you?'

She nodded, still trying to push the images of her future away.

'I like the red,' Lynx said, the hand on her waist snaking around her back. 'I haven't been able to stop thinking about you.' His eyes cast down to her lips.

No, he wasn't supposed to be thinking about her like this or looking at her like he really wanted to kiss her again. She didn't need any complications with a man like Lynx. She was going to stay here for a few months and get out. She was ignoring the future she had seen. The future was what you made it and if she wasn't here then none of that could happen.

She stepped out of his arms. 'I should go.'

He frowned in confusion as if suddenly realising where he had found her. 'Why were you in my house?'

'I was, umm... looking for you. Just to say that what happened in London stays in London and just because I'm here now doesn't mean it has to be weird.'

Although she was definitely making it weird.

'Your door was open so I thought you were in. When I saw you weren't, I came back out.'

'At a hundred miles an hour. What's wrong?'

'Nothing.'

He narrowed his eyes. 'Your ability to know things, to see things. Did you see something in there you didn't like?'

'You could say that.' Iris moved away from him, but he caught her hand.

'What did you see?'

She shook her head. 'It doesn't matter.'

'I think it does if it made you run out of my house like the hounds of hell were after you.'

'I can handle them. Look, if you must know, I saw your future and futures are funny things to see. They haven't happened yet so how do we know they will? There are a thousand different roads in front of you, every decision you make, no matter how small, is a fork in the road and can change your life irrevocably. So surely what I see is just one possible future, not *the* future.'

'I don't know if every small decision counts. What I have for dinner tonight is hardly going to change my life forever.'

'It could. Say you can't decide between beef stew and mushroom soup. In the end you opt for the mushroom but it has an ingredient in there you're allergic to. You get rushed off to hospital and you fall in love with the doctor that saves your life, you get married, have lots of babies. If you had gone with the beef stew, you would never have gone to hospital and never have met the love of your life.'

He smirked. 'That's some life-changing mushroom soup.'

'It might be an extreme example but life can change for us in a blink of the eye, so I don't think anything is set in stone.'

'I can understand that, but I can't understand why a glimpse of *my* possible future would upset *you* so much. Do I die a horrible death, hopefully non-mushroom-related?'

She narrowed her eyes at him. 'Maybe you will. I still haven't forgiven you for the way you stole the locket from me. I could think of many ways to ensure a very painful, long drawn-out death.'

He laughed. 'I'm sure you could. You're not going to tell me what you saw, are you?'

'Nope. If it happens, I'll tell you then that I foresaw it.'

'If I get eaten by a bear, you'll tell me then, oh yes, death by bear is what I saw, rather than telling me now so I avoid all bears.'

'Not too many bears in Cornwall.'

'But life can change in the blink of an eye,' Lynx said, obviously mocking her.

'You're an ass and I hope you do get mauled by a bear.'

She marched off and returned to her house, kicking off her shoes as soon as she was back inside. She needed some water therapy after speaking to him.

Morag was curled up asleep on the sofa and looked up at her when she walked in. 'Problem?'

'We may be staying here longer than I thought,' Iris said through gritted teeth.

Morag simply rolled her eyes and went back to sleep. Iris stormed outside and joined her nan who was still standing in the stream, her eyes closed. The water made her feel better instantly.

Ness didn't say anything at first but after a while she spoke. 'When a man gets under your skin like that the best thing to do is sleep with him.'

'I'm not sleeping with Lynx Oakwood.'

'Sure you won't,' Ness laughed.

'He's a witch. Why are you encouraging me to sleep with a witch when you've always made it clear you hate them?'

Ness shrugged. 'When in Rome.'

'Really? Thirty seconds in a witch village and now you love them?'

Ness opened her eyes and looked at her. 'You might

not be able to see your future very clearly, but I can. He makes you happy. Very happy. I can't hate that.'

Iris let out a groan of frustration and stormed back into the house. She hated feeling like she had no control over her life, like her whole future was mapped out in front of her and she had no say over it. One kiss and the rest of her life was decided for her. That was ridiculous. And yes, the kiss had been something so much more than she'd ever experienced before but that didn't mean she was ready to settle down, get married, have babies. She didn't even know Lynx. All she knew was that he had used the best damn kiss of her life as an opportunity to steal the locket from her. Could she really trust him?

But there was something about this man. Ness was right, he had got under her skin. She felt like a moth drawn to a flame with him. But would she get burned if she got too close?

She sat down next to Morag, sinking her hand into her soft fur. She thought about what she'd seen of Lynx's future, and even though it had only been flashes, she had seemed happy. Would she be a fool to turn her back on that? Wasn't it at least worth finding out if they had something more in common than an incredible kiss?

She sighed. She'd never been good at relationships. Making friends and having boyfriends had always been hard because she had this great big secret she couldn't really share. She remembered her first boyfriend, if you could really call him that. She'd been eight years old and they used to hold hands in the playground and sit next to each other in class. One day, they'd been out on the school field at break, making daisy chains, and she'd been brave enough to show him a bit of her magic, just a little bit, the daisies floating around her. He'd run away screaming and never spoken to her after that. Maybe she should have prepared the ground before she'd launched the magic on him, at least spoken a little about magic so he knew what was coming.

Years later, when she had been fourteen and hanging around with a group of friends at one of their houses, one of them had been upset over her boyfriend dumping her. Without thinking Iris had pulled a box of tissues to her from the other side of the room. The girls had completely freaked out, saying she was evil, a demon and a witch. The mocking had continued for many years, and she certainly hadn't been part of the friendship group anymore.

The last person she had told had been Jack. She had loved him so much, they had been perfect together. She'd been nineteen when they met and had dated him for two years, genuinely believing they would spend the rest of their lives together. On her twenty-first birthday he'd proposed and she'd said yes but the next day she'd realised she couldn't get married to him without telling the truth about who she was first.

She hadn't shown him any magic, not at first. She'd just told him that she was part kelpie and part witch. He hadn't believed her, thought she was making it up, and couldn't understand why she would say such a thing. So she'd shown him her magic and he had been horrified, running out of the house so fast she'd barely seen him for dust. He'd come back a few days later to tell her he'd done a lot of research into kelpies and believed she had charmed him to fall in love with her. He even threatened to sue her if she didn't remove the spell she'd cast on him – which would have been interesting if it had ever gone to court. Iris had been heartbroken that he could think that of her or that she was anything to be scared of. She was still the same person he'd loved for two years. She'd been put off having a proper relationship ever since.

That was until Christopher wormed his way into her life. She had loved him too and his betrayal hurt even more because of that. She didn't know if he had somehow heard about the locket and charmed her and her nan to get hold of it, or had simply seen it one night when he was having dinner with them and decided to take it. She kind of hoped it was the latter because the former didn't bear thinking about. She had made love to that man, he had told her he loved her. If all of that had been fake just so he could get the locket, that kind of betrayal burned in her gut. But either way, he was just another in a long line of people she had trusted who had let her down.

So she was wary of getting involved with Lynx, of trusting someone enough to not only not hurt her but to love her, all of her, exactly as she was.

Although at least her magical abilities wouldn't come as a surprise.

She supposed as she was going to be here for a few months it wouldn't hurt to find out what kind of man he really was.

And whether the second kiss would be just as good as the first.

CHAPTER 5

Iris decided to head out again as her exploring
had been cut short last time but as she opened
the door, Morag clearly decided to come with her.

'Might as well explore my new home. Doesn't look
like we'll be going back to Scotland anytime soon.'

'I wouldn't say that just yet,' Iris said. 'Nothing is
set in stone.'

'It seems your fate is tied to this man whether you
like it or not.'

'I don't know him to like it or not.'

'But you knew him well enough to kiss him.'

'That was a mistake.'

'Yet you're here, living in his village, two doors away
from him. And now you've seen his future, which is
inexplicably linked to yours.'

'It's a possible future, not the only future. Let's not

forget that I saw your future when I first found you and it did not end well for you. I changed that future and here you are all these years later, which shows our paths can be rewritten. Our fate is not laid out in the stars, we are in charge of our own destinies. If I stay here, it will be because I've chosen that life, not because I'm being forced into it.'

Morag made a noise of disbelief.

Iris was struggling to believe it herself. Her home was her beloved farmhouse, where she'd grown up, where she'd spent almost her entire life. Home was the beautiful, remote, rugged Scotland. It was hard to believe she could ever leave that permanently unless there was a really good reason. Falling in love and trusting a man with her future happiness was not good enough; she had been there and been burned far too many times.

They reached the village green to find lots of people milling around, chatting and laughing with each other. A few of them looked over at her curiously and she wondered if people knew she was part kelpie and what they made of it if they did.

She forced a smile on her face and gave them a little wave but she wasn't brave enough to go and talk to anyone, not yet.

A lot of people were heading towards one area of the village so she decided to go in that direction too.

She stopped at the entrance to Stardust Street. It

was evidently a street of shops but that wasn't what caused her to stop. There was magic everywhere. The shops themselves were magical with their impressive entrances, a giant cauldron in one with fire underneath, bright yellow liquid bubbling away inside, potion bottles moving around within the shop. Another shop had an oversized book out the front, the crinkled pages turning as if someone was actually reading it. Books moved around between different shelves in there too. The shops' wares floated out of the doors, either enticing potential customers to try the goods or to come inside to buy them. People were doing magic too, she could see it as they were talking to each other. How utterly wonderful to be able to just be completely yourself, to be so at ease to do magic whenever you wanted without fear or judgement. She had always done her own magic behind closed doors where no one could see.

'It's a lot to take in, isn't it.'

Iris turned round to see Star approaching her.

'I've never been anywhere like this before – not just the wonderful shops, but people using their magic so freely. I've always been taught to keep it hidden, that mundanes would never understand and my experience of growing up with them is proof of that. The few people I shared my magic with didn't want anything to do with me after that. But here people can just be themselves and it's a glorious thing to see.'

Star nodded. 'It is. People are happy here, you can see that. It's a very positive atmosphere. When I first came to the village, I was a wildling, I had no idea this magical world even existed. You can imagine how over-whelming I found it at the start. But people are very friendly here and very supportive. You'll make friends in no time.'

That was almost impossible to believe, Iris had never really made friends before.

Star glanced down at Morag and the fox offered out a paw. 'I'm Morag, pleased to meet you.'

Star's eyes widened and then, seemingly unfazed, she knelt down and shook Morag's paw. 'Nice to meet you too. We have a talking cat here called Viktor. He's a bit grumpy but there is a heart in there, I'm sure he will make you welcome once he's got used to the idea of not being the only talking animal anymore. Only, please don't eat him. Despite his continual sarcasm, I'm quite partial to him.'

Morag looked at her with disdain. 'I don't tend to converse with my food before I eat it.'

With that she stalked off, leaving Star smirking. She stood back up. 'Oh, she and Viktor are going to get on like a house on fire.'

'Your cat will be quite safe. Morag doesn't hunt. I raised her from a cub after I found her abandoned in the woods. I tried to release her when she was old enough but she didn't want to go so now I have a pet fox. Well, a companion, she doesn't like being referred to as a pet. But she prefers her food to be cooked and served on a china plate, not covered in fur and bones.'

Star laughed. 'When I first met Viktor he told me he liked his tea served warm, not hot, with a sprig of fresh lavender on the top. So I understand demanding animals.' She linked arms with Iris as if they were best friends, which Iris found a little unnerving. 'Come on, let's show you the shops.'

They walked through the wrought-iron gates into the street and a young man came hurrying over holding a clipboard.

'Star, is this a friend of yours?' the man said.

'Yes, Ezra, this is Iris McKenzie, she's just moved to the village with her nan, Ness.'

Ezra consulted his board, which Iris realised was some kind of electronic device. 'I wasn't aware of this.'

'It was very last minute but she'll be here for a few months at least. She lives at number sixteen Hazel Lane. I don't suppose she's been added to your system yet so can she just have a bracelet today for my account?'

'I can do that.' Ezra clicked his fingers and a little leather bracelet with a large rainbow-coloured stone on it appeared in his hand. He held it out for Iris and she took it in confusion. 'You use this to buy anything you want in the shops, or if you take any of the produce from the street it will be charged to your bracelet and money automatically deducted from your account. Or, for today, Star's account. So you never need to worry about bringing your purse or queuing up at the till, you just take what you want and walk back out and your bracelet will be charged.'

'So legalised shoplifting?' Iris said.

Ezra laughed. 'Something like that.'

She looked at the bracelet and could see the stone was swirling with different colours. It was clear everything here had been thought through. This community living was going to take a lot of getting used to. Whenever she went into her nearby village to go to the shops she could feel people were always wary of her. Most of them probably had no idea why, and didn't know or believe the rumours, but they knew Iris was different and that was enough. Iris had learned to get in, get what she needed and get out. Wandering aimlessly around the shops and chatting with people would be a complete novelty.

'Thanks Ezra. Come on, let's look around,' Star said, guiding her through the archway.

Iris looked all around her. It really was like walking into a magical theme park, with the imaginative shops displaying their magic so openly. The products moved, swirled and danced inside the shops, enticing customers to come in.

'Do you do potions, Iris?' Star gestured to the potion

shop. 'I have to be honest and say I don't know a lot about kelpies.'

'I have done some potion work but not a lot. I don't do a lot of spells, I haven't really felt the need. Obviously I do stuff around the house to make things easier, like washing-up or cleaning. If I'm sitting watching TV I might make myself a cup of tea without getting up or summon an apple from the kitchen. Sometimes I'll go into the village as someone else so no one will look at me and think, oh there's that weird girl from the farm again. I was not well liked growing up, none of my family were, so I never wanted someone to be walking past my home and see me standing over a bubbling cauldron.'

'No, I get that. If you ever wanted to learn more about potions, we have a potions club every week. It's a small group, only six of us, well seven if you include our teacher, Ashley. Everyone is very welcoming and it's always a fun night. There's also a lot of wine that gets drunk so you can see how seriously we take it.'

Iris laughed. 'I might come. All of this is going to take a lot of getting used to. I've never had magical friends before, witch or kelpie. I've not really had a lot of mundane friends either because they know that I'm different even if they don't know to what extent. Sitting around chatting and drinking wine with friends is not something I've ever done, let alone doing magic with someone outside of my family.'

'Then you must come. I was the same when I came here. Despite not knowing I was a witch, I always felt like I was different to everyone else and while I had some friends I didn't have a lot. But I've made some wonderful friends since I've been here. Come for that, even if you're not interested in potions.'

Iris chewed her lip. 'I'll think about it.'

An ice cream cone filled with white sparkly ice cream floated out of one of the shops. Iris grabbed it to stop it hitting her dress and felt her bracelet vibrate.

Star laughed. 'They are crafty about getting you to buy stuff here. I normally walk around with my hands in my pockets so I don't accidentally hold something. You might as well enjoy it now you've paid for it.'

Iris laughed at the audacity of charging people for protecting their clothes against ice cream stains. She took a small lick.

'Mmm, coconut, my favourite.'

'I think that might be magical ice cream, so it's any flavour you want it to be.'

Iris smiled. 'Now that is clever.' She took another lick, it was so creamy and delicious. 'I've never thought about mixing food and magic before.'

'I make a living doing just that. I make cakes to solve any problem: a broken heart, a cake to help with anxiety or to boost confidence, a cake to nail that job interview, or just a cake infused with happiness. I have an online shop called Witchy Bakes and Cakes and it's very popular, and of course I have a shop here on Stardust Street too. I could make you a cake to help you settle into Midnight Village, if you want?'

Iris laughed. 'I'm good thanks. I think the magical ice cream is enough for one day. There's actually a witch, Betty, who runs the bakery in the next town to where I live and she makes the most amazing tablet. It's sort of like fudge but more crumbly and tastes so much better. Her tablet is the best I've ever tasted, I've always wondered if she uses magic to make it taste so good. Though I've never asked her. She doesn't like me. She knows I'm magic but not exactly a witch, so she always views me with suspicion whenever I go in there. Although she's always happy enough to sell me her tablet. I suppose money is money no matter who it comes from.'

'You've had it rough if even the witches are giving you a hard time.'

'Yeah, I've been an outcast my whole life. Don't fit in with the mundanes, the witches don't want to know us and there is a distinct lack of kelpies.'

'Are there not many of you left?'

'None that I know of. I have a second cousin who lives in the Orkneys, she's half-kelpie too. But outside my family, I don't know any. Not to say they're not out there but we kelpies like to keep ourselves to ourselves so it's hard to know.'

'What part of Scotland are you from?' Star asked.

'Near Loch Fyne on the west coast. It's very beautiful, very remote. You can walk some of the hills and moors and sometimes not see a single person all day.'

'And you like that?'

'I love it. I'm not a people person, give me a sarcastic fox any day.'

'Life here is going to be so different to that. Everyone knows everyone's business, but they all mean well. I'd suggest trying to embrace the community vibe, talk to people – you might find you like it.'

Iris wasn't sure she would, she'd spent too long on her own, but she got the feeling she couldn't hide away in a place like Midnight.

A box of hot doughnuts floated out of one of the shops, but Iris made sure not to touch it this time and after a few minutes it floated away.

'Have you seen Lynx yet?' Star asked innocently.

Iris smiled at the question. 'Briefly. But I wouldn't get any ideas about some blossoming romance with him. It was a simple kiss purely to distract the guards, it didn't mean anything. I don't even like the man.'

Star smirked at this as if she didn't believe her. 'Well you certainly made an impression on him.'

'I'm sure it was the pretty blonde with the big breasts that made an impression on him, that's who I was when he kissed me.'

Although he'd looked at her the exact same way

when he'd met her as a redhead a short while before, with complete adoration.

'Lynx says you can see things. You know, things like a premonition. He told us about the premonition you had about our second child.'

'Yeah, sorry about that, I didn't mean to ruin the surprise.'

'I'm going to have to get a pregnancy test from outside the village to confirm if it's true. I couldn't possibly get one from in here, the whole village would know in less than an hour.'

Iris knew it was true, but she didn't say that.

'But that aside, I've had a few premonitions myself,' Star went on. 'Not many and I certainly don't have any control over it, but now I know where I knew you from. I've seen you in my future.'

'I think I've had enough premonitions for one day. If you're going to tell me that you've seen me happily married to Lynx with a baby, I don't want to hear it.'

'Ah, well in that case I better change the subject.'

They fell into silence for a minute and Iris tried to focus on the shops. There was a giant teapot pouring an endless cup of tea outside one café and a sparkling cake that slowly changed shape and flavour outside another, so that what started off as a strawberry cream tart one moment turned into a chocolate éclair the next.

'Is that what you saw?' Iris said. 'Me and Lynx together?'

'You said you didn't want to talk about it.'

'I don't. But what did you see?'

'I first saw you around eighteen months ago. You were very nearly the end of me and Wolf actually. We have a little holiday cottage called The Pearl, down by the coast. First time I went there in the very early days of mine and Wolf's relationship, I saw him playing with a red-headed baby, looking so happy, and then I saw you, standing in the kitchen, heavily pregnant. I made the assumption that the red-headed child must be his and yours, so I let him go so he could have that future and that happiness. I finally realised the child I'd seen was mine and we got back together but I've always wondered who you were. I've seen you a few more times since then. The first time, I didn't see your face, just the red hair and the pregnant belly. But the second time I saw you clearly. The third and fourth time I saw you with Lynx.'

'That doesn't even make any sense. Eighteen months ago I didn't know you or Lynx even existed. I hadn't even met Christopher then and he's the reason I'm here now. How could my future be so set in stone that every decision I've made has brought me here to Lynx? That's ridiculous.'

'I do believe in soul mates, that everyone has that one person they're supposed to be with. And some people never find theirs. If the stars have aligned for you to find yours, why not welcome it with open arms?'

Iris sighed.

'Did you have a premonition today?' Star asked.

'I did and I don't like it. I've never been able to see my own future, just flashes of other people's. But today I saw Lynx's future and it involved me and that bothers me more than it should.'

'Because you feel like you have no control over it.'

'Yes exactly,' Iris said. 'And my nan said she can see my future too and that Lynx makes me very happy and it all just seems like a fait accompli.'

'I could understand you fighting against it if it was a horrible future. But surely a guaranteed happiness is something to look forward to?'

'But I want a choice. I don't want to start dating him because my eyes are firmly on that future. I'd want to date him because I think he's nice, kind, funny and sexy as hell. If I believe in that future I might as well march round to his house and demand he marries me right now and skip all the dating malarkey altogether.'

'I do understand but no one can force you to fall in love with him, regardless of how it starts. Fate or destiny, or whatever you want to call it, can't change the way you feel.'

'But will I love him because of what I've seen? Because I've seen him holding my baby, our baby, and it was the most beautiful thing I've ever seen?'

'Ah, yes, I see what you mean.'

Star was silent for a moment.

'I don't even like him,' Iris added. 'What he did to steal the locket from me felt very underhand.'

'I know he feels awful about that. But if it helps, he really is a decent, kind man. He's been so worried about you since he met you in London and how he could protect you from this man you've got mixed up with. He's part of the reason Wolf offered you the house.'

Iris didn't say anything. Finding out Lynx was nice and protective was not helping her resolution not to let anything happen between them.

'What was the kiss like?' Star asked.

'The best damn kiss of my life. And if you tell him that I'll curse you so that every sweet thing you eat tastes of salt.'

'As my sole income is from making cakes, that would be a harsh punishment! But I promise my lips are sealed. My point is, you enjoyed that kiss before you saw those premonitions, which shows there's an attraction there that has nothing to do with any baby-related future you might have seen.'

'That's a fair point,' Iris said. 'But one kiss doesn't necessarily mean that I want to marry him and have his babies.'

'No, true. But surely a kiss that incredible warrants further investigation to see if you have anything beyond that?'

'I did think that earlier – that while I'm here for the next few months I should take some time to find out if he's the man of my dreams or not. But I'm still in denial right now. My nan thinks I should just sleep with him as that would get him out from under my skin.'

'That's certainly one way. Or you could just talk to him, see if he's someone you want to spend more time with.'

Iris nodded. She never wanted to regret the path not taken. She could talk to Lynx at least.

'What is it you do, for work I mean?' Star asked, thankfully changing the subject.

'I make jewellery out of water. I have an online shop called The Frozen North and I make icicles, snowflakes, bubbles and chunks of ice, or even frozen flowers or little animals, and then I magically preserve them so they never melt. I turn them into necklaces and other jewellery. Everyone presumes they're made from crystal or glass or resin but no, they're just water and a little magic. They sell well. I've had a couple of celebs find and wear my pieces so that always results in good sales.'

'How does that even work?'

'Well the one thing you should know about kelpies is our affinity to water. It's a massive part of who we are. We really need it to survive. I can't go a week without a swim in the loch or sea or at least paddling in open water. We start to feel really tired and run-down without it. Just like a lot of people get the benefit of vitamin D from being outside in the sun, we need the nutrients that the sea or other fresh water gives us. A lot of our magic is based on water too. So it's very easy to do something like this...'

She held her hand out with her fingers pointing down and a single drop of water dripped from her fingertips. She waved her hand, casting her magic over it, and before it fell into her other hand it had become magically frozen, forever. She passed the solid drop to Star who was staring at her with wide eyes. She held it up to the light.

'This is beautiful,' Star said in wonder.

'And something like this is a bit more complicated...'

Iris formed a small pool of water in her hand, chilling it fractionally so it was a bit more pliable, then lifted the edges to make small petals, before freezing it completely once she had formed a perfect flower. She handed it to Star.

'When I have my tools I can produce something a bit more intricate and detailed but you get the idea. I also sometimes freeze natural things like flowers, leaves, feathers or dandelion seeds within the ice, capturing them and preserving them forever.'

'Wow, I can see why these are so popular.'

'And every piece is unique, which is part of their charm.' Iris felt very proud of her jewellery but sharing how she actually made it was not something she'd ever done before. Maybe there was something to be said for this place where everyone shared their magic so freely.

'Actually, we could use your skills on the decorating team. We're getting ready for the summer solstice next week, which is really a celebration of the sun and fire, but also a celebration of nature. We decorate the village green with real flowers but we have other decorations too. Would you be willing to help?'

Despite Iris swearing to herself that she wasn't going to get involved with village life, she liked Star and the warmth and openness of the village was definitely growing on her. And perhaps it wouldn't hurt to become friendly with a few more people.

'What kind of stuff do you want?'

'I was thinking about some kind of solstice sun-catcher we can hang from the lampposts on the village green.'

'Oh yes, I can do that. We used to make those when I was a child and hang them all round the house.'

'Great. Maybe you can incorporate something inside them, like you do with the flowers and leaves, but with something a bit more solstice-themed. Could you put fire inside it? Oh, I'll leave it up to you and the other members of the decorating team.'

'OK.' Iris was already thinking of ideas.

'Brilliant. Can you be at the village green at nine tomorrow morning?'

'Sure. I can do that.'

They wandered on a little way and Star suddenly stopped her.

'You could have a shop here on Stardust Street selling your jewellery, I'm sure it would be very popular.'

'There's already a jewellery shop here.' Iris pointed to a shop they were passing called Fire in the Heart. It obviously sold fire-themed jewellery as every piece in the window glowed with red, gold or orange as if they made from pieces of the sun.

'But very different to yours. There are a few shops that sell cakes on Stardust Street too but I've never seen it as a problem. There's enough custom for everyone. The second floor of this jewellery shop is free, you could set up your shop upstairs and that way your customers will look at their stuff too and vice versa so you would be benefitting each other.'

'You want me to set up a competing jewellery shop in the same building as the current one? Talk about making a bad impression. I thought you wanted me to make friends here. They'd be chasing me out of town before I'd even had my first customer.'

'What if I told you that Lynx owns the bottom floor? When he's not charging round the world retrieving lost magical artefacts, he does this.'

Iris felt a slow smile spread across her face. 'So he would be the person I would be in competition with?'

'If that's the way you want to look at it, yes.'

Her smile grew wider. That was the kind of petty revenge she could get on board with.

'I take it that's a yes?' Star said.

'It's definitely a yes.'

'I'll talk to Wolf and make it happen. It will probably take a day or two to get it ready.'

'And can I be the person that tells Lynx?'

Star smiled and shook her head. 'Go for it.'

CHAPTER 6

Iris knocked on Lynx's door a while later, excited to be sharing the news with him. This was going to be so much easier than dating him. They were going to be mortal enemies instead, at least at work.

He opened the door and his face lit up when he saw her.

'I have some news.'

He folded his strong arms across his chest and leaned against the doorframe. The fact that his lips twitched in a smirk made the news that much more delightful to share.

'Go on.'

'I'm going to be moving into the shop floor above yours.'

He narrowed his eyes. 'Why do I feel like there's more to this and I'm not going to like it?'

She delivered her blow. 'I make and sell jewellery too. We're going to be in competition with each other.'

To her annoyance he wasn't angry, or shocked or even frustrated, he burst out laughing.

'So that's the way you want to play it?'

'You're not mad?'

'Why would I be, nothing like a bit of healthy competition.'

She was seriously disappointed with this reaction. 'That's right. We can have a competition. The first person to earn five hundred pounds wins. Once I'm open that is.'

'Fine by me. Same terms as our last competition? If I win, you'll have dinner with me.'

She let out a shock of laughter. 'I'm not sleeping with you if I win. That feels like more of a punishment than a prize.'

'Trust me, you'd enjoy it immensely.'

'Oh you're so smug. If I win you have to kiss my feet.'

He shrugged. 'I'm not really a foot man but OK.'

She cursed herself. She should have come up with something worse than that, at least for him. She suspected she might really enjoy it.

'Fine, I'll probably see you tomorrow then. I need to get the place sorted before I start.'

'I'll be there.'

She turned to walk away.

'Oh Iris, I have something for you.'

She turned back as he disappeared inside the house and returned a moment later with a box. She recognised the label instantly.

'Is that Betty's tablet?'

'Yes. I knew moving away from Scotland would be a massive change for you so I figured I'd get you something to remind you of home.'

She took the box. 'But... But how did you know?'

'I have several Scottish friends that now live in England and the one thing they always lament over is that England doesn't sell tablet. Apparently our fudge is nowhere near as good. So I looked up places that sell it near you and found Betty's. She's a witch so it's probably going to be good stuff.'

'It is. It's the best tablet I've ever tasted. But how did you get it here so fast?'

'I have my means.' He waggled his fingers and they sparkled with red and gold magic.

She stared at the box. 'Thank you, that's ... really thoughtful.'

He shrugged. 'No problem.'

She couldn't stop staring at the box and she knew she was making it weird. It was a really lovely gesture and she wasn't sure what to do with this kindness. She turned to go but then turned back, leaned up and kissed him on the cheek.

'Thank you.'

She quickly hurried away. She turned back again when she reached the bottom of his driveway and he was still watching her.

'Doesn't mean I'm going to go easy on you when I open my shop,' she said in an attempt to get back to some normality between them.

He grinned. 'Of course not. I'd be disappointed if you did.'

She smiled and shook her head in frustration as she walked away. That bloody man.

Ness finished the dinner that Iris had made for them and with a wave of her hand the dishes flew over to the sink and started washing themselves. She started fussing with the pearls on her bracelet. Iris wasn't going to be happy.

'Are you OK?' Iris asked her. 'I thought you were happier here since we discovered the stream at the bottom of the garden.'

'I am. It's just I really need that locket back.'

'OK, we can go and see them tomorrow.' Iris looked at her watch. 'I think it's probably a bit late now.'

'I forgot the evidence we need to prove it's mine,' Ness blurted out. She sighed. She hated this. Getting old was a cruel affliction. She was forgetful, body parts didn't work as well as they used to and, worst of all, her treasured memories were slowly fading away. That's why she needed her locket back. All her memories were tied up with that locket. But she had never explained how important the locket was to her granddaughter. Iris thought she just wanted the locket back because it had been a wedding present from her husband. She didn't know the truth. Ness didn't want Iris to think she was less than she was. She was a strong, powerful woman, she wasn't this doddery old fool who she saw in the mirror every day. When had she become this person that Iris felt the need to protect? When she was Iris's age she'd felt like she could take on the world. Now she forgot something ten minutes after Iris had told her and they'd travelled halfway across the country just because Iris didn't think she could handle some snivelly little mundane if he came a calling.

'What?' Iris said, in confusion. 'That's half the reason we're here, to get your locket back. How could you forget it?'

'I know, I know. I got it out of the drawer and I must have left it on the bed or something. I've checked all our stuff and it's not there. We have to go back for it.'

Iris shook her head. 'We can't. We don't know if Christopher will be there waiting for us. It's not safe.'

'But how will we get the locket back without it?'

'We'll talk to them. I'm sure once you start talking to them about the locket and how Pops gave it to you, they'll believe you. Plus there's the wedding photo of you and Pops inside. They'll have to believe us when they see that.'

Ness wasn't so sure. The photo was very old. She didn't look anything like the woman who had married the love of her life sixty years ago. But Iris trusted these people so she had to as well. And if they didn't give her locket back, she would have to come up with a plan to retrieve it.

Morag was sitting by the fountain, watching the water sparkling in the moonlight. She loved this time of night when no one was around.

Although her peace was ruined as she watched a black cat stalk across the green towards her.

'Morag, I presume,' the cat said. He had a very posh voice, way too posh for a common cat.

'I am, and I guess you must be Viktor.' She offered out a paw to shake which he ignored.

'Vik*tor* not Vik*ta*. Please work on your enunciation. Vik*ta* is not my name. Just like your name isn't Moorag.'

'My apologies,' Morag said, taking an instant dislike to this infuriating cat.

'Let's get something straight. I don't like you.'

'The feeling is entirely mutual.'

'I'm only putting up with your presence because your owner seems to be tied to Lynx's happiness and I'm quite partial to him.'

'Iris is not my owner, she is my friend. I am not a pet, unlike you.'

'I am not a pet either.'

'The collar you're wearing tells a different story.'

Viktor grunted his disapproval. 'As your *friend* would be upset if I gouged your eyes out, I suggest you stay away from me.'

He stalked away.

'Perhaps it is you that should stay away from me, kitty.'

Viktor mumbled something she didn't catch and she smiled to herself. She'd put that round down as a win for her. She was already looking forward to the next round.

CHAPTER 7

I ris walked towards the village green the next morning, ready to join the group of people making the decorations for the summer solstice. The village was just starting to come to life, with most people heading towards Stardust Street again.

She reached the village green and looked around. The fountain was a big, beautiful thing depicting potion bottles pouring into the cauldron below. There were Victorian-style lanterns surrounding the green with huge flower garlands already draped between each of the lamps ahead of the solstice celebrations.

But there wasn't a group of people that could be the decorating team. In fact, as her eyes swung around the green, Iris realised there was no one waiting there at all. She wasn't early, but she supposed that the others could be running late.

'Hey.'

She looked up at Lynx as he fell in at her side.

'Hey, what are you doing here?'

He smirked. 'I live here, remember?'

She looked away as she suppressed a smile. It was really hard to hate this man when he was so bloody likeable.

'I thought you might be queuing for a bus the way you were standing and waiting. Thought I'd join you. It's quite exciting, we never get buses here.'

She rolled her eyes, although she was having a real problem not smiling.

'I'm part of the decorating team actually, for the summer solstice. I'm just waiting for the rest of them to turn up.'

'Ah, that would be me,' Lynx said.

She looked at him. 'What?'

'Well the garland team have already done their bit, but Star wanted something else hanging from each lamppost. As the solstice is a celebration of sun and fire, she thought I could do something similar to my jewellery, but on a bigger scale. She mentioned about maybe doing sun-catchers. But I wasn't expecting an assistant.'

'I'm not your assistant. Star saw some of my jewellery and said it would be perfect for the decorations too. She asked me to work on the sun-catchers with the rest of the decorating team.'

'There's just me,' Lynx said.

'Ah,' Iris said, wondering whether she should bail out, leave him to it. But she didn't want to let Star down and maybe it would be a good time to get to know him better, see if there was anything between them more than just a crazy-good kiss.

'Do you think you can handle it?' Lynx said.

'I can handle it just fine. We're both adults. As I said before, it doesn't need to be weird between us just because we've kissed.'

'OK then. Shall we take a seat?'

He gestured to the large oak tree at the edge of the green and they wandered over and sat down next to each other under the great branches.

Lynx took his bag off his shoulder. 'So, Star wanted something fire-related as that's my speciality.'

'Oh yes, you're a fire witch'

'Yes.' He held out his hand and a large flame suddenly burst to life in his palm. He closed his hand in a fist and the fire went out without so much as a sizzle or a bit of smoke left behind. 'And you, as you're part witch, what's your strongest element?'

'I'd love to say it was air or fire, but rather predictably my mum married a water witch.'

'But that's still pretty cool. You can freeze things, right, produce snow from your fingertips?'

She held out her palm and it gently rained from it, as if she was pouring out a watering can. With a wave of her hand the rain turned to snow, gently swirling and dancing in the air.

'See, that's pretty awesome.'

'I hope so, this is the basis of my jewellery.'

She caught one of the snowflakes in her palm, waved her other hand over it and froze it forever. She passed it to Lynx who examined it. 'Now this is lovely.'

'I do the same for icicles, raindrops, bubbles, anything you can make from water, and then make them into pendants, earrings and other jewellery.'

'I can see them being very popular.'

'Popular enough for me to win the competition?'

He laughed. 'Maybe. I think my jewellery is a bit more masculine, so we probably appeal to very different audiences.'

'So you're saying there's enough room for us both and we don't need a fight to the death?' Iris said.

'Oh no, we definitely need the fight to the death. I'm still holding out for you to have dinner with me.'

She smiled but ignored that comment. 'So what are you thinking for the decorations?'

'I work with stained glass in some of my pieces of jewellery. I was going to make some sun-shaped sun-catchers to hang from the lampposts. But I can adapt to whatever ideas you have.'

'I used to make sun-catchers when I was a kid to celebrate the solstice. Just simple orbs like this that we'd hang up around the outside of the house.'

She formed a ball of ice in her hands, making it grow to the size of a small football. And just before she magically froze it forever, she added a small loop so it would be easier to hang. She passed it to him.

'This is wonderful,' Lynx said, holding the ball up to the light and smiling when the light fragmented through it almost as if it was a crystal.

'When I make something similar and a lot smaller for my jewellery I sometimes put flowers inside, or other natural elements. And Star suggested I do something like that but she suggested we entomb fire inside. I'm not sure if that will even work.'

'That's a good idea, fire plays such a big part in our solstice celebrations.'

'But fire and ice are not a great mix.'

'Are you worried my fire will melt your ice?'

She smirked at the double entendre. 'No, it's magically frozen, it's never going to melt. I was more worried that my ice would put out your fire.'

'I don't think that would ever happen,' he said, looking at her in a way that made her pretty sure he wasn't talking about the sun-catchers anymore. She smiled at his flirting. He was going to be impossible to work with.

He focussed his attention on the orb for a moment. 'My fire is magical too so let's give it a try. How would you put the flower inside?'

'I just hold the flower in my hand and form the ball of ice around it.'

'OK, I can do that. Hold your hands out as if you're going to form an orb of ice.'

She did that and to her surprise Lynx leaned over and placed his fingers on top of hers.

'I'll form the fire and immediately you produce the orb around it.'

She nodded.

A flame appeared in his hand that looked like the end of a sparkler. It floated fractionally off his hand and he quickly removed his fingers as she created an orb of ice around it. A few moments later the sparkle was magically encased inside the frozen orb.

'Wow, it's beautiful. I really didn't think it would work,' Iris said.

'OK, so we make a load of these and hang them from the lampposts. But as they will be quite high up I think they need to be a little bigger, around the size of a beach ball.'

'I can do that.'

'And I need a better position,' Lynx said, getting up and sitting behind her so he was leaning against the tree and her back was to his chest, his massive thighs bracketing hers.

She looked at him over her shoulder. 'Really? What was wrong with how we did it before?'

'This is going to be much easier. And kinder on our backs.'

'You sound like an old man.'

'That may be, but the amount of time I spend on the floor playing with Blaze, it's much easier to do it for long periods of time leaning against the sofa. Come on, relax into me, I promise I won't bite.'

She scowled but she knew he was testing her. He expected her to say no because she couldn't cope with being so close to him and there was a huge part of her that did think that herself.

'Are you going to pick my pockets again if I do?'

He laughed. 'I promise that was a one-time-only thing. That's not the normal way I introduce myself to women.'

'So it wasn't a chat-up line.'

'I'm sure I can do better than that.'

'Like asking me to lean against you when we're making decorations?'

He grinned. 'This is practical.'

'Really? So if you were making these decorations with Wolf, this is how you'd sit?'

He laughed. 'That's fair. Look, I'm going to sit here, against the tree, but you can sit however you want. But our hands obviously have to be touching so we're going to need to sit fairly close.'

She sighed, heavily, letting him know she was doing this under protest, then leaned back into him, ignoring the way his hard chest felt against her and his glorious spicy scent that wrapped around her. But he was right, it was definitely more comfortable to sit like this.

She held her hands out, palms up, and he placed his hands in hers with his palms up too while they started creating the orbs with the sparkles inside. There was something irritatingly intimate about this. Not just the way they were sitting, the way his legs were hard against her own, or the way their hands were touching, but creating something beautiful by uniting their magic. The completed orbs were almost a representation of them, his fire, her water – or ice in this case – and how incredible it could be if they came together.

'So how do you celebrate the solstice?' Lynx said, his breath warm on the back of her neck.

'When I was a child there were flowers everywhere. Inside, outside, hanging from the trees and parts of the house. We used to spend weeks gathering them, making them into garlands or little bouquets or posies to hang up. I remember the smell, it was heaven. I'd make these orbs to hang round the outside of the house and the trees to capture all the sunlight for the following weeks and months when the daylight got shorter, and then we'd hang the orbs back up on the winter solstice to release the sunlight on our shortest day as a symbol that the days would start getting longer again. It was kind of like decorating for

Christmas hanging those orbs, watching the sunlight sparkle inside them like tiny fairy lights.'

She finished the orb and placed it to one side before starting another.

'A lot of our celebrations involved swimming in one of the lochs, mostly naked.' Iris continued and smirked when Lynx cleared his throat. 'There is nothing better than floating on top of the surface of the loch as the solstice sunrise comes up, bathing your skin in that rose gold of the first rays. We do the same at sunset too and under the moon for some of our celebrations.'

'Sounds idyllic.'

'We get a lot of peace from the water. We swim in the lochs, rivers or sea almost every day. Well, I did when I lived in Scotland. It's restorative. We have a stream at the back of our garden now, which is lovely for water bathing, but I'll need to find somewhere to swim soon enough.'

'There's a couple of pools around the outer parts of the village. There are several streams that run through the village and also little lagoons or pools created by them. If you go to the far end of our road and keep going across the grass towards the trees there's a pool there just before you go into the woods. And the opposite side, that way, out the back of Holly Lane, you'll come to the woods quite quickly but you keep following the path through the woods and you'll come to a little waterfall and a freshwater pool there. It's one of my favourite places actually. I'll take you there. Most people here don't go beyond the main village and shops but the woods are lovely and very secluded as they are still within the private village boundaries. The pool is in a little glade, it's very beautiful. I love to swim there.'

'Naked?' she teased him.

'Well yes. But if we swim together, I promise to keep my clothes on. Well, some of them.'

'We'll swim together?'

'If that's OK? Or I can just stand awkwardly on the side and watch you swim in my favourite swim spot.'

'No, of course you can swim with me.'

Why did the idea of swimming together suddenly feel even more intimate than what they were doing here? Swimming and water bathing were such huge, important parts of Iris's life, and she'd never shared them with anyone beyond her family. Though she hadn't even swam with them since she was a kid, she preferred the peace of being alone. And it wasn't the potential nudity that made it intimate, she could easily keep her clothes on or swim in a bikini or swimsuit. It was sharing such a big part of her.

Lynx must have heard the hesitation in her voice.

'It's fine, I can show you where it is and leave you to it. If swimming is a private thing for you, I wouldn't want to intrude.'

'It's not a private thing. I've just always swam alone. I've never found someone I'd want to go swimming with or that would like to go swimming with me. A lot of people shy away from open water swimming, especially in Scotland where it gets very cold.'

'I get that. But I've always loved outdoor swimming. And I understand what it feels like to just enjoy that peace and silence. If you want, we can enjoy it together. But there's no pressure.'

'No, I'd like that.'

'OK. We'll go, maybe tomorrow?'

She nodded, trying to ignore the flutter of her heart at that thought. It didn't mean anything, it was just a swim. She decided to change the subject.

'How do you celebrate the solstice?'

'Well, it's a festival of the sun, we get up in the morning and watch the sunrise. Many witches go to significant places around the country like Stonehenge. On the morning of the solstice the sun rises exactly behind the Heel Stone, outside the main circle, and the sunlight is directed straight to the heart of the circle. We have something like that here, not standing stones that have been there for thousands of years, but the fountain in the village green. It was built in the exact right place to capture the sun's rays when it appears over the hills on the morning of the summer solstice. For a few minutes it reflects off the water coming from the potion bottles in the fountain and into the cauldron so it looks like a golden potion. One of our most popular gold potions is the one for happiness, so we believe that if the fountain sparkles with gold on the morning of the solstice then the village will have happiness for the rest of the year.'

'I like that.'

'Then we spend the day celebrating. There's always music, dancing and singing on the green and lots of food to eat. Some people prefer to celebrate with their own families, so not all the villagers will celebrate together and that's OK. We light a bonfire in the evening as the sun sets. Some people will write their wishes or resolutions for the year ahead on bits of papers, then throw them into the fire and the smoke releases their wish or goal so it can come true. When the fire starts to go out some people jump over it to bring them luck in love. Couples will often jump over it together.'

Iris smiled. 'I love the sound of a community celebration. We've never done anything like that. We've never been part of a community of witches or kelpies.'

'I do love that part of village life. There's a lot of nosy, interfering people here and everyone knows everything about everyone, but I do love how they all come together. And if you end up staying here, for good, you'll be able to get involved in the eight village celebrations that take place throughout the year.'

She smiled at that but then frowned. 'The plan was never to stay.'

'I know, but plans change.'

'Home is Scotland, it's the lochs, river and hills, it's the farmhouse where I've lived for almost my entire life. It's the memories and familiarity I have there. I like it here in Midnight but I'm struggling with the idea of leaving my home. Despite what I saw yesterday, I love my farmhouse too much.'

Lynx was silent for a moment. 'Despite what you saw?'

Iris cursed softly.

'You... saw yourself here in the future?' Lynx asked. 'Is that what made you run out of my house with such speed yesterday – because you didn't like what you saw of your future?'

She shook her head. 'I didn't run because I didn't like what I saw. I've never seen my own future before, that's not something I can do so that was a big shock in itself, never mind the content of the premonition.'

He was silent again.

'But yesterday, you said you saw my future. But now you're saying you've seen your future too.'

'I didn't see my future. I saw yours.'

'And you were part of it?'

'Yes. But it's not as straightforward as that. As I said before, what I see is only one possible future.'

'But one of the futures that's possible is us, together, here?'

The orb she was in the middle of making flopped uselessly around the spark and melted in a pool of slush. She quickly dropped it on the floor. What could she say? She didn't want to lie but saying yes almost felt like a lie too because what if what she'd seen never happened?

'Lynx, I can't tell you what I saw, because then it might become a self-fulfilling prophecy. You'll make it happen because it's been foretold, rather than it happening naturally because you want it to happen.'

He was silent and she didn't know whether he agreed with that or not.

'That's fair, I suppose,' Lynx said eventually. 'Can you at least tell me if we're friends in the future you've seen?'

She turned to look at him. 'The very best of friends.'

His smile spread across his face. Why was he so calm about this? She'd all but told him they were together in the future and he was just taking it in his stride.

'I have one more question and I promise not to ask anything else, but this one is the most important. Is your future a happy one?' Lynx asked.

She felt touched by that. He didn't want to know if he was happy or rich or successful, which most people would ask when faced with a premonition of their future. He wanted to know if *she* was happy in his future.

'Yeah it is, I seem ridiculously happy. Like I said, it's not that I don't want that future, it's just I'm battling with seeing everything laid out in front of me as if I no longer have a choice. I want to feel like it happens organically, not just because I've seen it.'

'I understand that. So it's not that you don't want it, it's more that you want to get used to the idea?'

'Yes, and feel like I'm still in control of my own life.'

He nodded. 'I get it. There's no rush to make that future come true, whatever it is. But *if* in some far-off distant future we do end up together, married or whatever, it doesn't have to be here. Or at the least we can spend half our time here and half our time in Scotland. Scotland is your roots, your heritage, it's who you are. I'd never want to take that away from you.'

She smiled, warming to him even more. 'I like that idea. *If* we get together.'

'Yeah of course.'

'I still haven't decided whether I like you.'

He grinned. 'I'll have to work on that.'

'You do that.'

CHAPTER 8

After going home to get changed into some old clothes, Iris walked towards Stardust Street a while later so she could make a start on getting the shop ready.

Wolf had been round the night before to explain the technicalities of owning a shop on Stardust Street and ask her what she wanted to make the shop happen. Having never owned a shop before, she hadn't really known what to ask for. All of her sales had been online so she'd never had to think about shop space before. Wolf had told her that most of the shops had themes, which she'd noticed in the impressively decorated entrances and interiors of the ones she'd seen. As her jewellery was made from ice, she'd suggested some kind of ice theme inside.

Wolf had showed her an really amazing magical

virtual reality program he'd created where she could wear a headset and see the shop in what he called augmented reality. She could build what she wanted in the VR program, using the shape of the empty shop as a guide, and then he'd make it come true for her. It all sounded very technical and exciting. She was looking forward to having a play with it in her shop.

She had spent the rest of the night before replenishing all of her stock so she'd have jewellery to sell in her shop. Making the frozen ice parts was easy, adding the fittings, clasps and settings was a bit trickier so that had taken her many hours.

She was excited to be starting off down this new road. It was going to be very different to anything else she'd ever done before. So this afternoon she was going to plan out her shop, transform it, at least electronically, into something beautiful and maybe she could open later on this week.

Lynx's shop was open so he must already be here. She stepped inside to find the shop was stunning, decorated to look like she'd walked inside an active volcano. The walls were lined with gorgeous rock formations, with bright red and orange lava seemingly oozing down the walls. There was even steam rising from the lava flows, too. Around the room, perched on top of rocks and pools of lava, were pieces of jewellery that gleamed with red, gold and orange. Some of them were made from metal, some from stained glass, some looked like they were made from fragments of fire or the sun. They were incredible.

She moved into the shop and saw Lynx working away at the back, with no top on, infuriatingly.

She knew she'd said too much earlier. She hadn't told him they were together in their future but he'd obviously jumped to that conclusion. She wondered if he intended to tease her and flirt with her constantly until she just gave in and dated him and this no shirt malarkey was part of that.

As he moved, the sunlight caught the muscles on his arms. Iris swore under her breath but Lynx must have heard her, despite the noise at the back of the shop, because he turned around and flashed her a big smile.

'Why are you working with no top on?' she asked and regretted it instantly. She didn't want him to know she'd noticed, but how could she not, the man was glorious. He was broad, with muscles on his arms, chest, and even the faint lines of a six-pack. Hair gathered around his belly button and trailed beneath the waistband of his jeans. And the whole beautiful package was sweaty and dirty and that just made him so much sexier for some reason. 'What would you do if I walked in here with no clothes on?'

The smile on his face grew to ridiculous proportions. 'Well, that's the kind of work uniform I could get on board with.'

She let out a groan of frustration and stormed off towards the stairs.

'Wait, Iris, if me not wearing a top offends you, I can put it back on. It wasn't done to piss you off, it just gets so hot back here.' He gestured around him and for the first time she realised he had two big furnaces burning away on either side of the shop. How had she not noticed them before? Oh yes, there was too much naked chest in the room.

He didn't wait for an answer. He summoned his t-shirt from across the room, used it to wipe some of the sweat and grime off his chest and then pulled it on, which was a huge disappointment, annoyingly.

'What are you doing anyway?' she asked, trying hard to not to pay attention to how good he looked in that white t-shirt, the material clinging to every curve in his arms.

'Well some of the jewellery I make is from using metal. Copper is one of my favourites as it has that beautiful rose-gold look to it. Do you want to come and see?'

She let out a huff. 'I suppose it would be quite interesting to watch your process.'

She moved closer.

'So right now I'm using a copper rod to make a leaf ring. I heat it up in the fire to make it soft enough to bend or mould.' He carried the rod over to the furnace and stuck it into the flames until the metal became white hot. He brought it back to the anvil. 'Now I continue hammering it until I get the shape I want. The more I hammer, the thinner it will get.'

He started banging it and it was fascinating to watch the metal take shape under his hands. He picked up a smaller hammer and started tapping away at the leaf part of the rod to make the veins in the leaf. It was so small and delicate, it was very impressive to watch him turn the metal into something else.

'This one is pretty much done, now I just have to shape it into a ring,' Lynx said.

He put the rod back in the fire again and then took it out and, using a pair of metal tongs, wrapped it round a metal pole, shaping it and twisting it until the ring had a leaf on one end and a curl of metal at the other that sat perfectly below the leaf. Then he used a wire brush to get all the black off the ring and it wasn't long before the ring was glowing with that gorgeous copper colour.

He pulled it off the metal pole and held it out to show her.

'Is that not hot?'

'The metal cools very quickly.'

She stepped closer to look at it. 'It's beautiful and so delicate.'

'Here, you can have it.'

'Oh no, I couldn't possibly.'

'Take it, I can make another just as easily.'

Iris hesitated and then picked up the ring, sliding it

onto her finger. It fitted perfectly. 'Thank you, it's lovely. You know, you make it very hard for me not to like you.'

'Well that's the plan.'

She moved her hand around so the ring caught the light. 'I would have thought, as a witch, you'd be sitting back, drinking a cup of tea and letting your magic do all the work for you.'

'I love the process of it. I find it very cathartic and relaxing. I do use magic for some of my jewellery but not stuff like this. And I do cheat a bit. The fires are witch fire. So they never go out until I want them to, I can control the temperature with just a wave of my hand and I can't get burned from them. Hence the not wearing a top and no need for protective gear.'

'Clever. Thanks for the ring. I better go and sort out the upstairs.'

'Well, I could come and give you a hand in a bit.'

'What, so you can nobble the competition?' she teased.

He laughed. 'Oh, I'm going to pull out all the big guns, whatever it takes.'

She rolled her eyes and made for the stairs. 'Feel free to take your top off again.'

His eyes widened with shock and joy at that comment. 'Did you like what you saw?'

Her cheeks flushed. 'I didn't mean for my pleasure. I meant, you should be comfortable in your own shop, I don't want you to feel like you have to cover up for me. You just carry on as normal.'

She was making it weird again, so she hurried up the stairs away from him.

'You didn't answer my question,' Lynx called after her.

She didn't reply, cursing herself for telling him to take his top off, what had she been thinking?

She walked through the door of what would be her new shop and looked around. It was dusty and in desperate need of a clean but three large windows let in a lot of light which would showcase her water and ice jewellery perfectly.

At the back of the space, hidden away, was a small kitchenette and a store cupboard containing various cleaning utensils.

She waved her hand and a bowl of hot soapy water started filling itself in the sink. She waved her other hand and the vacuum cleaner floated out of the cupboard, plugged itself into the wall and started vacuuming round the shop. Within ten minutes the place was spotless. Magic definitely had its benefits.

She lifted the virtual reality headset from the bag Wolf had given her and slid it on. She could still see the shop through the headset, but there was also a toolbar she could use. She'd never used a VR headset before but she had used several design programs for marketing her jewellery online, so these tools seemed familiar. She picked up the two handsets so she could access the tools. She selected a tool that looked likely and with a swish of her hand she painted an entire wall with ice. She laughed – it looked so real but she knew it was only on the VR headset right now. Wolf would make these images a reality later. She covered all the walls in ice, some of it dripping down the walls in frozen icicles, and added icicles over the windows too. Then she decided she would create little tunnels and separate ice chambers, one for earrings, one for necklaces, one for bracelets, one for rings and one for other jewellery like cufflinks or brooches. She started painting the room with ice walls and icicles, creating tunnels of ice that led to different ice chambers. She added ice tables or platforms to showcase her jewellery, then added lights, moving them around to get them in the exact right spots to show off her jewellery perfectly.

She looked around at the beautiful room she had created. It looked like she'd just walked into a cave in the deepest Arctic – all it needed now was a polar bear. Just for a laugh, she added one to the ice room and giggled when it sniffed and grunted as it walked around the room.

She heard footsteps on the stairs and after a few moments Lynx appeared, carrying two mugs.

She directed the polar bear towards him and laughed as it appeared to sniff at him. 'Get him, eat him.'

'Do I want to know what it is that you're encouraging to eat me?'

She laughed. 'Death by bear, just as I predicted.'

He laughed and she took the headset off, disappointed to see the shop hadn't changed to a beautiful ice chamber as she'd seen with the headset on. But it hopefully would soon enough.

'Can I see what you've done?' Lynx said.

She handed him the VR equipment and he looked around the room she'd created. 'Cute bear. Probably not too practical to have a real one here, but you could have everlasting ice sculptures.'

'Oh, good idea.'

He moved around the room and she saw him smiling as he took in all the tunnels and ice chambers.

'This looks spectacular,' Lynx said, handing back the headset. 'I can't wait to see it for real.'

'Me too. It's very clever, isn't it.'

'Wolf is great at stuff like that.' He handed her a mug. 'I thought you could probably do with a coffee and a break. It's hazelnut.'

'Thank you, that's very kind.' She took a sip. 'Ooh, this is nice.'

'All the coffees from Mystical Morsels are amazing and they do so many flavours of coffees. I had a pineapple one the other day.'

Iris smiled. It was still going to take some getting used to that she now lived in a place that had a potion shop; a shop that sold cauldrons, candles and everything else a witch could need; a shop that sold every herb and spice imaginable for potion or spell work; and, in the case of Star's shop, a place that sold cakes to help solve every possible problem. She wondered if Star had a cake to solve the problem of really liking a man when she really didn't want to.

'So you like living here?' Iris asked, taking another sip.

'I never used to. I was born and raised here. For a few years we moved to a mundane village when I was a child. My parents wanted to give us some normality rather than only knowing the world of magic but Wolf and I were bullied for being different, Wolf a lot more and a lot worse than me. Even our parents were treated as outcasts. When my mum got sick, no one helped my dad or us and it made us feel very alone. We came back here but shortly after my mum died and then my dad died when I was thirteen. Wolf was my guardian. He looked after me, and the rest of the villagers helped too.'

Lynx took a sip of his drink before he continued.

'Wolf's brush with the outside world made him wary of it. He closeted himself away and never wanted to leave, although of course as he grew up he did leave several times for one reason or another, but never for very long. But for me, I wanted so much more. I'd had a taste of it and I wanted to see it all. Yes there are dark, dangerous, scary parts of the world, yes there are people that are nasty and some that are downright evil. But there is also goodness and kindness and a desire to help people, and in my experience the good far outweighs the bad. There are parts of the world that are just incredible and beautiful and I wanted to see every little corner of it. So as soon as I could I left the village and travelled the world, saw so many wondrous things. I met other witches and learned more about my magic than I thought possible. But... I always loved coming back here, which surprised me. I thought I would hate it because it's so secluded and cut off from the world. I still want to visit and enjoy the world but this is home and I think it always will be. Unless of course, I marry a beautiful Scottish woman, then it will be home for half the year and the other half will be spent in Scotland, swimming in lochs and rivers.'

Iris smiled but decided to ignore his last comment. 'I can definitely see the attraction of Midnight. Having somewhere where you're safe and where you can be completely yourself is wonderful. And raising a family here, knowing your children would never be bullied or made to feel different, that's pretty special.'

Lynx nodded. 'When Wolf had Blaze last year, I fell in love with her instantly and I know without doubt this is the safest place for her. The weather being so warm lately, Wolf and Star are often out in the front garden with her. Blaze sits there trying out her magic in that way kids do, where they have no idea they are doing it, or what they are doing, and no one bats an eye. And I know if I ever have children, which may be a long way off, I'd want to raise them here.'

Iris smiled as the memory of her and Lynx holding their baby pushed its way to the front of her mind.

'And you want that? Children, marriage, the whole caboodle? Won't that interfere with your need to travel and see the world?'

'Blaze makes me broody. I want the life that Wolf has, happily married with the woman he loves, a child, probably another on the way. I don't know if that will ever happen for me but I'd like to think that one day it might. What about you, do you want the caboodle?'

She sighed. 'Yeah, I did. I mean I do. But I've never found someone... worthy enough to want forever with.'

'Worthy enough? What do they have to do to be worthy enough?'

'I don't think it's a big ask, not being a complete dick is a good start. I've only gone out with mundane men, been in love a few times too, but it never ends well.'

'That's where you're going wrong, you need to find yourself a nice witch man.'

Iris rolled her eyes.

'I don't mean me, just someone you can trust to be yourself with. I've dated mundane women too and I always felt like I wasn't being completely honest with them when I hid my magic. And what kind of relationship is that? The one or two women I did talk to about my magic, the relationship fell apart shortly after. They either thought I was pulling some kind of stunt and lying or were just completely freaked out by it. I'm not sure that witches and mundanes can ever have a real relationship or even a friendship if you can't be the real you.'

'That's it exactly, I've had the same issues with men. Jack even proposed after two years of dating and I said yes, I thought we were going to be together forever. But when I told him the truth he didn't want to know me. I was so hurt by that. I was still the same person he fell in love with, just with the added bonus of a bit of magic.'

'You want to be with someone who will love every single part of you,' Lynx said, softly.

'And that's what I mean by worthy enough.'

'No, I get it.'

'And that's why I said I *did* want that. I'm not sure if I'll ever find it,' Iris said.

Although according to the future she'd seen, she found it with Lynx.

'Yeah, me too. I don't know if it will ever happen and I would love to have a family of my own one day. I feel a bit sad that I've never met the right woman that I'd like to share that with.'

She chewed her lip. 'If you promise not to ask me

any questions, I'll tell you one thing that I saw in your future.'

His eyes widened. 'OK.'

'I saw you with your child in the not-too-distant future.'

A smile grew on his face. 'I have a child?'

'Remember what I said before, it's one possible future. Nothing is set in stone.'

Lynx stared at her and when he spoke his voice was rough. 'Is it... our child?'

'I can't tell you that. And you promised not to ask any questions.'

'But if you told me more details, like who the mother of my child is, then when I meet her, I could make sure I pull out all the stops to impress her, charm her with my brilliance.'

'If it's meant to be then it will happen without any interference from you. And what if you pulling out all the stops to impress her is the thing that turns her off?'

'How could she possibly be turned off by my brilliance?' he teased.

She smiled and rolled her eyes. 'You're so smug, it's not an attractive quality, you know.'

Although she knew that wasn't true. He didn't take himself too seriously and that made her smile.

'So no clues at all.'

'I've already told you too much. And it might never happen so don't get too carried away.'

'Five minutes ago, I didn't think it would ever happen, so I'll take a possible future over no chance any day.'

'Why do you think it will never happen?'

'I think my problem is I'm too picky. I date a woman, we have fun, but then I end it because I'm searching for something deeper, something more. And I don't even know what that looks like. I want that spark, that instant connection, and I've never felt that with anyone. Well, there was one woman but I probably pissed her off with my brilliance.'

She smirked.

'Maybe that crazy in love never really happens. Maybe I should just settle down with a nice woman and stop looking for the impossible.'

'Definitely not. Never settle for anything less than that head-over-heels-in-love feeling, that great big love story that fills your heart to the top. If you marry a *nice* woman you quite like, I guarantee you'll be divorcing her after a few years. Real love is the kind that lasts forever. Tell me about the woman you had that instant spark with.'

'It was you.'

Iris laughed. She'd walked straight into that one. 'You can't tell me you've fallen in love with me after one kiss.'

'One incredible kiss, the best first kiss I've ever had. But no, I never said that, I said I felt a spark. From the moment you took my hand I felt something I'd never felt before. Which is why I'd like you to go out to dinner with me to see if there's something more than just a spark.'

She had felt that too, that incredible connection, it was something special.

'I'll always remember that kiss too,' she said, softly, as she stepped closer to him. His eyes fell to her lips. Then she fixed him with a scowl. 'As the moment you stole the locket from me.'

She stepped away and he groaned. 'I do feel really crappy about that. But don't tell me if the situation had been reversed you wouldn't have taken advantage of the situation too.'

She knew she probably would have, but she wasn't going to admit that to him. She wanted him to feel bad about what he'd done.

'I just think the kiss can't have been as good as you claim it was if you had time to think about and execute stealing the locket. If I was enjoying the best kiss of my life, my attention would have been one hundred percent on that.'

Her attention had been one hundred percent on that, because she'd never realised he was stealing the locket.

'My attention was a hundred percent on you, but then I moved my hand to your hip and felt the locket digging into my palm and I... I am sorry, I never meant to hurt you.'

'Oh, I'm made of stronger stuff than that. But, I suppose, I forgive you.'

He smiled. 'So does that mean we can be friends?'

She thought about it and nodded. 'We can be friends.'

He stuck out his hand. She didn't really want to shake it, knowing she'd feel that connection all over again, but she couldn't exactly refuse. She averted her eyes when she took it, focussing on their hands rather than the jolt of awareness, the way her heart leapt, the spark that burned like fire and that ache of need for him. She released his hand and looked up at him and knew instantly he'd felt the same.

She was in big trouble.

CHAPTER 9

L ynx was working away at the back of his shop, banging the hell out of a copper rod. That woman was going to be the death of him. Iris might as well have dragged him to a watery grave, as the kelpies were known for, because he was done for. His every thought, every breath was filled with her. And when they touched it made it so much worse.

It was clearly just an infatuation, something he needed to get over, but he'd never felt this way about a woman before. And he was pretty damn sure that she felt the same too. Which begged the question, why was she fighting it so hard?

He knew he'd pissed her off when he'd stolen the locket from her, but that didn't seem enough of a reason not to at least investigate the spark between them. Although the fact they now lived in the same village was probably part of the problem too. If this was going to be her new home, she probably didn't want to get involved with him and make things awkward between them when they had to see and even work together every day. He could understand that. He'd never dated anyone from the village before. Not that he'd had strict rules against such a thing. If there had been someone he liked enough, he would have dated them but he could appreciate how awkward that would be if it all went wrong. But he and Iris were both adults who, he assumed, could be sensible about it if they did get together and then broke up.

Or was it the child she'd seen? There was a part of him that hoped it was their child, but if it wasn't, if she'd seen him happily married with another woman, then she might not want to get involved with him, only for it to end in a few months or years when he met his future wife.

He knew she was battling against what she felt was a predestined path and trying to prove that she had control over her own life, and he could understand shying away from that path to a certain extent. But what if that path was them together, married with children? Surely then she wouldn't avoid that just to prove she was in charge of her own destiny? That felt like cutting your nose off to spite your face. She'd said that her future made her ridiculously happy shouldn't she be running towards it, not away from it?

He sighed as he battered the copper rod beyond recognition. It didn't really matter her reasons. It was quite clear she didn't want anything to happen between them, not now at least, and he had to respect that.

The door opened and his friend Erin walked in. He had known her for way too long and generally their conversations revolved around teasing each other mercilessly.

'I hear you have a girlfriend,' Erin said with no preamble.

He frowned as he stared at his completely ruined copper rod. Only Wolf and Star knew about the kiss in London and he knew they wouldn't say anything to anyone. He doubted Iris would have told anyone, so he wasn't sure where Erin had got that information from.

He turned to look at her. 'I'm not sure what you mean.'

'Our newest resident, Iris McKenzie. Apparently the two of you were seen looking very cosy together under the tree on the green this morning.'

He cursed under his breath. He sometimes forgot how quickly rumours or embellishment spread in Midnight. He supposed he had looked pretty cosy with Iris but it certainly hadn't been the high drama Erin was making it out to be. Good job she didn't know about the kiss in London.

'That was nothing,' Lynx muttered.

Erin laughed. 'So why are you blushing?'

'Because of how it's been misconstrued.'

She studied him for a moment. 'You like her.'

'I don't really know her.'

But that didn't stop his need for her.

'But you'd like to,' Erin smirked.

'Did you come here just to annoy me?'

'Isn't that normally why I come here? But now I think I need to introduce myself to my new best friend. I hear she's opening a shop upstairs, another jewellery shop. That's got to be galling.'

'I don't mind the competition.'

'I bet you don't when it's a pretty woman.'

He grinned and shook his head. 'It's not like that. It's just been a big change for her, moving here from Scotland, and I want her to settle in and be happy. If opening up a jewellery shop helps her, I'm all for it.'

'Oh I really need to meet her, I can see she's made quite the impression on you. Is she upstairs?'

'Yes, but Erin, be kind. She's had a rough few days.'

'I'm always kind.'

'Not to me.'

'But where would be the fun in that?'

Lynx rolled his eyes as Erin ran up the stairs.

Iris was busy making some more jewellery. The shop was much bigger than she'd envisaged and she wanted enough things to sell to fill it.

She heard a female voice at the top of the stairs.

'Hello!' she called. The accent was Irish so it definitely wasn't Star.

'Hello,' Iris said.

A woman with long blonde hair streaked with blue walked in, a big smile on her face.

'Hi, I'm Erin.'

'Iris. Good to meet you.'

'I'm part of the welcoming committee.'

'Is there one?'

'Well, unofficially. Secretly, it's my opportunity to be super nosy about the newcomer.'

Iris laughed at the honesty.

'There are rumours about you and Lynx being an item already, apparently you two were seen cuddled up on the village green earlier. So I needed to come and meet you.'

Iris flushed. 'That wasn't... what it looked like.'

'Lynx said the same thing, but the word is that you two looked pretty cosy.'

'We were just sitting together making decorations for the summer solstice.'

Erin laughed. 'They always make something out of nothing here, but in my experience there's no smoke without fire.'

Iris smiled and shook her head. Village life was going to take a lot of getting used to.

'Will you come to potions club on Wednesday night? It's a good laugh and everyone is lovely, no one takes it very seriously.'

'I, umm...'

Maybe she should embrace the community spirit. She couldn't be anti-social if she was going to open a shop. Everyone was going to be curious about the new girl and her jewellery, which meant she had to practise being friendly, not closet herself away like she'd been doing for most of her life.

'I'm afraid I can't take no as an answer,' Erin said.

'Well in that case I suppose I better.'

'That's the spirit.' Erin stepped closer, looking at the jewellery that Iris was making, 'These are beautiful.'

'Thank you.'

'Lynx is going to have stiff competition.'

'That's the idea. I was hoping my presence here would piss him off but he seems to have taken it in his stride.'

Erin laughed loudly. 'I can see I'm going to like you. Why would you want to piss him off?'

'We met in London, before I came here, and he... well let's say he did something that deserves revenge.'

'Oh I definitely need more details.'

'I'm too embarrassed to tell them.'

'Is that why you moved here? For revenge?'

Iris laughed. 'No, I'm not so petty as to upend my whole life for revenge. No, sadly, I've got myself mixed up with what turned out to be a dangerous man, so Lynx invited me here to protect me. I was worried about my nan so I came here so she would be safe.'

'Oh, that's nice of him.'

'It is, rather annoyingly. So revenge has to be fairly low-level.'

Erin grinned, moving closer. Suddenly she gasped.

'Dear Gods. You're a kelpie.'

Iris's heart leapt. She hadn't been planning on telling anyone that, such was the bad reputation of kelpies.

'I, umm...'

'No need to look so alarmed. My best friend was a kelpie. Oh, we had such fun growing up, her with her water magic, me with my air and wind. I thought she was amazing. I was a little bit in love with her if I'm honest. Her family moved to Japan with her dad's work when she was sixteen and we lost contact after that. As soon as I got close enough to sense you, I could feel it. It's the same energy she had.'

'I... wow, I've never met another kelpie before, outside of my family. I never even knew there were any left.'

'Oh, I've never met another, so I think they're quite rare. But both her parents were, and her sister, so there are definitely some out there. Can you change appearance too?'

Iris changed from her normal self to a wrinkled, weathered elderly man.

Erin laughed with delight. 'Oh, I'm really going to like you. Kelpie magic and looking for revenge on Lynx, this couldn't be any more perfect. I think the man has a little crush on you.'

Iris changed back and decided that, as Erin had been so enthusiastic about her kelpieness, she would be a bit honest with her.

'Irritatingly, the feeling is mutual.'

Erin howled with laughter. 'Oh, this is too good. Rather than succumb to his charms, you'd rather exact revenge. It's going to drive him mad.'

'That's the idea.'

Although Iris wasn't going to be completely honest about all the reasons she was holding back, like her future written in the stars that she was currently fighting against.

'This is brilliant.' Erin glanced out of the window and cursed.

Iris followed her gaze to see a giant of a man walking past the shop. 'Who's that?'

'That's Storm Quinn. He's relatively new in the village too, been here a month. He's a right grump, doesn't like anyone, especially me. I don't particularly like him either but unfortunately for me I keep having sex dreams about him and I seem to bump into him every day with all his scowls and anger.'

Iris burst out laughing. 'Oh no, that's inconvenient.'

'It really is. I find it so embarrassing. Thankfully, they're only dreams and he doesn't know but that doesn't stop me blushing like a schoolgirl every time I see him. Right, I must go. I'll see you Wednesday, at potions club. It's at Ashley's house. Lavender Cottage, Sycamore Street. Seven o'clock.'

'I'll be there. But listen, could we keep the whole kelpie thing between ourselves? Wolf, Star and Lynx know but I worry how others will react to it. Kelpies don't have the best reputation.'

'My lips are sealed.'

Erin gave her a wave and walked back down the stairs. Iris leaned over the banister to hear what she'd say to Lynx on her way out.

'I think Iris is going to be my new best friend,' Erin said.

'Wonderful,' Lynx said, dryly, which made Iris snort.

But then she smiled. She knew Erin was being flippant and they weren't kids anymore, but she'd never had a best friend before and that thought made her feel warm on the inside.

Iris had spent the rest of the day tweaking the design and layout of the shop using the VR headset, adding ice sculptures, more lights and icicles until it was perfect. She had spent a lot of time making more stock too, trying new styles, different sizes, in the hope she would have something for everyone.

She grabbed her bags and went downstairs. Lynx was packing up ready to go too.

'How's it going up there?'

'Stock-wise, I'm ready. The room is finished on the computer program, Wolf just has to work his magic now. Depending how long that takes, I should be ready to open the day after tomorrow. Are you ready to have your ass whipped?' Iris said.

Lynx laughed. 'I am. I'm presuming we're only judging it on shop sales, not online?'

'That seems fair.' She glanced at a few price tags of his jewellery, forty pounds, fifty, thirty-five, very similar prices to hers. So he would have to sell approximately the same amount of jewellery as her to win. It would probably take a few days for both of them to get near to five hundred pounds too.

'Before you go, Wolf would like to talk to you about the locket.'

'Oh, of course. Should I go and get my nan? It's her locket really.'

'No, Wolf was quite adamant about only wanting to talk to you about it, not Ness. I'm not sure why, but we can go together if you want.'

'Sure, OK.' Iris was a bit confused by this but hopefully she could at least finally get the locket back for her nan. She just hoped they believed it was hers without any evidence, as that was still sitting up in Scotland.

They left the shop and, with a wave of his hand, Lynx locked it.

She glanced up and smiled when she realised the shop sign had changed. Instead of Fire in the Heart, it was now called Fire and Ice.

'Did you do this?'

'Yes, it needed a new name to reflect the new ownership. People need to know about you and your jewellery.'

'Thank you, that's really nice.'

He shrugged. 'No big deal.'

She couldn't help feeling touched by that, even if it was a symbol of their unity that she wasn't sure she wanted to advertise. She didn't want anyone else to think they were together.

They started walking back through the street towards the village green. Lots of other shop owners were leaving and making their way home and a few of them were looking over at her curiously. Or were they looking at them, wondering if they were together, just like Erin had said?

'Erin seems nice,' Iris said.

'She is, well most people. She generally loves to give me a hard time. But for the most part I give as good as I get.'

'And you two, there's no romantic history between you?'

'Oh no, I've known her for I think fifteen years, maybe more. She's like an annoying little sister to me. Besides which, Erin is dating a witch from outside the village, Greg I think his name is, he works in finance.'

Erin hadn't mentioned that when she'd talked about her inappropriate feelings for Storm earlier.

'She, umm... knows I'm a kelpie,' Iris said. 'Apparently her friend was one when she was growing up so she felt it as soon as she came near me. It wasn't really something I was going to share with anyone as kelpies have such a bad reputation, but I guess a lot of people might be able to sense that me and Ness are different to them.'

'They might. I certainly did, but I didn't think kelpie, I just presumed you were a witch. Your aura is completely unique but the world of magic is a curious thing, there are witches out there that can do things we never thought possible, so I wasn't concerned that you were different. But if anyone guesses and gives you a hard time about it, they'll have me to answer to. And

Wolf. As mayor of the village it's important to him that all witches are welcome here, regardless of their background, and that this is a safe place for them. He would want everyone here to treat you in the same way, so if you meet any resistance to you being here, you must tell us so we can deal with it.'

'I will, thank you.'

They approached a house which Iris assumed was Wolf's, although it wasn't any grander or bigger than anyone else's. Clearly being mayor didn't come with any trappings, or at least nothing showy to prove he was important.

Lynx knocked on the door and after a few moments Star answered it.

'Hey, how's it all going in the shop?' she asked, stepping back to let them in.

'Great,' Iris said. 'I've finished the design so it's ready for Wolf to make it into a reality and I have enough stock to fill the shop. I should be ready to open soon. And my competition has been annoyingly magnanimous.'

Lynx laughed.

They followed Star down to the kitchen to find Wolf there with a little girl on his lap. Iris assumed this was Blaze. He was feeding her something that was so bright orange it was likely to be pureed pumpkin.

'Iris, hello, thank you for coming to see us,' Wolf

said as he looked up from feeding time. 'Have you finished with the VR design?'

'Yes.' She handed him the headset and tablet. 'It's all in there.'

'Great, I'll get that done for you tomorrow morning. It should be ready for you to move your stuff in tomorrow afternoon.'

'Thank you.'

Just then a black cat jumped up on the table and eyed her suspiciously.

'You're Iris, I presume,' the cat drawled.

'Hello, yes, you must be Viktor.'

'I am. And you're a kelpie, I hear.'

'Part kelpie, part witch,' Iris said.

'I have met kelpies before in a previous life. I feel like they are misunderstood so I'm prepared to give you a chance,' Viktor said, haughtily, as if he was the one in charge of the village. 'Your fox on the other hand. I'm not sure whether I can let her stay.'

'Viktor,' Star said, warningly.

'I met her last night,' Viktor went on, completely unabashed.

'You did?'

'I did not like her.'

'Morag is lovely. A little bit blunt maybe, sometimes she's a bit grumpy, but you two have a lot in common.'

'I don't have anything in common with a fox.'

'Well fortunately we don't kick anyone out of the village just because you don't like them,' Wolf said.

'She will have to prove herself to me,' Viktor said.

'How can she do that?' Iris said, trying not to laugh that this cat was taking it all so seriously.

'I will be watching,' Viktor said.

'OK,' Iris said, slowly. 'I'll be sure to pass that on.'

'You do that,' Viktor said, before jumping off the table and walking out of the cat flap with his tail high in the air.

'Don't mind him,' Lynx said. 'He's filled with his own self-importance.'

'And he's a little upset he's no longer the only talking animal in the village,' Wolf said.

'He'll get over it,' Star said.

'Anyway, we wanted to talk to you about the locket and its history and your connection to it,' Wolf said.

'Well, as I said to Lynx, the locket is my nan's, she would certainly be able to tell you more about it than I could.'

'And I can talk to her if I feel I need more information about it, but I didn't want to worry her.'

'Worry her?'

Wolf stood up and passed Blaze to Lynx. Lynx's face lit up and the little girl reached out for his hair. Wolf went to a cupboard and took out a small box. He brought it back to the table and opened it to show the locket sitting inside. Iris had known it was safe in the

139

village somewhere, but seeing it now made her let out a little sigh of relief.

'Can you tell me what you know about the locket?' Wolf said.

'It was a wedding gift from my grandad to my nan. She wore it on her wedding day, over sixty years ago. Before her, my grandad's mum wore it on her wedding day and her mum before that. As far as I know, it's been in our family for around three hundred years but it could be a lot longer. It was listed in one of my ancestors' possessions when she passed in 1719, which is the first mention of it we can find. There is a drawing of it in a book of pressed flowers that is dated 1747. Beyond that I have no idea when or how it was made, and whether it was always in our family or how our family acquired it, but the women of the family have worn it on their wedding days as far back as we know. It's something my nan has worn every day since her wedding but she has always charmed it to look like something else. We don't know if the stones are precious, we never had it valued or authenticated, but we knew it certainly looked real, which would make it an easy target for thieves.'

Iris sighed as she reached out to touch the locket. 'I met Christopher about six months ago, we had a relationship, he was... lovely and there were many times he would come round to dinner and meet my nan. They got on like a house on fire. I guess one day she forgot to charm the locket, or she trusted him and so didn't bother, and he saw it for what it really was. One day, when I was out, he drugged my nan's tea and stole it. I'd like to think he was simply an opportunistic thief that saw the locket and took it, not that his relationship with me was all part of one big con to get it. But you lot had heard about the locket way before it was stolen so maybe he had heard about it too, which makes his betrayal so much worse.'

'We know about it because it's talked about in witch society. It's mentioned in our history books. As Christopher is a mundane he wouldn't have heard about it in that way, so I'd suggest it was the former rather than the latter,' Wolf said.

Iris nodded. That only made her feel a tiny bit better. It was still a betrayal. 'My nan was heartbroken. So as soon as I heard he was going to display it at an exhibition, I decided to steal it back for her. To find out he brought a gun to the exhibition because he knew I'd come for it is just... horrifying. I slept with this man. I told him I loved him. And he betrayed me and then planned to kill me.'

Wolf nodded. 'I believe the locket is yours. Unfortunately Christopher is claiming the locket is his and the police are involved. Because of the perceived value of the locket and the manner in which you took it back, it's been hailed as one of the biggest jewellery heists of the twenty-first century.' Wolf opened up his laptop, pressed a few buttons and turned it round for Iris to see. It was a CCTV video of her stealing the locket. 'This video is everywhere. It's been covered in the press, the TV news, the police are going nuts trying to find you. Fortunately, the person they are trying to find, this blonde woman, doesn't exist, so you have that in your favour. But if the police somehow do track you down, you'll need to somehow prove you have ownership of the locket. Do you have the pressed flower book and the list of possessions you were talking about?'

'Not here, they're still up in Scotland along with half of our lives. We were supposed to bring them with us but in the rush to pack they somehow got over-looked. But I can go back for them.'

Lynx shook his head. 'No way. I'm not risking you like that. We have no idea if Christopher is waiting for you.'

Iris found his protectiveness endearing and infuri-ating at the same time. Christopher wouldn't be there twenty-four/seven and if he was she was pretty sure she could handle him.

Wolf nodded. 'I don't see how they can ever find you or the locket here so I'm sure it's not anything to worry about. It will all die down eventually and be forgotten. I just wanted you to be aware what was happening out there.'

'Well I appreciate it. As you said, we have no links to Midnight prior to coming so they can't possibly know we're here, but if they did turn up, we do have proof it's ours. Nan has one of her wedding photos inside the locket, it's magically seared to the metal, kind of like it would be if it had been lasered on, so there's no way Christopher could have removed it.'

Wolf frowned in confusion.

'You didn't open it?' Iris said.

'We tried. The locket appears to be permanently closed.'

Her heart leapt in alarm. 'What?'

She picked up the locket, lifted the tiny gold latch and... nothing, the locket didn't budge at all.

She examined it. 'What the hell has he done to it? This was never stuck. Do you have a magnifying glass?'

Star hurried to a drawer in the cupboard, and brought one back to the table. Iris looked at the seams.

'I think he's superglued it together. Why would he do that?'

'Well I guess because of the photo,' Lynx said. 'If no one can see that, you can't prove your ownership.'

'Dear Gods, my nan is going to be gutted about this. She would look at that photo every day and stroke it. Can anyone magically remove it?'

'I could obviously magically force it open, but I would worry about the damage that could do to the locket,' Wolf said.

'I could melt the glue with my fire,' Lynx said. 'There's pretty much nothing I can't melt, but again I'd worry about melting the locket or causing some irreversible damage.'

'I'm sure there is something we could use to chemically remove it,' Star said. 'Like acetone, nail varnish remover, vinegar. I bet if we were to google it we could find something.'

'I'd be worried what kind of damage nail varnish remover would do to the gold though,' Iris said. 'Are you telling me, with all your great power, there's not some magic spell you can utter that could just get rid of it?'

'There's not a spell I know,' Wolf said and Lynx shook his head too. 'But there's lots of magic that I don't know or can't do. Normally in these situations, magical brute force works well enough for me.'

'I bet Ashley could come up with something,' Lynx said. 'She's our potions queen, she can come up with a spell, charm or potion to solve pretty much any problem. It may take her a few days to do it but I'm sure she'll manage something.'

'OK, I think I would trust magic over acetone or vinegar.'

'Come to potions club the day after tomorrow, you can meet everyone and then talk to Ashley after about the locket,' Star said.

'Erin has already persuaded me to come.'

Star laughed. 'I bet she did.'

'But I may go and see Ashley tonight, I'm keen to get this back to my nan as soon as possible.'

'You're free to take the locket back to Ness, even if it isn't in quite the same state it was when it was taken from her,' Wolf said. 'And we'll keep you posted about any developments outside the village. But before you go, can I ask, does the locket hold any power?'

'No, well none that I know of, and my nan certainly hasn't said anything about it if it has. It obviously has a magical energy but I think that comes from being worn by kelpies and part witches for the last few hundred years.'

'The stories we've heard involved the locket being used to control the seas and rivers. That's why we were so keen to make sure it didn't fall into the wrong hands.'

Iris smirked. 'No, that's us, the kelpies. We have that power, not the locket.'

'Oh,' Wolf said. 'You can control the seas?'

'If we wanted to. It's not something we ever do, we respect the water and the wildlife that lives in or around it, so we don't just cause tidal waves and tsunamis for fun. But yes, if you've heard stories of people wearing the locket and controlling the rivers, using the water as some kind of weapon, that's kelpie magic, not the locket. Though I have to say, I've never heard of anyone in my family doing something like that before. There was once a kelpie who caused the land to flood after a massive drought, but that was trying to help the farmer so he didn't lose his crops, it certainly wasn't malicious. And I don't think they were one of our family anyway. The kelpies obviously got caught up in the witch hunts and the stories tell of them causing great torrents on the rivers to escape the mundanes that were chasing them, but I think that's as far as it goes.'

'Wow,' Lynx said. 'Remind me never to piss you off.'

'You already did that,' Iris said, she made her hand into a gun shape and squirted water at him as if using a water pistol. It hit him square in the face and Blaze let out a squeal of laughter.

Lynx chuckled and wiped his face, looking as if he was plotting some terrible revenge and that gave her a delicious thrill.

'Well, I should go.' Iris put the locket back in its box. 'I'm sure my nan will be delighted to get this back. Thank you for letting me know about the investigation.'

'I'll walk back with you,' Lynx said, handing his niece to Star.

Iris said her goodbyes to Wolf and Star and walked out with Lynx.

'Are you worried about all this police stuff?' Lynx asked.

'Not really, they can't possibly know I'm here. But even if they did, it's not like I'm going to be carted off to jail for stealing back my own property.'

'You'd have to prove it's yours, though.'

'If we can get the locket open, then we'll have all the proof we need. If not, then I need to work out another way to discredit Christopher. We may have to go back to Scotland at some point to get the evidence.'

'No, that's too dangerous.'

'I could go in disguise.'

'I don't want you anywhere near that man. If we need it, we'll go mob-handed to go and collect it. There's safety in numbers.'

'I'm not worried right now. I think this will fade away quite quickly when there are no leads.'

They left Wolf's road and started walking up theirs.

'Want to come in for a coffee?' Lynx said.

She thought about it for a moment but she was sure she could be in his house for half hour without suddenly wanting to marry him or freaking out if she saw that she did. 'Sure, OK.'

She followed him inside his house, which she noticed was still unlocked. 'Are you not worried about break-ins here?'

Lynx smiled. 'Not here.'

She moved into the lounge, trying not to look at the dreaded sofa that she deliberately didn't touch. She didn't need any more visions.

She glanced around the room. She hadn't had a proper chance to look around before, because of the glimpses of her future she'd seen. But now she could take her time. There were a few artefacts from different countries in the world, showing Lynx's love of travelling. There were photos too, some of big tourist destinations, some of places that were definitely off the beaten track.

In a green glass bowl were three black stones with the iridescent rainbow glow of petrol and oil. She could feel a weird energy coming from them and she knew they were obviously magical.

'What are these?'

'Witches have different names for them. Some call them journey stones, or roaming stones or even holiday stones. I've always known them as key stones, as they are the key to different destinations. You hold them in your hand, close your eyes, think of where you want to go and, when you open them again, you find yourself there.'

'That easy?'

'Oh no, I wish it was, it takes a lot of energy and power to do it. And it's kind of like travelling on a twisty rollercoaster, you arrive feeling sick and dizzy, which is why it's recommended to shut your eyes. You have to really know your destination well, to take that leap; sometimes I can be standing here for ages trying to get a lock on the place, so I have to watch a ton of videos and look at loads of photos of the location before I try and travel anywhere with them. So it's not easy or enjoyable. But the effects wear off after a while. I also have to be careful about going to public places, like the Eiffel Tower for example. That's always filled with tourists, so I can't just appear out of thin air.'

'Yeah, I get that. I've never heard of key stones before.'

'They're quite rare. There are various different ways to travel through the fabric of space but none of them are easy or particularly pleasant. I find using the key stones to be the easiest. But you got down here quickly from Scotland, I'm presuming you used some sort of magic to expedite your journey?'

'Ah that's kelpie magic. We can travel via the rivers, lakes and lochs. They all have a magical energy about them and we tap into that energy to travel to different locations. I'm not sure how to explain it. It's kind of like creating a portal that we drive through in the car at the start of a river and there's a wormhole type thing that takes us to the end of the river or loch. But we can only go as far as the end of the water source then we'll drive a little way to pick up the next river and then we can jump to the end of that too. It's not an instant travel solution like your keystones because we travel in increments, but it makes a ten-hour journey around two hours instead so well worth doing.'

'That's fascinating. I've never thought about using the rivers as roads. I wonder if that's something us witches could try or whether that's exclusively a kelpie thing.'

'I'll have to try and teach you one day. It's easier to create a portal for one person than it is to create one big enough for a car. But travelling by water doesn't make me dizzy or sick, so it's worth a go.'

'I'd love that. I love learning about new magic, so much of it has been lost over the years and we're constantly finding new or better ways to do things. Let me make us a drink.'

She followed him down to the kitchen.

'Tell me more about being a kelpie,' Lynx said as he started magically making two mugs of coffee.

It was a funny thing, being able to talk about it so openly for the first time in forever and not face any judgement or fear either.

'Well, we can see perfectly underwater without the need for goggles and we can hold our breath under-water for a really long time.'

'How long?'

'Two or three hours.'

He turned to look at her in shock. 'What?'

She shrugged. 'Just one of our special skills.'

'I'm beginning to realise there's a lot of special things about you.'

She smiled. 'Let's not get carried away, we still have our fight to the death to endure.'

He carried the two mugs through to the lounge and placed them down in front of the sofa. He sat down and, with no other seating available, she reluctantly sat next to him.

'I'm also starting to understand why you're shying away from a relationship with me.'

Her heart leapt. 'Hang on, since when was a relationship with you even on the table?'

'You can't deny we have a connection.'

'There is no connection.'

'When we kissed, when we touch, it burns bright between us, but you keep pushing it away. And now I know why. You've been let down so many times, with Jack who you were engaged to, and Christopher who betrayed you in the worst possible way. You don't want to take a risk with your heart again.'

'I don't want to damage your ego but maybe I'm just not that into you.'

'My ego is fine. If a woman isn't interested in me, I'm OK with that. And if that's the way you want to play it, I promise I'll say no more about it. But we both know there's something between us. And I get that you're scared of getting hurt again but I would never hurt you in that way. I can't speak for our future, I don't have that gift, but don't you think we owe it to ourselves to find out if we have something beyond one amazing kiss?'

She'd be lying if she said she didn't want to find out, that she hadn't thought about kissing Lynx one more time. But there was a big part of her that was still fighting against her predetermined future. She wanted to feel like she had some control over it.

'Maybe the kiss wasn't really that amazing.'

'You seemed to enjoy it at the time.'

'Maybe that's it. Maybe it was just the adrenaline of the moment, stealing the locket, the guards looking for it, hiding in darkened corners. Maybe we just got caught up in the thrill of it all. I bet if I were to kiss you right now, we wouldn't feel a damned thing.'

He shrugged. 'I'm happy to put that to the test. And if we don't, we know we can finally put these maybes to bed once and for all.'

Iris really didn't want to kiss him, she knew one more kiss would change everything between them and she wasn't ready for that.

She quickly backpedalled away from it. 'I didn't mean I wanted to kiss you right now. I'm just saying, if we did, it wouldn't be anywhere near exciting as you hope it would be.'

'Let's see.'

She bit her lip and his eyes darkened as he watched her. OK, she could do this. If she could have one simple, meaningless kiss with no emotional reaction, then maybe he'd leave her alone and she could get on with her life without this great big Lynx complication hanging over her. Maybe she could just pretend she was kissing a frog. That would do it.

'Fine, one kiss and we're never doing it again.'

He nodded and moving quickly, perhaps before she talked herself out of it, he bent his head and kissed her.

The second their lips touched, feelings exploded through her. A need for him, desire, passion, hunger, but above it all was this feeling of happiness and peace, the same kind of feeling she got from water bathing, that sense of being where she belonged. What she'd hoped would be a brief, chaste kiss very quickly turned into something so much more.

She stroked his face, he cupped her neck, she slid her hand down the open neck of his shirt, feeling the strength and warmth of his chest. He moaned against her lips and then hauled her closer against him, but not close enough. She knelt up and straddled him without taking her lips from his.

He slid his hands up her back, his fingers grazing her skin at the top of her dress. It was crazy to feel this way, this insatiable need, but she wanted so much more. She undid one of his shirt buttons and moved her hands inside, caressing the muscles on his chest. He shifted his mouth to her neck and she gasped. Her breath was heavy as if she'd just swam a hundred miles. He slid his hands up her dress and round her bum as he moved his mouth to her breast.

Suddenly she remembered one of the flashes of Lynx's future she'd seen before. Making love on the sofa just like this, even wearing this dress. This was the moment she'd seen, or at least a few minutes before it.

With more determination than she thought she had, she pulled away from him, trying to catch her breath. He looked at her in confusion, his eyes clouded with desire.

What was she thinking? She'd known she couldn't kiss Lynx sensibly and not have any reaction to him, so why the hell had she done it?

She climbed off him and stood up. She grabbed her coffee and took a big swig and realised she was still trembling with need for him. She started pacing the room. She couldn't exactly say it meant nothing to her now when she'd undone his shirt and straddled him.

'I think you proved your point. Yes, I'm attracted to you, yes I want you as much as you want me, happy now?'

He stood up. 'Iris, I'm so sorry. I never meant to take it that far. It was only supposed to be a quick kiss, I didn't keep going just to prove a point. I've never met a woman that makes me feel the way you do, I just lose all control with you.'

'The feeling is very mutual.' She rubbed her hand over her face, trying to clear it of the need to finish that kiss. 'Please don't apologise. You didn't do anything I didn't want you to do. And if I listened to my heart, I'd be making love to you right now. I just...' she trailed off. How could she even begin to explain she was fighting against a beautiful, perfect future? It didn't even make sense in her own mind. Stopping the kiss, stopping that particular flash of his future from happening, made it feel like she was still in control of her life, like she was in charge, not on some predetermined path. But the decision she'd made to not let it happen wasn't something she wanted, so it didn't exactly feel like a triumph.

'It's happening too fast?' Lynx said.

'A little.'

'I'm sorry. I shouldn't have pushed it. After what Christopher did, I can understand you being cautious and not wanting to get involved with someone.'

'I trust you in that regard. But I feel like if we did get together, our relationship would be something serious and life-changing, and I need to get my head around that, not rush in, all guns blazing, just because we've now had two earth-shattering kisses. I should have been honest and said I wasn't ready, not pretend this thing between us didn't exist.'

He stepped closer and wrapped his arms around her. She leaned into him, sliding her arms round his back. He kissed her forehead and she looked up at him.

'There's no rush, I can wait as long as you need.'

'Thank you.' She smirked. 'You know, if we do eventually make love, it's going to be explosive.'

'Oh, I don't think we'll survive it.'

She laughed. 'I better go, I want to talk to Ashley about the locket tonight.'

He let her go and she stepped back slightly from

him. She reached out and did the buttons back up on his shirt. The way he was watching her made her mouth go dry.

'Can I take you to the pool tomorrow? Wolf will be transforming the shop and I don't want to get in the way of that. I promise I won't be naked or try to kiss you again. I'll be the perfect gentleman.'

She nodded. 'I'd like that.'

'I'll come and collect you at nine.'

'OK.'

She went to the door and he followed her. He opened the door for her and she stepped outside but then she turned back. Why was she running away from this? Every fibre of her being was telling her to go back inside the house and finish that kiss properly. Sex didn't need to be a relationship. Why couldn't she just have some fun with Lynx? Just because she'd seen that future, it didn't mean it would play out like that. Surely she could enjoy herself without focussing on that predetermined path. If she hadn't seen that future, if she wasn't trying to run away from it, she'd probably be having the best sex of her life right now.

'What if I just want sex?' she blurted out.

She heard a splutter from next door and felt her cheeks heat. They both looked round to see Lynx's elderly neighbour, just coming out of her house.

'Evening Elizabeth,' Lynx said.

'Evening.' She gave him a wink.

He turned his attention back to Iris. 'I'm definitely OK with that too.'

She hurried away, embarrassed, and every time she looked back, he was still standing in his doorway watching her go. Who was she kidding? There could never be anything casual about her relationship with Lynx Oakwood.

CHAPTER 10

L ynx sat down on the sofa, head buzzing and heart racing. He'd never experienced a kiss like that. But he'd pushed Iris too far. If they were going to date then she had to be ready for it.

There was a sudden banging on his door. He got up to answer it, wondering if Iris had changed her mind and come back to properly finish that kiss.

He opened it and sighed to find his grandmother, Zofia, on the other side.

'I thought you were on holiday,' Lynx said, standing back to let her in, because there was nothing worse than discussing his love life on the doorstep for all the neighbours to hear and that was likely to be the only reason she was here.

'I was, but I cut my trip short when I saw. Well, where is she?'

She looked around the lounge as if he was hiding Iris behind a plant pot perhaps. He knew exactly who Zofia meant and that she had likely seen the explosive kiss. Although if Iris had been there he probably *would* be hiding her, just so he wouldn't have to double down on the crazy by her meeting his grandmother.

'I'm not sure who you mean.'

'Don't play dumb with me. Iris McKenzie of course. I've been so desperate to meet her and I've waited so long. I was almost tempted to get you to go to Scotland and find her but I knew I had to wait for you two to meet naturally, for fate to bring the two of you together. And now she's here and I'm so excited.'

Lynx let out a deep breath, rubbing the bridge of his nose. Whereas Star and Iris seemingly only had flashes of the future, his grandmother was like an omniscient being and claimed to know everything. Clearly she'd seen Iris and if Zofia had cut her holiday short because of her, she must have seen something significant. But he really didn't want to talk about this with her.

'I don't think you're going to help matters by interfering.'

'I'm not interfering.'

'Yet you cut your holiday short to come back and see her.'

Zofia dismissed that with a wave of her hand. 'You two have kissed, right?'

'Yes.'

'And you've slept together?'

'Zofia, I'm not discussing that with you.'

'I'll take that as a yes.'

'It's a no actually. I've only known her a few days.'

Zofia scowled. 'What have you done to upset her? Don't you mess this up, do you hear me?'

'I haven't done anything.'

'But she's seen your future, she's seen...' Zofia trailed off.

'I have no idea what she's seen, she won't tell me and I don't want you to either.'

He wasn't going to mention Iris had told him he had a child. Although now Zofia was here making such a big deal out of it, he wondered if she'd seen his child too and whether Iris was connected to that in more ways than she was saying. The thought made his mouth go dry. He'd thought that the baby might be theirs as soon as she told him he had a child but had eventually dismissed that idea. Now he wasn't so sure. Was that really what she was running away from?

'But she likes you?' his grandmother asked.

'Yes, very much so.'

'Well that's something. You need to pull out all the stops to make sure she falls in love with you. Take her to dinner, buy her flowers, buy her books, whatever it takes. You need to fight for her.'

'We have nothing to fight for right now. And no, I'm not badgering her into this. What I need to do is wait for her to be ready. She's been burned badly with past relationships. She needs to choose if she wants to be with me. And if she decides she just wants one night with me, that's OK too. All of this needs to be her choice.'

Zofia stared at him. 'Oh actually, that's good. Giving her space and patience, I bet she'll find that very attractive. Great idea.'

'It's not a ploy. It's the right thing to do. She should have the final say over it, not just go ahead with it because you've seen she has a part to play in my future. Besides, if you're so sure in what you've seen, why not just sit back and let it happen?'

'Because you're not known for successful, long-term relationships and I worry you're going to screw this up. She makes you happy and I want that for you.'

Lynx smiled. 'Maybe I haven't been successful in long-term relationships because I've never found the right woman before and it had nothing to do with my ability to screw it up. We have to find our own way with this, just like we do with all aspects of life. And we may make mistakes but hopefully we'll grow because of it.'

'Oh when did you get to be so wise,' Zofia said. 'Normally that's my job.'

'I don't know if cutting your holiday short to interfere with my love life is the wisest choice, neither was the advice you gave Star when she first arrived here, which nearly finished her and Wolf forever.'

She flushed. 'Yes, well that was a mistake.'

'And I don't want you to make any similar mistakes which could drive a wedge even further between me and Iris. Go back to your holiday and leave us to cock this up on our own.'

His grandmother muttered something that sounded like, 'We'll see about that,' and flounced out.

Lynx sighed. He could try to protect Iris from any judgemental opinions about her kelpie heritage and he would fight to the death to protect her against Christopher, if their paths should ever cross again. But he couldn't protect her against the force of his grandmother when she decided to interfere in his love life.

Iris had just had a shower and got dressed when she heard her nan and Morag return, happily chatting to each other.

She ran downstairs.

'Hey, where have you two been?'

'We spent the day exploring our new home,' Morag said.

'And the shops,' Ness said. 'They are wonderful. I still can't believe all these people practising magic so openly.'

'If you were round the shops, you should have popped in and said hello,' Iris said.

'Oh, we didn't want to interrupt anything,' Ness said, her eyebrows waggling mischievously.

'There was nothing to interrupt. I was upstairs and Lynx was downstairs for most of the day.'

'So there's nothing going on between you?' Morag said.

Iris flushed as she remembered their hot second kiss. 'I didn't say that, just that nothing was happening in the shop. Did you do anything else today?'

'We traced the stream that runs through the garden all the way to the very back of the village, near the woods, and there's a gorgeous little waterfall there,' Ness said, dreamily. 'The water was deep enough to swim in too, so we both had a little paddle. Scared some old bloke half to death who had gone up there to do some fishing and found me naked in the pool. He grumbled that I'd probably scared the fish away, but I certainly didn't see any in there.'

Iris snorted with laughter. Her nan would always swim naked in the lochs and rivers. Iris tended to have a bit more caution when it came to showing her bits. She loved a naked swim, but she had to choose her locations carefully.

'Listen, I have some good news and bad news,' Iris said, going to the table and picking up the box with the locket in. She'd already decided not to tell her nan about the police interest in the jewellery heist, she didn't want to worry her. 'I spoke with Wolf today about the locket and he gave it back to me after I explained it was yours and the history of it.'

Her nan's face lit up. 'You've got it back.'

'Yes, but there's a problem.'

Her face fell. 'What's the problem?'

'Christopher has glued it together, probably with superglue or something else impossible to shift.'

'But I need what's inside. That's more important than anything else.'

Iris frowned in confusion. 'You mean the wedding photo of you and Pops?'

Ness nodded vaguely.

'We'll sort it out, I promise.' Iris showed Ness the locket and she took it out of the box, her hands trembling. Her nan tried to open it and tears filled her eyes.

'It's ruined.'

'No it's not. There are lots of things we can try, like nail varnish remover or vinegar, but Lynx thinks we can magically open it. There's a lady in the village called Ashley who apparently knows every kind of spell, potion and charm there is. Lynx thinks she will be able to come up with a solution that won't harm the locket. I'm going to go and see her now and ask her to take a look at it.'

Ness handed the locket back. 'Can she be trusted? I don't want to lose it again.'

'Lynx wouldn't have recommended her if she wasn't trustworthy. And did you know, he never locks his front door, he says he knows they'll never be a break-in here. So I guess he trusts everyone in the village.'

Ness grunted and Iris knew that in her eyes trust had to be earned, not presumed.

'I promise, we'll find some way to fix this.'

Ness nodded, sadly. 'Thank you,' she said, quietly, before heading outside to the garden and Iris knew she was going to stand in the stream again.

Iris sighed and turned back to Morag.

'You need to be careful with this Lynx,' Morag said. 'The last man you brought into our lives was a jobby-flavoured fart lozenge.'

Iris snorted. 'He was.'

'A complete bawbag.'

'Yes.'

'And because you trusted him, fell in love with him, we had to leave our home.'

'Thanks for the guilt trip, I'm aware all this is my fault.'

'I didn't mean it like that, I don't want to see you get hurt again is all. And you're not the only one at risk,' Morag nodded in the direction of Ness.

'I know I've not been the best judge of character in the past, but there's something about Lynx that makes me feel safe. And I think if you met him, you'd like him too.'

Morag scowled. 'I'll be the judge of that.'

She slunk off into the garden and Iris sighed.

She put the locket back in its box and slipped it into her bag, then headed off for Ashley's house. It was a gloriously sunny evening and the streets were still alive with people moving around and chatting. The village was so charming, each house different to its neighbours, painted in a different bright colour so the overall effect was like something from a picture postcard. She found Ashley's house easily enough with its purple front door, flowers growing up the walls and its rustic-style brass lanterns, and knocked on the door.

A blonde woman answered, giving her a huge smile. 'Iris McKenzie,' she said. It was clear from her accent that she was American. 'I've been looking forward to meeting you. I'm Ashley Dougan. Come in.'

She stepped back to let Iris in. The room had a large horseshoe-shape sofa with brightly coloured satin cushions. There was a large shelf filled with multi-coloured potion bottles of all shapes and sizes and candles flickering everywhere, lending a golden glow to the room.

Ashley studied her for a moment. 'You have the most unique magical energy. I've never felt or seen anything like it before. You're a witch, I can feel that, but there's something else there.'

'I... umm... I'm part kelpie.'

Ashley's eyes widened. 'I've never met a kelpie before. Of course we've heard of them, and the stories, but this is quite exciting.'

'The stories aren't true.'

'They never are.'

'You know, every witch I've ever met, before I came here, has always been suspicious of us. But since I've come here, everyone has been so kind and welcoming.'

'I have no doubt that some people will be a little concerned when they find out your heritage, but most of us here have open minds and big hearts.'

Iris liked that.

'I wonder if I could ask for a bit of magical advice actually.' Iris took the locket out of her bag. 'This is my nan's, and my asshole ex-boyfriend stole it from her and glued it together. Is there anything you could do, magically, to remove the glue without damaging the locket? It's very precious to my nan.'

Ashley took the locket and studied it. 'Yes, I'm sure there is. I did a potion once to remove a stain from my favourite sweater, and it came up better than new, so I'm sure I can come up with something similar to remove the glue. Maybe dandelion and sage, picked under a full moon. That could work. Or stardust and honeysuckle. If you're happy to leave it with me for a few days, I promise I'll take very good care of it.'

Iris hesitated for a few moments. She was desperate

to get the locket fixed for her nan but trusting strangers didn't come easily. But Lynx trusted Ashley and that was good enough for her. 'Yes, thank you, that would be great.'

Ashley carefully put the locket back in its box and then moved over to a small cupboard that was secured with five completely different locks. She waved her hands and the different locks started turning and whirring by themselves and finally the door opened.

'I keep all the dangerous potion ingredients in here. I don't use them very often but I'd never want them to fall into the wrong or uneducated hands, so I keep them under lock and key. Your locket will be very safe in there.'

Iris watched Ashley place the box next to a bottle of red, glowing liquid that looked like sparkly blood before the door was closed and the locks magically secured the cupboard door once more.

'Thank you,' Iris said.

'Well, if you don't have to rush off, would you like a cup of camomile tea and perhaps we could talk a bit more about kelpie magic?'

Iris smiled. 'I'd like that.'

Ness was just settling down to watch her favourite programme on TV when there was a knock on the door. Morag lifted her head suspiciously and Ness got up to answer it. Outside was an elderly woman about the same age as Ness, perhaps a little older.

'You must be Ness,' the woman said.

'I am and you are?'

'I'm Zofia, Lynx's grandmother.'

'Ah, you best come in then.' Ness shuffled back to let her in. 'Can I get you a drink? Tea, coffee?'

'Whisky if you have it?'

Ness smiled. 'Only the best kind, from Scotland.'

'That's the only kind that counts in my opinion.'

Ness grabbed a bottle and two glasses from the side. She looked at Morag. 'Do you want one?'

Morag shook her head. 'I'm off out now anyway. I have things I need to do.'

She slunk out of the open door and Ness waved a hand to close it behind her. She poured out the glasses and handed Zofia one. She gestured for Zofia to sit down. 'What is it you want to talk about?'

'I know you have the gift of foresight, just like I do.'

'That's right.'

'So you've seen Iris and Lynx, their future, their children.'

'I have.' Ness took a sip of her whisky, wondering where Zofia was going with this.

'And Iris, she's seen it too?'

'Her gift is not as clear as mine. And even I can't see everything. If I could, I'd have seen that little bawbag steal my locket and I would have stopped him. But Iris never sees her future, only other people's, and it comes in flashes and sometimes doesn't come at all. So seeing her future was a shock for her. I know she's seen something because she came back here and said we may be staying here and she wasn't happy about it.'

'Why wasn't she happy about it? From what I've seen of their future they have amazing chemistry together.'

'Iris is finding this whole future-set-in-stone thing a bit overwhelming. She feels like she wants control over her life, not to have it all laid out in front of her. She says she wants a choice.'

'That's silly. Fate isn't forcing them to be together, no spell, charm or potion or any kind of magic can make two people love each other. What Iris is seeing is just what will happen. And if she hadn't seen it, it would still happen.'

'I know that, but she sees her and Lynx's future, marriage, babies, and she doesn't even know the man.'

'Well that's what I want to talk to you about. With Iris actively trying to avoid that future and Lynx being a gentleman and patiently waiting for her to be ready, I'll be dead by the time they walk down the aisle – if they ever do. I think they need a little nudge.'

Ness took another sip of whisky as she thought.

'You can see how happy they make each other,' Zofia said.

'I can.'

'Then it wouldn't hurt to give them a little help.'

'OK, what are you thinking?'

'Poker.'

'Poker?'

'Let me explain...'

Morag was sitting outside her house, enjoying the cool of the evening as the sun disappeared behind the hills, when she saw a black shadow skulking down the road towards her.

'Good evening Vik*ta.*'

'Moorag.'

She suppressed a smirk.

'Still here, I see,' Viktor said, sitting down next to her.

'Where else would I be?'

'I was hoping Scotland.'

'Wherever Iris is, I'll be too.'

'Well, I thought that she and Lynx would have had their little fling by now, he'd have broken her heart and she'd have gone back to Scotland, taking you with her.'

'We can't go back to Scotland, not yet anyway. The

last man she dated turned out to be dangerous, so we have to stay here until it all blows over. And why do you think Lynx will break her heart?'

'He's not known for his longevity. He's had more girlfriends than I've had hot dinners. And as someone who remembers every one of my many past lives, that's a lot of hot dinners.'

Morag examined one of her claws as if bored by this conversation but now a seed of doubt had wiggled its way into her mind. Was Lynx the right man for Iris? She didn't want to see Iris get hurt again.

'Look, you don't want to be here and I certainly don't want you here. If we were to make sure Lynx and Iris don't get together, we'd both get our wish. You'd go back to Scotland.'

Morag had heard enough. She pounced on Viktor, pinning him to the ground, and his eyes widened in shock.

'How dare you manhandle me like this. Unhand me at once.'

'If you do anything to interfere with Iris's happiness, I'll have you assassinated.'

'Assassinated? Just how do you plan to do that?' Viktor said, scathingly, clearly believing she didn't have it in her.

'Perhaps a draught of poison in your lavender tea.'

'How do you know I drink lavender tea?'

'I listen, I hear things. I also know you like cake, I

could easily put poison in one of those.'

'This feels like a little bit of an overreaction on your part.'

'Or maybe I could smother you with a pillow or push a gargoyle on your head.'

'This is all sounding rather macabre,' Viktor said, sounding bored. 'I merely suggested we throw a few spanners into their relationship. I don't think that warrants a death sentence on my part.'

'There'll be no spanners, no plotting to break them up or keep them apart. Iris deserves to find happiness for once in her life and, according to what she's seen, Lynx is the one who gives her that. So if I hear you've interfered in any way...' Morag dragged her claw across her throat threateningly. 'If you dislike me that much, we can draw a line down the middle of the village and never the twain shall meet. Failing that, you'll just have to man up and try to like me.'

'After this, never.'

Morag sighed and climbed off him. 'I mean it, stay away from them.'

Viktor scrambled up and started cleaning himself as if that whole thing hadn't happened. He was the most infuriating cat Morag had ever met. Maybe killing him would be easier than putting up with this crap.

She crossed over the road. Maybe it was time to meet the man himself, see if a relationship between Iris and Lynx was really worth fighting for.

Lynx was reading a spy story when there was a knock on the door. He got up to answer it but when he opened the door there was no one there. Confused, he was just about to close it again when he heard someone politely coughing to get his attention. He looked down and a fox stared back up at him.

'Hello.'

'Good evening,' the fox said.

He blinked in surprise. 'You must be Morag, Iris's...'

The fox glared at him as if daring him to say pet.

'Friend,' Lynx said and she seemed appeased by that.

'I am and I've come to see what kind of man you are and whether you're good enough for Iris.'

'Well in that case you better come in.'

He stepped back and Morag gracefully trotted into his house.

'Please take a seat,' Lynx said and watched her jump up onto the sofa easily, looking like a pet dog as she made herself comfortable. 'Would you like a drink?'

'A tea will be fine, chamomile if you have it.'

'Sure.' He bit his lip. 'In a mug or...?'

'Do I look like I have opposable thumbs? A bowl will be fine.'

'Of course.' He waved his hand and heard the drink

being made in the kitchen. He sat down opposite her. 'How can I help you?'

'It seems that Iris's future happiness is tied to you, at least her immediate future.'

'That's what I hear too. My grandmother who, from what I can gather has more precognitive abilities than Iris does, has also seen something. Although I don't know what she's seen as Iris hasn't told me and I refuse to hear it from my grandmother when Iris hasn't told me herself.'

He really needed to talk to Iris about this. Just what had she seen? He was happy to wait for Iris to be ready but he really needed to know what he was waiting for.

'How do you feel about it?' Morag asked. 'It could be marriage, babies. That's a lifelong commitment. Most men in your shoes would be running a million miles in the opposite direction if a woman they'd just met had suggested marriage.'

'Well she hasn't suggested it. She's the one trying to run away from it right now.'

'That doesn't really answer my question.'

Lynx suppressed a smile just as the bowl of chamomile came floating out of the kitchen and landed in front of Morag. He watched her delicately drink the whole thing, then she lifted her head, looking at him expectantly, clearly wanting an answer.

'I really like Iris and we share a connection I've never felt before. And if something develops between us and that turns to love, I'd be very happy to marry her. According to my grandmother, she makes me very happy so why would I want to run away from that?'

'But do you make her happy?'

'I could only be happy if she was happy.'

'Good answer. Ever been unfaithful?'

'Never.'

'Ever broken a woman's heart?'

Lynx frowned. 'It's unlikely. I've never had a serious relationship before.'

'Ah, why is that?'

'Never found the right woman.'

'Not because you like playing the field?'

'I've dated a few women in my life, but they never lasted because they weren't looking for something serious or because I was looking for something special.'

She nodded. 'Ever stolen from someone?'

'No.'

'Ever been intimidated by another person's magic?'

'No, why would I be? I can do things other people can't. Other people can do things that I can't. That's how magic works. I've never been jealous about other people's abilities.'

'Ever hit a woman?'

'Dear Gods, no.'

'How would you protect Iris if someone meant her harm?'

Lynx held his hand out and a large flame appeared in his palm. 'That normally does the trick.'

Morag narrowed her eyes at him as if trying to think of other questions to ask.

'Favourite colour?'

'Blue.'

'Favourite food?'

He chewed his lip. 'Fox stew.'

Morag actually smiled at this. 'Very good. Funny and handsome.' She hopped down from the sofa. He followed her to the door and let her out. She turned back. 'I'm keeping an eye on you, Lynx Oakwood. If you hurt her, you'll have me to answer to.'

He nodded. 'And I take that very seriously.'

He watched her cross the road and vanish from view.

The Spanish Inquisition from a fox was the last thing he'd been expecting from this evening. He smiled, shook his head and went back inside.

Iris let herself back into her house to find Ness and Morag sitting quietly watching the TV.

Ness paused the programme. 'Did Ashley think she can fix the locket?'

'She does, she thinks dandelion and sage picked

177

under a full moon might do it, or stardust and something. Anyway, she's going to look at it over the next few days and come up with something that doesn't damage the locket.'

Ness sighed heavily. 'I was hoping it was something she could do straightaway. I really need that locket.'

'I know, it'll just be a few days.'

Ness nodded. 'I had a visit tonight from Lynx's grandmother.'

'Zofia? What did she want?'

'Just... to welcome me to the village.'

'Ah, that was nice.'

'She wants to come round tomorrow to play poker.'

'Oh lovely, that will be nice for you to make some friends here.'

'Will you come?'

'Oh, I'm not particularly good at poker.'

'I just want you there for moral support. You know what I'm like with making friends, you can stop me making a tit of myself.'

Iris smiled. 'I'm sure you won't but I'm happy to come and play badly.'

'Excellent. Five o'clock.'

'I'll be here. I'm going to read for a while before I go to bed. Goodnight.'

She leaned over and kissed her nan on the cheek, waved goodnight to Morag and went upstairs.

CHAPTER 11

Iris walked out of her house the next morning with her towel tucked under her arm to find Lynx already sitting outside waiting for her.

'Hey, you ready?' he said, hopping to his feet.

'Yes, I'm excited to see it. I feel a bit bad because when I told Ness I was going for a swim, she wanted to come too.'

They started walking towards the village green.

'She could have come with us, I don't mind,' Lynx said.

She smiled. He really was a decent man. 'Well I did say that to her but when I told her I was going with you, she said she didn't want to get in the way of our date. I did say it wasn't a date but she refused. And I feel bad because I'm secretly quite glad it's just the two of us. Anyway, she found the other pool at the end of our road yesterday so she's going to go back to that again instead.'

They reached the village green and started walking up one of the roads on the opposite side.

'That one's nice too, and a much shorter and easier walk to get to. And while I'm always happy for Ness to tag along, I'm secretly pleased it's just the two of us too.'

She smiled up at him. 'It's not a date.'

He smirked. 'I never said it was. Although there will be quite a bit of nudity.'

'Is that what constitutes a date for you?'

He laughed. 'No, and if this was a date I'd be trying harder. There'd be flowers at least.'

He clicked his fingers and a bouquet of peonies appeared in his hand.

She laughed as he passed them to her. 'It isn't a date. We're just going for a swim.'

'So you don't want these?' He clicked his fingers again and some chocolate-covered strawberries appeared in his hands.

'These are from London,' Iris said, recognising the shop name.

'I bought some for myself when I was there. But I'm happy to share them.'

'Maybe you should save them for an actual date.'

He shrugged and clicked his fingers and they

vanished again. She felt a bit silly for complaining because they had looked really delicious.

'Maybe we have them for after the swim,' Iris said.

'Is that when the date starts?'

She laughed. 'Stop it.'

'OK, OK, I'll be on my best behaviour from now on.'

'You're going to have to teach me that click your fingers thing. It would be handy to do.'

'Oh it's a summoning spell. You have to be able to see the item clearly in your head and exactly where it is. It's quite hard to do to start off with. It's a lot easier when you've been doing it all your life but I tried to teach Erin how to do it once and she didn't have much success. But I'm happy to try and teach you one day, you might have more luck. It takes a lot of work and a lot of patience, it took me weeks to learn when I was a kid so don't be put off if you can't do it straightaway.'

They reached the end of Holly Lane and she could see woods stretching out either side.

'Does all this belong to the village?'

'Yes, the woods on this side go quite far back before you reach the village boundary.'

They followed a path into the woods where the cover of the trees blocked out a lot of the sun so only tiny sparkles of light filtered through the leaves. It was lovely and peaceful.

'And no one comes in here?'

'They do but not many of them come this far. And

I've been at my little pool hundreds of times over the years and I've never seen anyone else there.' Lynx took her hand. 'It gets a little bit uneven from here on in.'

She smiled at the tactic, she was quite sure she could navigate walking through some woods easily enough, but she didn't let go of his hand.

'How did you find the pool?'

'I was just a bored kid exploring the village and I stumbled across it one day. I love the fact that no one else appears to know it exists. Everyone else is content to just stay in the main village so it really does feel like it's mine.'

'And now you're sharing it with me?'

'Of course. If swimming is so important to you, I want you to have it so you have somewhere beautiful and peaceful to come and swim.'

They walked through a gap in the trees and there it was, the most beautiful little pool Iris had ever seen. The sunlight glimmered through the leaves here, casting a gorgeous green glow over the glade. Water tumbled over rocks at the far end, sparkling like diamonds in the sun.

'Oh Lynx, this is lovely.'

'I'm glad you like it. It's a special place.' He started laying out a blanket.

'Is it deep?'

'Yes, surprisingly so. Especially that side, though it's quite shallow over here.'

She quickly stripped down to her bikini and dived in, immediately feeling the healing power of the water seep into her skin and her bones. She swam right down to the bottom and smiled at the fish, newts and frogs that had made their homes here. This was glorious. She stayed underwater for a while, enjoying the feel of the water surrounding her, the coolness on her skin, the way the sunlight sparkled through the water.

Suddenly she got a flash of her future here – or rather Lynx's, it was impossible now to say whose future she was seeing as they were so intrinsically linked to each other. She saw the first time they made love in the shallow side of the pool under a setting sun, she saw herself giving birth to their daughter here on the banks of the pool, her daughter's first swim when she was a few weeks old, Lynx hovering like an overprotective dad. And instead of freaking her out, these images of her future made her smile. This was a happy future, why was she running away from it?

The images faded away and she was left with a warm glow.

She looked up and saw Lynx treading water above her. His thighs were big and muscular and she was enjoying seeing his chest again without the embarrassment of him seeing her ogling him.

She swam to the top and surfaced in front of him.

'I was just beginning to wonder whether I needed to swim down and rescue you,' Lynx said.

'I can hold my breath for a really long time, remember.'

'I know, but it's still a little disconcerting to witness it.'

'Were you worried about me?'

'Of course. I worry about you a lot. I worry that you're safe, that you're happy, I worry about you meeting my grandmother and running away because she is all kinds of crazy.'

She laughed. 'I'm meeting her later today actually. She and Ness are playing poker at five and Ness asked me to come along for moral support.'

Lynx groaned. 'I've been asked to come along for the same reason. I thought it was a bit dodgy. My grandmother is the last person who needs moral support.'

She laughed. 'Oh. I didn't see that coming. My nan told me Zofia had been round, I thought she was just being nice welcoming Ness to the village.'

'This is a set-up, they're trying to get us together. Zofia loves to interfere, she thrives on it. She's seen us together in the future and doesn't want to wait for fate to take its course.'

'She's seen us too?'

'Yeah. I wouldn't let her tell me anything though, I thought you should be the one to tell me, if and when you're ready.'

She sighed. So much for not revealing too much about his future. 'So what are we in for tonight?'

'I told her that it's your choice whether we have a relationship or not and that I wasn't going to badger you into it. She didn't like that so this will be some attempt to get us together.'

'And she's roping my nan into her shenanigans too.'

'We can just tell them no.'

'We'll see, I may just come up with a plan of my own.'

He grinned at that.

Iris sighed. There really was no getting away from the plans fate had in store for her. If she believed the visions she'd seen, one day she would be happily married to Lynx, with children, maybe living here in this perfect, safe little community. And if she ran away from that future, avoided it like the plague, it seemed Zofia and Ness were going to pull out all the stops to make it happen.

'Please don't think I'm rude, but would you mind if I just floated for a while?'

'Oh yeah, go for it, do what you need. I'm going to have a little swim, but after, do you mind if I float with you?'

'Not at all.'

He swam away from her to the far side of the pool. Iris starfished on her back, staring up at the sun filtering through the leaves, enjoying the silence. And it was lovely to enjoy the silence with someone else. No expectation to talk, just be together. She'd expected it to be weird to share this with someone else but there was something about being with him that made her feel so peaceful.

She needed to make a decision about Lynx. After that incredible kiss the night before, it was very clear they had a mutual attraction. She also just really enjoyed spending time with him. He was a kind, patient man and she liked he wasn't pushing her about this, even though he must have questions about the future she and Zofia had seen.

He swam back towards her and turned over onto his back next to her, and it made her smile so damn much when he took her hand so they were floating together. It reminded her of two otters, holding hands while they slept on top of the water so they didn't float apart.

She had often watched the otters on the sides of lochs and rivers and found herself envious of them because they had mated for life. It seemed otters didn't spend years trying to find their other half, drifting through unsuitable partners, being betrayed by them, they somehow just found the one. That simplicity of finding their life partner, that person that would be there for them through every up and down, their soul mate, had always appealed to Iris. She had always told herself when she met him she would know. The connection between her and Lynx had been instant from the moment they'd met and, according to the future she'd seen, he was her forever, so why the hell was she holding back?

She rolled up so she was standing shoulder-deep in the water and he did the same, facing her.

'I've been constantly second-guessing everything since I've come here because all roads lead back to you. I stopped us making love last night because I'd seen that exact moment and I thought by stopping it I was proving I was in control. But I'm really not. We were fated to be together years ago. Did you know Star saw us together eighteen months ago? How crazy is that? We didn't even know each other existed then. How could we be destined to be together when we'd never met?'

'Ah, you're the mystery red-head that nearly drove Star and Wolf apart?'

'It's mad, isn't it. And for the last few days I've been trying to decide what to do. Whether to give in to it because I'm pretty sure you'll be the best thing that's ever happened to me, or keep fighting it, live a life of misery just to prove I'm in control of my own life. When I say it like that, there is only one choice. When I'm with you, when I'm kissing you or cuddled up to you, it just makes so much sense. And you're so laid-back about it all, you're not fazed by our future together. I just want to be with you and feel that way too and stop worrying about what's going to happen. I didn't want to tell you about what I saw because I've been freaked out enough as it is, coming here to see my whole future laid out in front of me, and I didn't want you to be freaked out too. But if you want to know, I'll answer your questions. I shouldn't be the only one deciding whether I want that future, you should get to decide too.'

'OK, I'm not sure I want to know it all, there is some fun in finding it out for myself, but...' he reached out and ran his fingers through one of her curls. 'What colour is my baby's hair?'

She smiled at the way he was going with this. 'I can't tell you that.'

'Then you kind of already have.'

'I can't tell you because in the flashes I've seen of her here, growing up, she has green hair, blue, pink, gold, purple. She changes it every day, although I think she quite likes the purple.'

His eyes widened. 'She... she's a metamorph?'

'Yes she is.'

He stared at her in shock.

'And now I've freaked you out too. But yeah, that's what I've been struggling with for the last few days.'

'I'm not freaked out.' His voice was choked.

She laughed. 'Sure you're not. You thought we'd have a few dates, have a good time, and now you realise you're playing with fire, I'm the mother of your child, surprise!'

'I've been playing with fire my whole damn life. You don't scare me, Iris McKenzie.'

'You... you're OK with this?'

'I felt our connection was something special and beautiful the second we touched. This explains why.'

'But—'

Lynx stepped closer and stroked her face, then gave her the briefest, sweetest kiss that made her melt into him. 'I get that you're scared by this and that's OK. I'll be here waiting, if and when you're ready. And if you're not, that's OK too. It's one possible future, right? If that future includes marriage, or children, or whatever else you've seen, if we're going to bring a child into this world, then it will be in a loving relationship. If I ask you to marry me, it will be because I love you, completely and utterly. If I'm going to spend the rest of my life with a woman, I want to know she's there for the right reasons. That she loves me and I love her. Knowing this *possible* future doesn't change that. No one is going to force you into doing something you don't want to do.'

Iris stared at him. She hadn't been expecting him to be so calm about it.

'Come on, let's go and chill out over here for a bit, I'm sure it's time for that box of chocolate-covered strawberries,' Lynx said.

She followed him out of the pool, dried off a little and cheekily pulled his shirt on while he was still drying himself. He had a lot more to dry than she did and it was all muscle.

He turned round to see her wearing his shirt and smiled. 'That suits you.'

They lay down on the blanket and he clicked his fingers so the box of chocolate-covered strawberries appeared between them. She took one and it tasted delicious.

He bit into one too. 'That is good.'

He stroked her hair again. 'Listen, you don't have to decide now between all and nothing. It's not like we're going to be walking down the aisle tomorrow. It doesn't need to be a big deal.'

'It doesn't?'

'We can go out for dinner, have a few dates. If you're willing I'll make love to you.'

'I'm very willing.'

'And we see how we fit together. We can see if we like each other for something more. It doesn't have to end up with marriage, babies and a happy ever after. We'll just see how we go. But at least we'd know and we can stop worrying about the future.'

'You make it sound so easy.'

'It kind of is. It's just a few dates. No big deal.'

'But what if it ends with marriage, babies, the whole caboodle?'

'Then it will be because we've both fallen in love with each other, not because fate has decreed it so.'

Iris smiled. He made it sound so simple and she wanted that, she really did. 'OK.'

His face split into a huge smile. 'Really?'

'Yes, we can date. Maybe it's how you make me feel when I'm with you, that it just makes sense. But I'm not running from you any more. I'm not saying I'm going to suddenly start trying for a baby, but I want to give us a chance and see where this goes between us. And that includes dinner tonight.'

'Excellent. How about a picnic instead? I've taken you to my favourite place, you could take me to yours.'

She sat up. 'In Scotland?'

'Yes, I'll show you how to use the key stones. As long as it's nowhere near your house, I'm not risking you by going back there, but maybe a loch or beach or somewhere that's special to you.'

'I would love that and I know the perfect place.'

'Great, it's a date.'

She smiled and leaned forward to give him a sweet kiss. 'It's a date.'

Lynx pulled back. 'And I want you to know that it'll just be dinner, we'll talk, maybe kiss. But I absolutely promise not to take it any further than that, not tonight, so you don't need to worry about sex.'

'Unless I want to.'

His smile grew, then he shook his head. 'No, not tonight. I want to get this right and I don't want to rush things and—'

She put her finger on his lips to stop him talking. 'Relax. In the spirit of ruining things for you, the first time we make love is right over there near where the willow tree touches the water, the sun is setting, painting everything rosy gold. It's quite lovely. It won't happen on a beach in Scotland.'

He smiled. 'Right there?'

She nodded.

'Wow, this place is going to become a lot more special for me.'

She laughed. 'You have no idea.'

Iris opened the door to Fire and Ice and walked upstairs, excited to see what Wolf had done with the place.

She had left Lynx in his house after their swim and she was buzzing with excitement about their date that night. She really liked this man and it was silly to hold back just because she'd seen their future.

She stepped inside the shop and gasped. It looked exactly as she had designed on the VR headset but so much better. The design had looked digital, while this looked so real, she could almost feel the cold. She reached out to touch one of the ice walls and it did feel cold and wet to the touch. It really looked like she'd walked into a cave in the deepest Arctic. The ice sparkled and glittered in the natural light coming from the windows and from the little spotlights that would hang over the displays. Icicles hung over the windows and in stalactite and stalagmite type shapes around the room. But the pièce de résistance were the ice sculptures in the corners and at the entrances to each ice chamber. They looked so real, even down to the fine lines of the animals' fur.

She wandered through the different ice chambers and knew it would look spectacular once all the jewellery was in place.

'Hello!' Star called from the entrance to the shop and Iris came out of the tunnels to see her. 'What do you think, is it OK?'

'It's wonderful,' Iris said. 'Wolf has done an incredible job, I can't believe this is the same place that was four dusty walls yesterday.'

'He is very clever. He built the whole of Stardust Street himself, obviously with a lot of magic but you have to have that creative ability to pull something like this off.'

'I agree, it's incredible.'

'I'll tell him you're happy. But if you work here for the next few days and realise something is missing or in the wrong place, it will be very easy to change it.'

'OK, thanks.'

'And you should probably know you were right

about the baby. We took the test this morning. Several in fact.'

'Congratulations.'

'Thanks,' Star said, nervously. 'We're excited but it is a little worrying. Blaze is only seven months and she is into everything. The fact she's magical makes it even more exhausting, you have to have eyes everywhere. And she's brilliant and funny and I love her so much, but having two under the age of two is going to be a rollercoaster.'

Iris smiled. 'Well, I'm always here to help, and I'm sure Lynx will lend a hand too.'

'I know, he's already helped so much. And thank you, I might just take you up on that offer. But living here has been wonderful, I can't imagine what it would be like to raise a magical child out there in the mundane world. Here it's safe. She can set fire to our plants in the front garden and no one bats an eye. She made Wolf's car fly the other day and everyone coos how cute she is. She'll never have any fear or judgement or hatred from those that don't understand or know about our world. It's a haven here and I feel so lucky to have it.'

Iris nodded, knowing she felt the same. It was silly to think that far ahead when she was having her first date with Lynx tonight, but if everything played out how fate had shown her, she would be bringing a child into the world in the next year or so. Despite what Lynx had promised her about spending half the year here and half the year in Scotland, she wanted to raise her daughter here, where it was safe, where she wouldn't have to grow up like Iris, keeping the best part of her hidden. This was going to be her home and, although she'd miss Scotland and they'd have to visit often, she couldn't be happier about staying here.

Lynx was walking towards Stardust Street with a big smile on his face. Iris was going to be the mother of his child? When she'd said it, he'd been quite calm about it, but now it was really starting to sink in.

He'd always been a believer in people having a soul mate, the one person they were supposed to be with. And after watching Wolf and Star get together, he now believed in it a whole lot more.

When he'd dated other women, he'd always felt that he had been missing something with them although he'd never known what it was he was looking for. He'd told himself he wanted a deeper connection, without knowing what that looked like. And then, *there* was Iris McKenzie and he suddenly felt like he'd found what he'd been searching for all his life. To find out they were fated to be together kind of made a lot of sense. Although it was still going to take a bit of getting used to. A few days before he'd had no idea this whole life was laid out in front of him and now it looked like he was going to spend the rest of his life with her, and he couldn't help smiling about that. But only if she was willing to let him in.

He saw Ashley coming towards him.

'Hey, Ashley, did Iris talk to you about the locket?'

'Yes, she did.' Ashley was looking worried.

'What's wrong?'

'Lynx, something is very wrong with that locket.'

'What do you mean?'

'I could feel it, lying in bed last night, this weird energy in the house. I went downstairs to see if I could locate it and it was coming from the cupboard where the locket was. I took it out and I could feel this bad energy coming from inside the locket.'

'Some kind of magic?'

'I don't know. If it is it's certainly nothing I've ever come across before.'

'Iris said the locket wasn't magical, that the only energy it had was from being worn by someone magical.'

'Well she's either lying, or she doesn't know. Or the man that took it from her did something to it, maybe a curse. I can't be sure until I open it.'

'A curse? Her ex-boyfriend is a mundane. And when she used her magic to steal it back from him, it was quite clear he'd never seen magic before, so I can't see it would be that.'

Which meant it could only be the first two options.

'Look, I like Iris,' Ashley said. 'I can just get a feeling for someone and I've never been wrong. She's a good person, I can feel that. But there is something dodgy about that locket and it gives me a really bad feeling. I suppose what I'm feeling could just be kelpie energy from her nan wearing it, and its kelpie heritage, but it didn't feel like the energy that I felt from Iris, nowhere close. And the kelpie energy I feel from Iris isn't bad, just different.'

Lynx pushed his hand through his hair. 'I trust Iris.'

Ashley smiled. 'I do too. It's the locket I don't trust.'

'I need to talk to her about this.'

'I agree, maybe she can shed some light on it. And I need to talk to Wolf and tell him we could potentially be dealing with a cursed item here. We'll have to put some protective spells around it once I can open it. I have a spell I'm going to do on it at midnight tomorrow, under a full moon, which should get rid of the glue but it will take a few hours for the spell to kick in, normally twelve, so it will probably be ready at lunchtime the day after.'

'OK, we'll be there.'

She nodded and hurried away.

He swore under his breath that he'd now have to talk to Iris about them having brought a potentially cursed item to the village.

He walked into the shop and could hear her singing

upstairs. He stopped and listened. It was sweet and melodious and beautifully haunting. He could easily imagine her sitting on the side of the loch, singing, and how that would charm passersby.

He walked upstairs and looked around in awe at the incredible ice cave. The villagers were going to get a big kick out of this. She was tweaking the displays of jewellery. She looked up at him and her face broke into a huge smile.

'Hey, I'm going to be ready to open tomorrow and whoop your ass.'

He laughed. 'Are we still doing the competition? I've already got a dinner date for tonight, so it kind of already feels like I've won.'

She moved over to him and, wrapping her arms around him, leaned up and kissed him. This was so much nicer than her running away from their attraction.

'If you win, I'll give you dessert.'

He laughed. 'Then you need something better than me just kissing your feet if you win.' He ran his finger over his lips as he thought and then fixed her with a dark look. 'I'll think of something.'

She laughed. 'You know I have a slight advantage. As it'll be opening day people are going to be curious about the new shop, I'll probably get a lot more footfall tomorrow than an average day.'

'That's OK, it feels like a win for me either way.

Besides, extra footfall for you means extra footfall for me too.'

'True.'

He stroked her hair from her face and she looked so happy. There was no way she was hiding some dark secret from him. He trusted her completely.

'Listen, we need to talk. Ashley has sensed something bad about the locket.'

She frowned. 'What do you mean?'

'She says she felt this bad energy last night and traced it to the locket. She doesn't know what it is as it's not any kind of magic she's ever felt before, but she thinks there's something inside the locket and whatever it is she has a bad feeling about it. She wondered if the locket might even be cursed.'

'Cursed? Surely if Ness had been wearing it every day for the last sixty years, opening it daily to see the picture of her and her husband on her wedding day, we would have let the curse out by now or felt it, or seen it or reaped the bad luck from it? And I can't see her husband giving a cursed locket to her as a wedding gift. That doesn't sound romantic to me.'

'Could Christopher have done something to it?'

'He's a mundane, he doesn't know anything about witches or kelpies or magic.'

'Something is wrong with it.'

Iris frowned as if remembering something.

'What's wrong?'

'I don't know, just something my nan said last night. I need to talk to her. This doesn't make sense. I didn't feel anything and neither did my nan when I gave it back to her briefly.'

'I didn't feel anything either. Well, I felt it had an energy when I first saw it, but as we said that was just residual kelpie energy from your nan wearing it. It would be infused with that energy, just as any item of jewellery would be after being worn by someone magical. But kelpie magic or energy isn't bad. Even so, I have to trust Ashley's instincts about this. If she says there is something bad inside that locket, then I believe her. Is it possible Christopher has hired a witch to put some kind of protective spell on it? There are witches all over the internet offering their services. Most people don't believe in witches and magic but that doesn't stop desperate people paying for a spell. That locket is worth millions, that would make someone pretty desperate to protect it.'

'What do we do?'

'There is nothing we can do right now. Ashley says she is going to do a spell on it tomorrow night at midnight under the full moon, to cleanse the locket of the glue, and that we'll probably have to wait until the day after for it to kick in. Then we open it and... we'll see what's inside. Whatever it is, we'll deal with it then.'

'I hate this, I don't want to do anything to curse the village or hurt anyone.'

'There's no point worrying about this until we can open it. And we have some very powerful witches in the village. I'm sure we can deal with it safely.'

Iris nodded and he hugged her. Whatever it was, they'd face it together.

CHAPTER 12

Iris had spent the afternoon laying out all her stock and getting it ready for the big opening the next day, although her heart wasn't in it.

She was excited for it but she couldn't stop thinking about the locket and the fact that Ashley had sensed something bad coming from inside. What if they had brought something awful to the village inside that locket, something that could threaten the safety of the villagers? She also kept on thinking about what her nan had said the night before when she'd found out that the locket was glued together. She'd said, 'I need what's inside,' which Iris had thought was a weird turn of phrase, but she'd assumed her nan had meant the wedding photo of her and Pops. Now she wasn't so sure. Surely her nan hadn't been hiding something cursed and dangerous all this time and never told her?

Iris had sworn to Lynx, Wolf and Star that the locket wasn't magical, that it held no powers, but what if that was a lie?

She heard footsteps on the stairs and Erin came in with a big grin on her face. 'I hear you and Lynx were seen coming out of the woods this morning looking very loved-up and holding hands.'

'Is nothing secret in this place?' Iris laughed, putting away her fears over the locket until she could do something about them. 'I wouldn't go so far as to say loved-up, but yes, we were holding hands.'

Erin gave a little squeal of excitement. 'What happened? I thought you were holding back for revenge purposes.'

'Well, you know there's a mutual attraction. We've decided to date and see how things go.'

Iris really didn't want to mention that if it went well there'd be marriage and babies within a few years. She trusted Erin to a certain extent but she didn't want the whole village to know about her future before it had happened, although Zofia might tell everyone anyway.

'Now that is exciting. Although I am a bit sad I don't get to see you exact your revenge on Lynx.'

Iris laughed. 'He's too nice for me to hold a grudge.'

'Yeah he is, which is very annoying. How's it going in here?'

'Really well. I've never had my own shop before and I'm really enjoying getting it ready. Fear of rejection and judgement, of not fitting in, has had such an impact on my life and how I lived it. I would never have been brave enough to do something like this out there in the real world.'

'Yeah, I didn't fully appreciate how wonderful it is to never have to worry about someone seeing your magic until I came here. I own the seafood restaurant at the end of Stardust Street, the one shaped like a pirate galleon, and everything is so much easier to do when you can use magic freely. I used to own a café out there in the real world, as you call it. The Black Cat Café. It was a novelty café, all decked out with cauldrons and witchy paraphernalia. When I did magic like floating their meals out of the kitchen onto the tables people loved it, thought it was all some really cool special effects.'

Erin pushed her hair back from her face. 'I got carried away, I thought I could do any magic and people would be fine with it, because it was part of the gimmick of the café. But people started to get a bit uneasy about it all. When the tables would clear themselves, plates stacking themselves and floating back off to the kitchen, it was too much for their mundane brains to take in. People stopped coming. And then there was the fear, the hatred, the comments. Maybe if I'd been in a big city I would have got away with it, but living in a little seaside town, they definitely weren't open to it. Now, here, everything is done with magic. I can even mow my lawn with a wave of a hand without having to worry what the neighbours think. There really is a lot to be said for being your true self.'

'You're right,' Iris said. 'And I think that's important in a relationship too. I've never been with a man I could be a hundred percent myself with either.'

Erin nodded and then her face lit up. 'Wait, have you never been with a witch before?'

'No, generally I had very little to do with witches. I always found they were suspicious of us, as they knew we weren't proper witches. And my nan was always suspicious of them as historically the witches have not been kind to the kelpies.'

'Oh wow, you're in for a treat,' Erin said.

'What does that mean?'

'When two witches have sex they connect on a magical level. His magic and yours, they become one. It's very intimate because you're sharing a part of yourself that no one else gets to touch and it really is quite beautiful.'

Iris stared at her. 'Are you joking?'

Erin grinned. 'Once you've had witch sex, you never go back.'

Just then Lynx walked into the shop. He stopped when he saw her.

He turned to Erin. 'Why does she look like a rabbit in the headlights?'

'I was just trying to explain about witch sex,' Erin said, innocently.

'Ah yes, I was just thinking about that.'

'You were thinking about witch sex?' Iris asked.

'I think this might be my cue to leave,' Erin laughed. She gave them a wave and hurried out.

Lynx walked over to Iris and put his hands on her shoulders. 'Since you mentioned that our first time will be in the pool, I've been having trouble focusing on anything else. Not witch sex, just me and you, together. And there's no rush for that, but I can't deny I've been thinking about what it will be like to touch you, to feel your body against mine. And while I was working in my shop just now, letting my mind wander, I did think about what it will be like to connect with you on that magical level. And then I remembered you'd said you'd never dated a witch before, so I thought I should come up here and talk to you about it.'

'You want to talk to me about sex? This isn't my first rodeo, I don't need a diagram about which bit goes where.'

Lynx laughed. 'The mechanics of it are all the same but there is a point when our magic will connect too and it can be quite a shock if you're not expecting it. Can I show you?'

'Now?' Iris looked around in alarm.

'Not sex, just a little bit of what it feels like when our magic connects.'

She frowned and then nodded. 'OK.'

He took her hands in his. 'OK, close your eyes.'

She flashed him a look. 'No funny business.'

He laughed and she closed her eyes.

'So I'm going to touch your magic with mine,' Lynx said.

She knew the second he had done it as she could feel him everywhere, inside her, surrounding her, almost as if he was a part of her. She opened her eyes to look at him. It was so intense, so intimate, almost as if she was standing naked in front of him. She felt like he could see every single part of her. She could feel his magic, this bright burning fire spreading through her. He was strong and powerful. She felt like he was consuming her and she was surprised how much she wanted that.

He released his hold over her and she let out a breath. He seemed breathless too.

'That was incredible,' she said.

'Yeah, for me too. And when we make love it will be so much more. It's a lot more powerful than that.'

She reached up to kiss him, cupping his face, and he wrapped his arms around her, holding her close. She pulled away fractionally, feeling his heavy breath on her lips. 'I can't wait.'

He grinned and kissed her and she loved the way his fingers played up her back as he held her.

She pulled back and rested her hands on his chest.

Downstairs, she heard Lynx's shop door open.

'Hellooo!' came a woman's voice from the bottom of the stairs.

'Oh crap,' Lynx said. 'That's my grandmother, Zofia. I thought she'd be content with waiting until the poker game tonight to meet you but clearly not.'

Iris laughed.

They heard footsteps on the stairs.

'Can I hide you somewhere?' Lynx asked.

'She can't be that bad.'

'Trust me on this, she'll be asking if we've slept together yet, how many orgasms I gave you, whether I'm the best sex you've ever had. And then it will quickly turn into when do you want to get married and how many children do you want. Come on, hide out the back.'

'How about in plain sight?' Iris quickly changed so she looked exactly like Storm Quinn, towering over Lynx.

Lynx let out a bark of laughter.

'Wait, where does he come from?' Iris said, in a man's voice. She could do a generic man's voice pretty well but she wasn't great at accents.

'I think he comes from Spain originally but—'

Suddenly Zofia arrived in the room with them, her eyes lighting up at the potential of meeting Iris. Zofia looked around and Iris watched her shoulders slump when she couldn't see her.

'Where is she?'

'Hi Zofia,' Lynx said, wearily. 'Iris is on a break. She popped out to the coffee shop, I think.'

'I thought I'd come and show my support to the new shop,' Zofia said.

'I'm sure that's why you're here,' Lynx said.

Zofia eyed Iris. 'Hello Storm, how are you settling in, dear?'

Iris cleared her throat in preparation for trying her best Spanish accent. 'Hello Zofia. Fine thanks.'

Lynx's eyes widened and Iris knew it had been bad. Even Zofia's eyes narrowed suspiciously.

'Umm, Storm was just telling me he's had a throat infection for the last few days,' Lynx said.

'And I was just leaving,' Iris said; even she could tell how bad her accent was.

'I'll walk you out, dear. I'm glad I bumped into you. I wanted to talk to you too.'

'Oh, I'm in a bit of a rush,' Iris said.

'It won't take long.'

Iris gestured for Zofia to go ahead of her. She flashed Lynx a look of desperation and he shrugged helplessly before she clomped after Zofia down the stairs and out on to the street.

Zofia threaded her arm through Iris's. 'Have you had much chance to meet some of the other villagers?'

Iris remembered that Erin had said that Storm was

grumpy and rude to everyone so she figured she could get away with short answers.

'No,' Iris said.

'Erin's a lovely girl, have you had a chance to talk to her?'

'No,' Iris said again. Although it was curious that Zofia would try to matchmake Erin and Storm. Iris wondered if she knew about the dreams Erin had been having.

And if fate was watching all this unfold, it suddenly decided to make an awkward situation ten times worse, as Storm stepped out of one of the shops in front of them and came face to face with... himself.

'What the hell?' Storm said, clearly angry.

Iris burst out laughing and quickly changed back into herself. 'I'm so sorry.'

He stepped back, eyes wide, and Zofia looked stunned too.

Iris took a step back, keen to avoid Storm's wrath. 'I should go, but you two should talk.'

With that she hotfooted it back to her shop, giggling at their faces.

'That little minx,' Zofia said.

Iris burst back into the shop and Lynx looked up from where he was working.

'Abort, abort,' Iris said.

'What happened?'

'We ran into Storm.'

Lynx laughed loudly.

'Are they going to be mad at me?'

'Zofia won't. She'll definitely see the funny side. Storm, not so much. I haven't seen him crack a smile yet.'

The shop door opened and Storm barrelled in towards her.

'Oh crap,' Iris said.

Inexplicably Lynx moved in front of her. Lynx was a big man but Storm was a giant – if this actually ended in a fight, it would be over very quickly and probably not in Lynx's favour. Although Lynx was a powerful strong witch, and could probably defend himself if need be, Iris felt her magic rise in her. She would wipe Storm out with a torrent of water to protect Lynx.

'Now there's no need to be angry,' Lynx said. 'It was just a joke at Zofia's expense. We didn't mean any harm to you.'

'I'm really sorry,' Iris said.

'I don't care about that,' Storm said, urgently, his eyes only on hers. 'Are you a kelpie?'

Dear Gods, was this about to become her first time encountering kelpie hatred in the village? She knew the horrible reputation that preceded them, and that some witches were wary of them because of it, but everyone had been so lovely about her heritage so far. Should she lie, deny all knowledge?

'Because the only person I've ever known who

could change shape like that, completely melt into another person, was a kelpie. So are you?' Storm asked.

'Wait, you... you've met a kelpie before?' Iris asked, hoping his experience had been a positive one.

'Yes,' Storm cleared his throat. 'My wife. She passed away a year ago.'

'I'm so sorry.'

'She used to...' he smiled slightly. 'She used to do me. When I was in a bad mood, she'd change into me and stomp around like a belligerent teenager. She'd say, "I'm Storm, I'm a big grumpy man." And it always used to make me laugh.'

Iris stepped around Lynx, letting go of her magic. 'I'm sorry, I didn't mean to upset you with memories of her.'

'It's OK. They're good memories. So, are you?'

Iris nodded. 'Yeah. I've never met another kelpie before, outside of my family, I had no idea there were others out there. But Erin said her childhood best friend was one and now I find out you were married to one. There are obviously more of us out there than I realised.'

'I've never met another either,' Storm said. He held out his hand. 'Storm Quinn.'

'Iris McKenzie.' She took his hand and shook it and suddenly had a flash of his future. Surprisingly it was linked with Erin. Maybe Zofia had seen more than she'd let on when she'd thought she was talking to Storm a few minutes before.

'I take it you can see my future too. Amelia could do that as well.'

'Yes, just flashes.'

'I don't want to know,' Storm said, quickly.

'I don't blame you, I was freaked out enough when I came here and saw my future was tied to Lynx.'

Storm glanced at Lynx and smirked. 'The first time I met Amelia she told me we were going to get married. Surprisingly it didn't scare me off. It just sort of... made sense. I had never before believed that love at first sight was possible until I met her.'

'I know what you mean,' Lynx said. 'Iris and I had an immediate connection too, and when I found out we were fated to be together forever, our connection made so much more sense.'

Storm nodded and turned his attention back to Iris. 'You don't know how happy it makes me to meet another kelpie. I've been living under a dark cloud for the last year and meeting you has felt like the cloud has lifted slightly. Would it be OK, with you both, if I came back here to talk to you again?'

'Of course,' Iris said. 'I've just moved here and I don't know many people. I'm always happy to make new friends.'

Storm turned to Lynx. 'Is it OK, this isn't anything romantic or—'

'Absolutely, I'm totally fine with it.'

Storm nodded. 'Thank you.'

With that he walked out.

Iris wrapped her arms around Lynx. 'Big sexy man wants to be my friend and you're OK with it?'

Lynx shrugged. 'Why wouldn't I be? If you wanted to be with him, you'd be with him. But I trust in that future you've seen. If we love each other enough to get married and bring children into the world then no one else will ever come close. And if it doesn't get that far because you've found someone else, then I'd want that for you because he obviously makes you happy.'

She slid her arms round his neck and kissed him. 'That's very confident.'

He kissed her. 'I know I can make you very happy.'

She laughed at the dark look in his eyes. 'I'm looking forward to it.'

The door to Lynx's shop was pushed open and a customer came in.

'I must go and finish getting ready for the opening tomorrow, see if I can win this competition,' Iris said.

'Well don't try too hard.'

Iris laughed and ran up the stairs.

'How are we going to play this poker game?' Lynx asked as they walked back to their road.

'Badly, going by my previous experience of playing poker,' Iris said. 'I know how to play and understand the rules, I've played quite a bit with Ness over the years, but I never win.'

'No, I mean, with our interfering grandparents. Should we just tell them we're dating so we get them off our backs?'

'No, I think we make them work at it. We go in there and be nothing but polite to each other, no affection at all. Really make them think they have their work cut out.'

He grinned. 'I like it. Also Zofia has chosen poker for one reason: she's really good at it. I suspect she wants to win so we have to kiss each other or something absurd as a forfeit. So if that's the case we'll just give each a really chaste kiss.'

'A peck on the cheek.'

Lynx laughed. 'That will infuriate her.'

'Perfect.'

'But I've lost a lot of money to her over the years at poker, so I've been brushing up on my skills every opportunity I've had. It's been a while since we played so she won't be expecting it. If she's going to win tonight, she'll have to work hard.'

'Or cheat.'

'Now I wouldn't put it past her. Nor would I put it

215

past her to have cheated in the past. But fortunately, on my travels, I came across an anti-cheating spell so that should put a stop to any little tricks she has up her sleeve.'

Iris laughed. 'OK, I look forward to it. I'll see you shortly. I need to talk to my nan about the locket.'

He nodded and waved goodbye before heading over to his house.

She took a deep breath and walked up the path of her house. She had a feeling this conversation was going to end up in confrontation and she wasn't looking forward it.

She walked into the lounge to find a poker table she didn't know they owned or had brought with them, with some casino-style chips in the middle. There were also snacks on little side tables; her nan was obviously taking this thing very seriously. Or Zofia was.

Her nan was sitting doing her crossword.

'Hello, how's the shop looking?' Ness asked, peering over her glasses.

'It's looking really good, I'll be ready to open tomorrow.' Iris sat down next to her. 'Nan, I need to talk to you about the locket.'

'What about it, has something happened to it?'

'What's inside the locket?'

Her nan looked alarmed and Iris immediately knew she hadn't been truthful with her. 'I don't know what you mean. Nothing is inside the locket, just an old wedding photo, nothing else.'

'Nan, don't lie to me.'

'I'm not.'

'You are, I can tell.'

'Why do you think there's something inside the locket?'

'Because Ashley said she can feel something dark from it.'

'That's rubbish, there's nothing bad inside that locket.'

'Nan, if there's something dark about that locket, you need to tell me, we can't let Ashley or anyone else open it if someone is going to get hurt. This village is a safe place, we can't ruin that. Last night when I told you the locket was glued shut, you said you needed what was inside. What did you mean by that?'

'Just... that I wanted to be able to see my wedding photo again.'

'Nan! This is serious, these people have trusted us, they've looked after us, protected us. We can't bring something bad into their home.'

'Why won't you believe me?'

'Because I know you and you're a terrible liar. You're hiding something about that locket and I don't know why you won't tell me the truth.'

'Because I don't want you to think less of me,' Ness blurted out.

This silenced Iris. 'There is nothing in this world that would make me think less of you. Unless that locket is made from the bones of dead puppies, I love you and I could never ever think less of you.'

Ness sighed. 'It's not dead puppies.'

'Dead kittens?' Iris teased.

'Stop it,' Ness grumbled.

'Just tell me.'

'Iris, I'm eighty-six years old.'

'I'm very aware of how old you are.'

'And my mind isn't what it was. I forget things. I'll go into the kitchen to get my book or a drink and I'll forget what I went in there for.'

'I do that all the time.'

'I forgot to charm the locket so Christopher wouldn't see it.'

'That's an easy mistake to make and we both thought we could trust him.'

'I forgot to bring the evidence we needed to prove the locket was ours.'

'Well I was rushing you to leave the house, that wasn't your fault.'

'And I've forgotten what your mum looks like.'

Iris swallowed a lump in her throat.

Ness shook her head. 'My only daughter and when I think about her I can't picture her face anymore. I can't remember her smile or the way she laughed. I can't remember what she smelled like, I can't remember how her eyes changed colour when she was happy. I know they did, but I can't remember what colours. There are other memories too, my wedding day, the way your grandfather looked when I told him I was pregnant. You being born.' She cleared her throat as it was clear she was struggling to talk. 'Everything that is important to me is fading away. Sometimes it comes back to me, as clear as day, and then it's gone again the next second, slipping through my hands like water. So over the years, I've stored them in my locket. All the important memories I still had but didn't want to lose, or whenever a memory would come back to me fleetingly, I stored each one inside a tiny crystal and added it to the rim of the locket. Every day, I'd sit slowly running my fingers over each crystal so I could see the way your mum laughed again, so I could see your grandad crying with happiness when I walked up the aisle. Those are things I never want to lose.'

Iris took her hand. 'Oh Nan, why didn't you tell me?'

'I didn't want you to think I'm weak.'

'I would never think that. You're one of the greatest women I know. You're strong, badass, you can take on the world.'

'So why have you not told me about the police looking for you and that every news programme is carrying this story?'

Iris sighed. 'Because I didn't want to worry you.'

'There was a time we told each other everything,' Ness said. 'Good and bad and we dealt with it together.'

Iris nodded. 'How about we make a promise that from now on we'll be completely truthful with each other?'

Ness held out a hand and Iris shook it. 'I promise.'

'I promise too. And in the spirit of that promise, want to tell me what's going on at this poker game tonight?'

Ness sighed. 'I knew it was a bad idea. Zofia is desperate to get you and Lynx together and she coerced me into helping. When she wins, she's going to give you a forfeit that you have to go out on a date tonight.'

Iris laughed and shook her head. 'As we're being completely honest, I already have a date with Lynx tonight. We've kissed a few times too and I've told him about his daughter, our daughter. But we're not going to tell Zofia any of that. We're going to make her work hard to get that date.'

Ness laughed. 'I'm happy for you and I'm more than willing to help.'

'Although we're not going to drag it out too long, I want time for our date too.'

'Got it. So back to the locket. There's no way Ashley is sensing my memories and could possibly think they were something bad.'

'I agree, but I'll have to tell her about the memories just in case. Maybe she's sensing the magic involved in making those memory crystals and jumping to the wrong conclusion.'

'Either she's got it wrong or Christopher has done something to the locket.'

'I don't think she's wrong.'

'Then what the hell did he do? I swear, if he's done something to my memories I will hunt him down and chop off his balls.'

Iris smiled. 'That's the Ness I know. I think we'll just have to wait and see. Ashley is doing a spell on it tomorrow night and we'll be able to open it at lunchtime the day after that.'

There was a knock on the door.

'For now we have some poker to win.'

CHAPTER 13

Lynx knocked on Iris's door and looked around at Viktor, who had randomly decided he wanted to play poker with them too, and Zofia, who was humming with excitement.

'If this is some kind of set-up, I'll be really annoyed,' Lynx said, knowing full well it was.

'Of course it's not,' said his grandmother. 'I just thought it'd be nice to welcome them to the village.'

'With poker?'

'Why not. Ness said she loved poker.'

'I just think you're barking up the wrong tree with me and Iris. I like her, but the more time I spend with her, I can't see a future there at all. I think we had that initial fizz of excitement when we met but that's well and truly fizzled out now.'

'Now this is music to my ears,' Viktor said.

Zofia looked horrified. 'Are you serious?'

Lynx shrugged. 'She doesn't really do it for me. Also, I think she and Storm have become quite friendly after what happened today. I think they like each other. I'm happy for her, he seems like a good man.'

'No, no, no, this won't work at all.'

'No, it won't work,' Viktor said. 'If she ends up with Storm, she'll still be here and so will that bloody fox.'

Lynx frowned in confusion.

'It won't work because Storm is supposed to end up with Erin,' Zofia said.

'Erin and Storm?' Lynx said in surprise. He hadn't seen that coming.

'Forget I said that. You and Iris are fated to be together, the sooner you get on board with that idea, the better.'

'You can't force them together if they don't like each other,' Viktor said.

'Exactly,' Lynx said. 'You've always said there's no spell or potion in the world that can make two people fall in love. I think you've made a mistake with this one. Maybe your skill is getting a bit rusty in your old age.'

'I'll give you old,' Zofia snapped.

Just then the door opened to Ness. 'Oh hello, thank you all for coming.'

'Ness, we haven't properly met yet, I'm Lynx.'

'Oh, nice to meet you. Iris has told me all about you.'

'She has?' Zofia's eyes lit up.

'Well yes, mostly how infuriating and annoying she finds you. But she said you were a nice enough man.' Ness gave his shoulder a consoling pat and Lynx had to suppress a bark of laughter. Iris has clearly been planting seeds of her own.

'Well come in, come in,' she ushered them inside. 'Oh hello, you must be Viktor.'

'I am. And thank you for pronouncing my name correctly. Your pet fox couldn't seem to get it right but then I've always found foxes a little stupid.'

'Viktor, don't be rude,' Zofia snapped. 'It doesn't make a good impression.'

'I am nearly two thousand years old, I stopped trying to impress people a long time ago. I know I am impressive, if people can't see that then they really are stupid.' Viktor stalked inside.

'Sorry about him,' Zofia said as they followed him inside.

Iris was waiting inside with Morag, who scowled at Viktor as he glowered back at her. This was clearly going to be an entertaining night.

'Hello Zofia, sorry about earlier,' Iris said.

'Oh no, it was all good fun,' Zofia chuckled. 'It's nice to properly meet you.'

'And you.' Iris turned her attention to him. 'Lynx,' she nodded, politely.

'Iris.'

Out the corner of his eye he could see Zofia nearly blowing a gasket at their complete indifference.

'Well, let's get down to business,' Ness said. '*Midsomer Murders* is on at seven and I can't miss that. Five-card draw, I'll deal.'

'Oh, I thought I would deal,' Zofia said, meaningfully, nervously holding the pack of cards. She definitely had a few tricks up her sleeve.

'Why don't I deal,' Lynx said, swiping the deck of cards out of her hand. He knew Zofia was going to find a way to deal at some point in the night, but he just needed to touch the cards to place his anti-cheating spell on them first. Although he'd only tried it once so he wasn't entirely sure how effective it would be. Nevertheless, as he shuffled the deck, he placed his spell on the cards and hoped for the best.

'Well, I think we can all take it in turns to deal,' Zofia said. 'But by all means Lynx, you can deal to start with. The night is young.'

They all sat down at the table and Morag and Viktor jumped up onto opposite corners, glaring at each other.

Lynx dealt out five cards to everyone including himself.

Iris looked at her cards. 'Oh, good hand, but I'll twist.'

Lynx smirked but hid it behind his hand of cards.

'That's pontoon,' Zofia said.

'Or blackjack,' Ness pointed out.

'You do know how to play poker, don't you?' Zofia said.

'Of course.' Iris studied her cards. 'Are aces high or low?'

'Both,' Zofia said.

'Oh that's confusing.'

'This is going to be a walk in the park,' Zofia muttered.

'So I was just telling Zofia, you have a thing for Storm,' Lynx said to Iris.

She looked blankly at Lynx for a second before nodding. 'Yes, big sexy man, what's there not to like.'

'Surely you would prefer to be with someone you connect with on a much deeper level?' Zofia said.

'I suppose,' Iris shrugged. 'But I've not met anyone here that I have that with. I bet Storm could show me a good time.'

'No,' Zofia snapped. 'I mean. There's a lot more to a relationship than sex.'

'But sex is always a good place to start,' Ness said.

Zofia looked at her in confusion, as did Lynx. He hadn't been expecting solidarity there.

'I'll take another card,' Iris said, sliding one of hers along the table to Lynx. He dealt her another one.

'I'll take one too,' Ness said.

'I'll take another,' Iris said, which wasn't strictly allowed but Lynx did it anyway.

'So to be clear, you two haven't had sex yet?' Viktor asked.

'Oh no,' Iris shuddered with disgust.

Lynx pulled a face and shook his head. 'Definitely not. She's not my type.'

'Well, that is good news,' Viktor said.

Morag glowered at him, making throat-slitting gestures.

'Aha, rummy!' Iris said, laying down her hand of cards to show everyone.

'We're not playing rummy,' Zofia said, exasperated. But everyone looked down at Iris's cards to see she had a royal flush.

'She can call it what she wants, that still trumps everyone else,' Morag said.

'This is going to be a long night,' Zofia mumbled.

Iris was having trouble not laughing. Zofia was looking thoroughly dejected and Iris almost felt sorry for her. Almost. Lynx's grandmother had tried every trick in the book to try and get her and Lynx together. She'd started off telling Iris all Lynx's good points, how he travelled the world, how he gave a lot of money to charity, how he'd saved a baby rabbit and how he'd even donated his bone marrow to one of the witch kids in the village a few years before. All of this had undeniably made Iris fall for him even more but she had to look like she was completely bored by this information.

Zofia had then spent a good deal of time talking about fated love stories and how it was always perfect when two soul mates found each other and how theirs were always the happiest marriages because they were two halves of a whole reconnecting again. Iris had told her she didn't believe in any of that stuff and Lynx had agreed.

Throughout it all, Viktor was getting happier and happier and Morag, who they hadn't had time to tell what they were up to, was getting more and more confused and annoyed with Viktor. Iris had spent a long time trying to pretend she didn't understand the rules of poker but despite that Zofia had lost every single round.

Because of Iris's supposed lack of knowledge when it came to poker, and to speed things along a little, Zofia had soon decided they should play in teams. Of course, that meant that Iris was now paired up with Lynx, which they both had objected to. But now she was sitting very close to Lynx so they could look at the cards together and his citrusy spicy scent was wonderful and his hand had secretly been resting on the bare flesh of the inside of her knee for the last half hour, which was utterly delicious. So much so, she wanted the game to come to an end so she could finally spend some alone time with him.

'This has been fun,' Iris said. 'But I have some work I need to get done tonight ready for the big opening tomorrow, so I'm going to bow out now.'

'Me too,' Lynx said, a bit too quickly. 'I mean, I have things I need to do too.'

'One more game,' Zofia said. 'And why don't we make this interesting,' she added, right on cue. Iris had been waiting for her to reveal her hand.

'I can't afford to play for real money,' Iris protested.

'I wasn't talking about money.'

'I'm not playing strip poker,' Lynx said.

'No, whichever team loses has to pay a forfeit,' Zofia said.

'What kind of forfeit?' Iris said.

'Just whatever we come up with you have to do,' Zofia said.

'I want to know the terms before we agree,' Iris said.

'OK. If you two lose, you have to go out on a date tonight,' Zofia said.

'I'm not agreeing to that,' Lynx said, folding his arms.

'It's just dinner, a picnic, maybe on the village green or in the woods. We'll provide all the food and drink so you don't have to lift a finger. If at the end of the night you decide you don't want anything more to do with each other then I promise to leave you both alone from now on.'

'Now that's the kind of arrangement I could get on board with,' Lynx said. 'No more interfering, no comments, no stalking us.'

Zofia nodded. 'I promise.'

'OK, I'll agree to that. But what are you going to do if you lose?' Lynx said. 'I know, you'll both walk through the village, stark naked.'

'Fine by me,' Ness said, who was more than used to getting her kit off.

Zofia cleared her throat. 'OK. If that's what you want.'

Ness dealt the cards and Lynx and Iris studied their hand. It was a full house, which was a good hand, probably capable of winning, although there were a few other hands that would rank better.

'Place your bets,' Ness said.

Lynx and Zofia both tossed their chips into the middle, Lynx throwing a big handful to intimidate his grandmother, or at least make her sweat.

'Any replacements?' Ness asked.

They both shook their heads and Zofia and Ness didn't replace any of their cards either.

'Any further bets?'

Iris looked at Lynx and fractionally shook her head.

'We fold,' Lynx said, throwing his cards face down onto the table.

'We won?' Zofia said in surprise. 'We won?'

'You won,' Iris said.

Zofia stood up to do a little victory dance and then clicked her fingers. A large picnic basket appeared in her hand and she offered it out to Iris.

'Wow, so you didn't plan this at all then?' Lynx said, sarcastically.

'You agreed to the terms,' Zofia said.

'Fine, we'll go out on a date, but no one said anything about enjoying it.'

'No, but you could at least try to be nice,' Zofia said.

'Come on, let's get it over with,' Iris said, taking the basket.

Lynx let out a huff of annoyance and stood up. He took the basket from her, opened the door and ushered her out.

They walked across the road in silence just in case Zofia was watching and quickly went inside Lynx's house.

Immediately he took her in his arms. 'Well, that was a fun night.'

Iris laughed. 'I loved seeing Zofia getting more and more desperate. Although I was sorely tempted to try and win that round, just to see her really getting her comeuppance.'

'Me too. We've probably thrown her off the scent for a day or two but her all-seeing ability will catch up with us soon.'

'Well, let's make the most of it and go on our date.' She let go of him and bent to pick up the picnic basket.

'No leave that, I can call that to us once we're there.' Lynx went over to the key stones and picked up a medium-sized one. 'OK, this part won't be fun. But the travelling only lasts for a few seconds and the after-effects wear off after a minute. It's going to feel like you're on the worst rollercoaster in the world, but it'll be worth it to go back to Scotland.'

Iris nodded, taking the stone.

'Nowhere near your house, remember.'

'I promise. There aren't even any houses or roads near where we are going, we'll be quite safe.'

'OK,' he wrapped his arms tight around her. 'All you have to do is feel the energy in the stone, picture that place in your mind, see it, smell it, feel it, as many details as you can, and then connect your magic to the stone's energy and we'll be there. Whatever you do, don't let go of the stone.'

She nodded, closed her eyes and wrapped her free hand tightly in Lynx's shirt, picturing her favourite spot in the world. The image of it came easily and then she felt a sucking sensation as if she was being ripped from Lynx's lounge with the force of a hurricane. He held her tighter as they tumbled through the fabric of space, twisting, turning, spinning so fast and so hard, and then suddenly they were spat out the other end, stumbling a bit as they landed.

Iris opened one eye to see the beach and the loch and quickly closed it again as her head was spinning.

'That was horrible.' She clung to Lynx.

'I know, sorry,' he muttered, taking the stone from her and holding her close.

'I think I'm going to pass out.'

He scooped her up in his arms and sat down with her in his lap. 'It's OK, just take some deep breaths, it will pass in a second.'

Her fingers were still wrapped tightly in his shirt and she found some comfort in that, as if he was anchoring her in one place. She took some deep breaths and, after a few moments, the dizziness started to fade. She opened one eye and then the other to see Lynx was looking at her with concern.

'Are you OK?' he stroked her face softly.

She smiled. 'I am now.'

She leaned up and kissed him and that feeling for him erupted in her as soon as their lips met. The taste of him was glorious and she moaned softly as she felt his tongue touch her lips. He stroked his hand up her back, touching the bare skin above her dress. She realised her fingers were still wrapped tight in his shirt, so she released them, sliding her hand inside to feel the warmth and smoothness of his chest. He let out a groan and moved his mouth to her throat, kissing across her hammering pulse.

'I've been wanting to do this all night,' Iris said, as

his mouth moved lower. 'And instead, I had to pretend I didn't even like you.'

'Me too. All I kept thinking about was our date when I could be alone with you and kiss you.'

She kissed him again and he moved his hand to the back of her neck. It was so utterly wonderful, she had never been kissed like this before, with so much adoration and need. She knew she was falling for this man.

Lynx pulled back slightly and gave her a sweet brief kiss on the lips. 'We need to stop before I break my no-sex rule.'

She laughed and he leaned back and looked around. She looked around too, trying to see it from his eyes. The white sandy beach they were sitting on was small and enclosed either side by high hills. The loch was surrounded by purply hills undulating along the whole length of it, the water glittering with a pink hue as the sun started its slow descent in the sky above them. There was not a single house or building in sight, although there were plenty further up the loch, but right here it was secluded, private.

'This is one of the most beautiful places I've ever been,' Lynx said.

She looked at him. 'Really? I've always thought so myself but you've travelled the world.'

'This is raw and rugged, I love it.'

She stood up and took his hand. He got up too and they walked to the shoreline. 'Down there to the far right, is Inveraray Castle, which is a gorgeous old castle. We can't see it from here, but I'll take you there one day. Over here to the far left is Tarbert on the opposite side of the water and that's where the loch goes out to the sea, in the Firth of Clyde. And up there, in the hills in front of us, behind that big lump of trees, is my home.' Iris saw him frown. 'Don't worry, it's about a twenty-minute walk through the woods and over the hills down to the loch from my house, and then probably a half-hour swim to get to our side. I used to make that journey several times a week to get to here and it's quite the trek. Christopher wouldn't even set foot in the woods for fear of ruining his shoes, and he never wanted to go swimming here or anywhere outdoors, so we're quite safe.'

'Why did you come here, specifically? I mean, it's beautiful but I imagine there are many beautiful places around here you could swim.'

'It's so secluded here, no houses or roads on this part of the loch so I can swim naked without fear of being seen. But it's probably the wildlife that's the biggest draw. I often see otters on the rocks over here and seals that seem to spend all their time sleeping on the shores; for some reason they all prefer this side. The loch is a lot deeper this side than the other so we'll often get dolphins and sometimes whales as they come in from the sea.'

'You get whales here?' Lynx asked.

'Yes, not often but we get a sighting at least a handful of times in the summer. There are whale and dolphin cruises that go round the loch and out in the sea just round the corner from here and they seem to see them all the time in the warmer months. Orcas occasionally too, though I've never seen one. I've only seen a minke twice, though that was impressive enough. One had a baby with it so that was pretty cool. And I never tire of seeing the dolphins and they're here all the time.'

'It sounds incredible. What a brilliant place to grow up.'

'In terms of wildlife and beauty, yes. This was my playground, I'd spend hours out here exploring the hills, forests and lochs, watching the deer, the red squirrels, the sea life and just enjoying all this peace and quiet. But growing up half-kelpie, half-witch, surrounded by mundanes that know you're different even if they don't know why, led to a lonely existence. I was either out here alone or tucked up in my favourite armchair in my beloved farmhouse reading a book alone. I'm envious of what you had growing up: that safety, that community. I wish I had that.'

'You have it now.'

She smiled. 'I know.'

'And regardless of what happens between me and you, there will always be a home for you in Midnight.'

'Thank you. Knowing that I can come back here any

time I want in the blink of an eye helps making that decision a little bit easier. Even if the journey is awful.'

'You can use the key stones whenever you want, as long as you don't go back to the farmhouse alone. We can go together in a few months once all of this has blown over.'

She nodded and wrapped her arms around him. 'You'll love it, it's so rustic and cute, and such a warm, happy home. It has great views of the hills and the loch. It'll make the perfect summer house for us. One day, if things work out between us, that is. Although we may need a nursery at some point too. Or am I jumping too far ahead? This is only our first date and I'm already talking about decorating the nursery.'

He cupped her face and kissed her. 'I can't wait to see it. And decorate the nursery if and when the time comes.'

'You're really not freaked out by this?'

'No, I'm not. Shall we go and see what's in the picnic basket?'

They turned away from the shore and Lynx clicked his fingers to bring the picnic basket to him. He placed it down and opened it up.

On top was a blanket which he spread out on the beach and they sat down on it. Inside the basket Iris could see quiche, cheeses, crackers, cold meats, strawberries, grapes and even some sparkling elderflower and a carton of orange juice.

'Wow, your nan thought of everything.'

'I'm surprised there's no champagne. Not that I drink that much but champagne is much more her style than sparkling elderflower.'

'Ah, I don't drink a lot either so the elderflower and orange juice is probably Ness's input.'

'Was she on our side tonight?' Lynx took out two plates and started unloading all the food onto the blanket.

'Yes, we had a big heart-to-heart before you guys came. It turns out we've both been keeping a lot from each other. We agreed to be more truthful with each other from now on, including not going behind my back with Zofia's shenanigans.' Iris popped a grape in her mouth as she thought about whether to tell Lynx about what her nan had told her, but they needed the full picture when opening the locket. 'Last night when I told her that the locket was glued shut, she said she needed what was inside the locket, which made me worry when you told me what Ashley said. I talked to her about the locket and how Ashley thinks there's something bad in there. It turns out she's been storing her memories in there – her wedding day, when her daughter was born – because she keeps forgetting the important stuff. She puts each memory inside a tiny crystal and attaches them to the inside of the locket.'

'I'm sorry she's going through that, that has to be hard for her.'

'Yes, it has to be awful. I think she's embarrassed about it too, so don't talk to her about it. I'm only telling you because you need to know what we're dealing with before we open the locket. I'll tell Ashley too, just in case that's what she's sensing. Maybe she's not expecting something magical and she can feel there's magic inside.'

'I hope that's all it is.'

'Me too.'

Lynx was lying on his side chatting to Iris, the sun just disappearing behind the hills, when suddenly she sat up in alarm and pointed to the loch.

'Look!'

He sat up and saw a huge greyish brown shape gliding along the surface of the loch. That thing had to be easily seven or eight metres long. His first thought was that maybe the Loch Ness monster was real and had perhaps moved lochs until he saw the huge dorsal fin sticking out of the water.

'Is that a whale?'

'It's a shark,' Iris squealed in delight.

To his shock, she stood up, kicked off her shoes and pulled off her dress so she was only in her underwear and started running towards the water.

'Iris, what the hell! Are you going swimming with a shark?'

'It's a basking shark, they're completely harmless. Do you have goggles and a snorkel back at your house?'

'Yes but...'

'Get them, trust me.' She ran into the water.

He swore under his breath, clicked his fingers for his snorkel gear, yanked off his t-shirt and jeans and ran into the water after her, pulling on the goggles.

He watched her dive gracefully into the cold water and then she disappeared under the surface and didn't come back up. He quickly followed and saw the basking shark slowly swimming up the loch with its mouth wide open. It was quite possibly the most incredible thing he'd ever seen in his life. This massive, gentle giant of the deep. It was as big as a single-decker bus.

Lynx surfaced briefly to get some air and then dived back down again, joining Iris. She was staying a respectful four or five metres back from the beast, but the shark had seen them and was slowly heading in their direction. As it reached them, it closed its mouth just briefly before gently nudging its nose into Iris. She let out a squeal of pure joy as she stroked the top of its nose and Lynx wondered if the shark could sense she was a kelpie. It slid past Iris and gave Lynx a gentle nudge too, like a dog greeting its owner. Lynx tentatively stroked its nose, feeling the coarse roughness of its skin, before the shark moved on, reopening its mouth and gliding off up the loch.

Lynx moved back to the surface and Iris did too, laughing with delight at what she'd seen.

'That was magnificent,' Lynx said, trying to catch his breath.

'What a privilege,' Iris said. 'I've never seen one before, aren't they so beautiful? And he was so gentle.'

'Did he know you were a kelpie?'

'I think so. The animals know we're not mundanes, they can feel it.'

'Yeah, I thought that too. I could feel this peace from him, he knew we weren't going to hurt him. That was the most amazing experience of my life,' Lynx said, shaking his head.

'Did you see all the fish too? There must be loads of plankton in the water to attract the shark, and the sprats also feed off the plankton. The mackerel, the bigger silver fish, they go after the sprats and they in turn will bring in the dolphins. I wouldn't be surprised if we see a few of them tonight.'

Lynx thought they were unlikely to see much more now. The last slivers of sunlight had just disappeared behind the hills, leaving behind a deep rosy twilight which would probably last another half hour, maximum, before the darkness of the night rolled in. The hills were already silhouetted against the dusky sky, the moon was out and stars were starting to appear above them.

But it seemed they wouldn't have to wait any longer as, hot on the shark's tail, clearly chasing after all the fish, was a massive pod of dolphins.

'Look!' Lynx said, pointing at them as they jumped through the water.

'Oh wow. There's so many of them,' Iris said. 'Do you surf?'

'Yes but—'

Iris suddenly formed a surfboard out of ice and climbed on, gesturing frantically for him to get up too. He quickly hauled himself up behind her.

'Hold on tight,' Iris said and he wrapped his arms around her waist, still confused how they were going to propel themselves forward when there were no waves to move them. But he should have known magic would be involved. She stretched out her hand in front of them and propelled the board through the water alongside the dolphins. The creatures were completely unfazed by the magical see-through board that was suddenly racing up the loch beside them, in fact, they moved closer, jumping either side of the board. Some of them started getting really excited and jumping clean out of the water by their side. It was utterly exhilarating. Iris let a whoop of excitement, holding both hands in the air.

Suddenly one of the dolphins leapt out of the water

and flipped the surfboard to the side, causing both Iris and Lynx to go tumbling into the water.

They surfaced, coughing, spluttering and laughing as the dolphins disappeared up the loch.

'Are you OK?' Lynx asked, although it was quite clear she was. She was practically glowing with happiness, her smile so huge, her eyes sparkling, as she wrapped her arms around his neck.

'Best first date ever.'

'Well, I'm not sure I can take any credit for that.'

She leaned forward and kissed him and he forgot any more protests, forgot how brilliant the last ten minutes had been because being with her was the most magnificent thing in the world.

Lynx was lying on the beach, staring up at the stars, as Iris cuddled into his chest. It was a beautiful night, with millions of stars peppering the inky sky and the moon covering the loch with a silvery blanket. There were bats fluttering through the cloudless sky, flying low over the water and then off up over the hills. It was so peaceful and quiet, though the warmth of the day had well and truly gone by now and he could feel Iris's skin was cool to the touch. They would have to go home soon, but he was so blissfully happy right now.

Lynx cleared his throat. 'Iris, since we've met, you've turned my life upside down in the best possible way. I never realised I could feel this happy. I know this is only our first date but I'm excited about our future. I know it's all come as a shock to you and your whole life has changed over the last few days, leaving your home, coming to Midnight, seeing your future. But if you stay, I promise you we will find a way to keep Scotland in your life. I know it's important to you and I can see why, but we can come up here every weekend if you want. And there's no pressure, I'm happy for you to take as much time as you need to decide whether you want a future with me. And if you decide you don't want that, that's OK too, but you have to know, I'm falling in love with you.'

There was silence from Iris and he cursed that he was probably moving too fast for her. He lifted his head to look at her and realised she was fast asleep. He smiled; it was probably just as well.

He shook her gently awake and she stirred. 'Oh sorry,' she mumbled.

'Don't apologise. Shall we go back to Midnight?'

She nodded.

He slipped his hand into his pocket and pulled out the key stone. He wrapped his arms tightly around her and she held onto him as he thought of his bed back home. A second later, they were ripped from the beauty of the beach and tumbling through space, flipping upside down, twisting, turning. He felt Iris's arms tighten around him and then they landed hard on his bed.

'Urgh, I feel sick,' Iris muttered, clinging to him.

'I know, sorry.'

'Are we home?'

He smiled at that, although he knew she probably didn't mean it in the way he wanted her to. 'Yeah, we are.'

He took a few deep breaths, trying to clear his head. Then he clicked his fingers to call the picnic basket, the blanket and their shoes to them. He put them down by the side of the bed, pulled the duvet over the two of them and she snuggled back into his arms again as they both drifted off to sleep.

CHAPTER 14

Iris woke up the next day and smiled to see she was lying in Lynx's bed wrapped in his arms. Seeing she was awake, he gave her a kiss on her forehead, making her smile even more.

'Thank you for a lovely date last night.'

He stroked her hair. 'You are very welcome. I had so much fun and not just because we ended up swimming with sharks and dolphins. I love spending time with you. We just click in a way I've never had with anyone before.'

'I feel the same.' She looked up at him and she knew she was falling hard for this man. There was a part of her that wanted to hold back. She'd loved and been hurt before and didn't want to get hurt again, especially after Christopher's betrayal. And there was a part that just wasn't ready for marriage and babies yet, but there was a bigger part that wanted to go all in and not worry about any of that, to just enjoy it.

'Why don't you come here tonight and I'll cook you dinner?'

She slid a finger along his chest. 'And dessert.'

He grinned. 'I would love that but we don't have to rush into anything. I can walk you home and have you tucked up in your own bed alone by ten o'clock, or we can do this again. Just sleep together.'

'I like this.'

'I do too. I've never just slept in the same bed as a woman before. I enjoyed it.'

She smiled and leaned up and kissed him and it was the sweetest kiss he gave her back: slow, gentle, loving. She knew she wanted to take that step with him.

She suddenly pulled back. 'Oh no, I can't, I promised Erin I would go to potions club tonight.'

'That's OK, you can always come round after, to sleep, or for whatever you want.'

She smiled. 'I choose, "whatever I want",' she said, meaningfully.

'Don't, I'll never get through the day knowing that's waiting for me at the end of it.'

She kissed him, trailing her hand down across his stomach towards the waistband of his shorts.

His phone buzzed with his alarm.

'Sorry, I'll turn it off.'

She looked at the time. 'No, it's OK. It's opening day for my shop, I need to get there and get ready.'

She gave him another brief kiss, then got up.

'You could always have a shower here,' Lynx said.

'Thanks but my clothes are at home and my nan will probably be wondering where I am, although she knows I'm with you so she won't be worried.'

'And what about Morag?' Lynx said.

She looked at him curiously. 'Did she say something to you?'

'She came round the other night to give me the third degree.'

Iris laughed. 'Of course she did. I am sorry about her.'

'It's no bother and you'll be pleased to know I think I got fox approval.'

Iris smiled. 'You could charm the birds from the trees.' She leaned over to give him another kiss. 'I'll see you at work.'

She left him looking very happy with himself and she walked out of his house with the biggest smile on her face.

Iris let out a little huff of breath. She hadn't stopped working all morning. Word had clearly spread that there was a new shop open on Stardust Street and what felt like the whole village had turned out to see what she had. And while not everyone had bought something, they'd all been really supportive and enthusiastic about her jewellery. Although some people had blatantly been more interested in her than the jewellery; they'd clearly come just to meet the new girl. No one else had guessed she was a kelpie but some were curious about where she'd come from and her magical abilities, perhaps sensing she was different to them. But no one had been judgemental or mean to her, everyone had been very welcoming.

She heard footsteps on the stairs and she smiled, ready to welcome another customer. After a few moments Zofia appeared.

'Hello, just thought I'd come and see how you're getting on now the shop is open.'

Iris smirked. Zofia was clearly trying to keep to her promise of not interfering, but she was obviously desperate to know how the date had gone the night before. Iris was surprised Lynx had let his grandmother come up here, unless she'd managed to sneak past him without him noticing.

'That's very kind of you,' Iris said. 'It's going well. I've had lots of customers, made lots of sales. I'm going to have to make some more jewellery this afternoon to replenish my stock.'

'Well that's great news.'

There was an awkward pause while Zofia battled with the real reason she was here and Iris wondered how long she could drag out her torture before she put her out of her misery and told her how spectacular the date was and how happy she and Lynx were together. But then would come all the questions about when they planned to get married and when they should have children and she wasn't ready for that yet. Maybe she should enjoy the peace for a few more days.

She heard the shop door open downstairs and Lynx calling hello to Storm. A few seconds later she heard footsteps stomping up the stairs and then Storm appeared in the shop carrying a bunch of flowers. This couldn't have gone any better if she'd planned it. She was pretty sure the flowers weren't for her, and if they were they were only platonic, but this just backed up what Iris and Lynx had been saying the night before and Iris decided to run with it.

'Storm, hello,' she gave him a big, warm smile, possibly a bit too big. She wondered if a hug would be too much and suppressed a snort of laughter. She imagined it would be way too much for the quiet, withdrawn Storm who was only just venturing out of his shell.

Zofia stared at Storm and the flowers in horror. 'I don't understand, this isn't what I've seen.' She shook her head in despair and left. Iris nearly felt sorry for her.

Storm put the flowers down on the counter; clearly they weren't for her. 'What's up with her?'

'She's getting annoyed because her interference in our love life isn't going according to plan.'

'Ah, you've got to love a meddling grandparent. I just wanted to pop by and wish you luck for the opening.' He looked around. 'This place looks great, and the jewellery is beautiful. Amelia would have loved them. She used to make a star like this for the top of our Yule tree every year.' His voice caught and he swallowed a lump in his throat. 'It's our anniversary today, she loved sunflowers so it seemed fitting to buy these for her today.' He nodded to the flowers.

'They're beautiful. I'm sure she would have loved them,' Iris said, her heart breaking for him. He was clearly still deeply in love with his wife and she guessed he probably always would be.

'I also wanted to say, I've been watching the news and I've seen all the stuff with the stolen locket and your name getting bandied about a lot. I don't understand what went on there but if there's anything I can do to help, please let me know.'

'What happened is my ex-boyfriend, Christopher, the asshole *victim* in all the news stories, drugged my nan's tea and stole that locket from her neck while we were still dating, and then put it in that exhibition where I stole it back. I have no idea whether the multi-million-pound value is really what it's worth, or whether the stones on the outside are really as precious as he's making them out to be. Diamonds, sapphires, jadeite, seems a little unrealistic to me. But if it's true, or at least if others believed it was true, it would have made him a multi-millionaire and so you can imagine how angry he is about losing it. He brought a gun to the exhibition to try and stop me taking it and now I'm worried for my nan's safety, which is why we're here.'

'Wow, what a mess.'

Iris nodded. 'And now Ashley believes there is something dark inside the locket and I just don't know what Christopher could have done to it to make her feel that way. Lynx wonders if he might have employed a witch to put a protective spell or curse on it. I just hate the thought that our family locket could have brought something dangerous to the village.'

'I'm sure Ashley will find a way to get rid of it or diffuse it. There isn't a spell or potion she doesn't know. And Wolf and Lynx are powerful witches, whatever it is they'll be able to control or destroy it.'

Iris nodded and sighed. 'I know. But I also know Christopher. He isn't going to stop looking for the locket. The police may give up and stop looking at some point but he won't. If he comes here—'

'If he comes here I'll teach him a lesson he won't forget.' Storm looked thoughtful for a moment. 'Actually, if he did come here we could easily make him forget.'

She thought about that for a moment. Memory modification was not something she could do, but she was damn sure one of the witches in the village could. 'That's not a bad idea. Although I'd prefer it if he never came here at all.'

'I'm sure he wouldn't be that hard to find.'

The thought of seeing her ex-boyfriend again turned her stomach but it was an option. Iris couldn't do anything about the countless numbers of police who were involved in the investigation, but if she could discredit Christopher somehow and make them lose interest in the locket, then she could take care of Christopher once and for all. Maybe she needed to take back control of her life, not hide out here for the rest of it. She knew she had to wait and see what was inside the locket and deal with that first, but then she was going to come up with a plan. And if it included revenge, even better.

Iris looked round her shop with a smile. She had sold almost half of her stock that day. She knew that not every day would be like this, and it was only because it was her opening day that it had been so successful, but she was still really pleased.

She heard Lynx come upstairs. He'd called up a few

minutes before to say he was closing up, so she knew it would be him.

'That's it, your first day is over,' Lynx said, appearing with two fabulous-looking cocktails, with sparklers sticking out of slices of pineapple. She laughed, they were very over the top.

'Erin sent these over, she's trialling some new cocktails for the summer solstice. This is called Firework Fury. These are non-alcoholic, but I felt like we needed something to celebrate.'

She took the glass he offered her which was fizzing with gold and red. Once the sparkler went out, she clinked her glass against his and took a sip. It tasted like sparkling pineapple, it was delicious.

'Have you enjoyed running a shop today?' Lynx asked. 'I know it's a bit different to just doing online sales.'

'I've loved it. I've never been a people person but I've really enjoyed chatting with all the customers. I hope me being upstairs hasn't taken away too much of your custom though.'

'On the contrary, I've had the best day I've had in a long time thanks to you. I think we make a good team.'

Iris watched him, remembering the promise she'd all but given him that morning. 'Yeah we do, and I think we can celebrate a bit better than this.'

'What did you have in mind?'

'I think we should go for a swim in the pool and make fireworks of our own.'

Lynx stared at her for a second, then took the drink off her, placing them both down on the counter, before grabbing her hand and marching down the stairs and out of the shop. He waved his hand to lock the shop behind them and walked quickly down the road. She giggled at his haste.

They were soon in the woods, racing along the path. She pulled him to a stop and reached up and kissed him hard, sliding her hands round the back of his neck. She laughed when he bent down and scooped her up in his arms. He carried on along the path, still kissing her until they reached the pool, sheltered under a canopy of green.

He placed her feet back on the floor, cupping her face and kissing her again. He pulled back slightly and clicked his fingers and a blanket appeared in his hand, which he tossed on the floor. He clicked his fingers again and a box of condoms appeared.

She laughed. 'A whole box.'

'I'm just being prepared.'

'Actually, I'm on the pill and I had a health check after that arsehole betrayed me.'

He stared at her. 'I had one too, a few weeks ago. I'm clean.'

She gave him a little nod and he clicked his fingers once more. The condoms vanished and she reached up and kissed him again. He let out a noise that sounded like a growl at the back of his throat. She stepped back, got quickly undressed, keeping her eyes on him the whole time as he watched her. As soon as she was naked he reached for her but she let out a laugh and dived into the water to avoid him.

She surfaced and watched him trying to get his clothes off as quick as possible and then he was wading out to join her, gloriously and spectacularly naked. She stood up in front of him, tracing her wet fingers over his warm chest as he stared at her, his eyes filled with emotions she couldn't read. Then he bent his head and kissed her hard. He lifted her and she wrapped her arms and legs around him, holding him close as the kiss continued. She felt him move through the water and he sat her down on the edge of the pool and stepped back.

'You said, that if you won the competition, you wanted me to kiss your feet.'

'I have no idea if I won or not.'

'Right now, I feel like I've won, and I want you to feel that way too.'

'I already do. And you said you weren't a foot man.'

'Oh, I could definitely be a foot man when it comes to you, or a breast man,' he placed a gentle kiss on her breast. 'Or a stomach man,' he kissed her stomach. 'Or a thigh man.' She smiled as he kissed her thigh. 'But let's start with the feet. We didn't discuss how many kisses or how long I should kiss your feet for, so when you think I've delivered your prize, you just tell me to stop.'

She nodded, suddenly nervous. He was looking at her as if he wanted to eat her.

Lynx took one foot in his hand and her heart leapt at his gentle touch. With his eyes firmly on hers, he kissed the arch of her foot. The feel of his lips on her skin made her stomach clench with need.

He stroked a hand gently up her leg as he moved his mouth towards her ankle. She let out a soft gasp. It felt so good. He shifted to her other foot, kissing below her ankle and just above it, then trailing his hot mouth slightly higher. She let out a shuddery breath as he continued upward, slowly moving up her calf, then kissing the inside of her knee. He didn't take his eyes off hers for a second as he kissed slowly up her inner thigh. Need for him coiled in her stomach, her breath heavy as she watched him reach the top of her legs.

He gently pushed her legs apart and she let out a heavy breath as he kissed her right there between her legs.

'Dear Gods, Lynx,' she ran her hand through his hair. It was as if he had known her body for years. His touch was so familiar and confident, he knew exactly what to do to make her go weak. There was none of that fumbling around that she'd had with a new partner in the past, trying to find what the other one liked, he instinctively knew and he was driving her crazy. He clearly wasn't in the mood to make this quick either. That feeling kept on building, driving her to the very edge, and then he'd kiss her thigh or her stomach until it started to ebb away and then he was relentless in building it back up again until she was desperate for that release.

'Lynx, please, I need...'

She felt him smile against her, obviously relishing in her torture. But then the sensation tightened in her stomach, spreading out to every part of her body and exploding through her so fast and hard she could barely catch her breath. Yet still he was relentless, wringing out every ounce of pleasure from her.

He stepped back. 'Have you had enough?'

She shook her head. 'No, I want more.'

'How much more?'

She reached for him under the water and her eyes widened in shock. 'A whole lot more apparently.'

He laughed.

She ran her hands across his chest, tracing the curves of his body. 'You're so beautiful.'

'I was just going to say the same thing. You are the most incredible woman I've ever met.'

He gathered her legs around him, kissing her hard, and moved inside her, making her gasp. It was both too much and not enough, this overwhelming feeling of this being where she belonged, here with him. She wrapped her arms and legs around him, holding him close, sliding her hand up to his hair and making him groan against her lips. Every touch, every stroke, every movement was perfect, as if he'd been made just for her. He pulled back to look at her, his breath heavy on her lips, staring right into her eyes, and she felt something pass between them, something so much more than she expected. She stroked his face and he smiled.

Suddenly she felt the moment their magic collided like the force of a tsunami, relentless, unstoppable, powerful, and completely beautiful. A glow surrounded them, blue interwoven with gold. It was like swimming underwater on a summer's day, the sunlight dappling through the water, creating rays of light around her. The woods, the pool, the rest of the world, faded away, there was just the two of them in this blue and gold cocoon, as if they were floating in the water. It was utterly blissful.

Lynx kissed her again, then moved his mouth to her throat and she felt her need building for him, filling her, her body spiralling with pleasure, as Lynx took her higher and higher, the golden-blue light around them getting brighter. For a moment it really did feel like they were floating. She clung onto him as he took her over the edge and she felt him fall too, saying her name like a mantra as he fell apart around her.

He kissed her softly, stroking her hair as the blue and gold glow slowly faded away. She stroked his face.

'That was incredible. I've never felt that way before when I've been with a man.'

'That was without doubt the best sex I've ever had in my life,' Lynx said.

She grinned. 'Well, you definitely delivered on my prize. And now I know why you were so confident about me being friends with Storm.'

'Ah, just what every man wants to hear. Another man's name mentioned a few moments after sex.'

She laughed. 'I just meant that, after that, there's no way I could ever look at another man again. You've ruined me.'

He laughed. 'I should hope so.' He gave her a kiss on the forehead. 'We belong together. Come on, I need to feed you after that.'

He carefully stepped back, out of her arms, and she enjoyed watching him walk out of the pool naked to where his clothes had been scattered.

He was right, they did belong together and that fact didn't scare her anymore. The reason she could never look at another man was because she was pretty sure she was falling in love with Lynx Oakwood.

CHAPTER 15

Iris hopped around putting her shoes on. She'd come home to have a shower and get changed, while Lynx was going to cook her dinner before potions club.

She heard the door open downstairs and leaned over the banister. 'Hello?'

'Hello dear,' Ness called up.

Iris frowned slightly. Her nan sounded really happy.

Iris put on some lipstick and ran downstairs to find Ness sitting on the sofa with a big smile on her face.

'What's made you so happy?'

'I've just had the most amazing sex.'

Iris sat down on the chair with a thump. 'What?'

'I know. I'm as surprised as you are. I was swimming in the waterfall again and that man turned up,

Charles, complaining that I was naked again. I told him to come and join me and he did. Just stripped straight off and walked in. I felt like a silly teenager again watching him and he walked straight up to me and asked if I liked what I saw and I told him I did. And then he kissed me. I haven't been kissed by someone since your grandad passed away over twenty years ago and I thought I might have forgotten how to do it but he obviously enjoyed himself. The next thing, we were having sex, underneath the waterfall, and it was wonderful.'

'Oh wow, Nan, I, erm... I'm happy for you. So you like this man?'

'It was just sex darling, it didn't mean anything. But if he wants to do it again, I wouldn't be opposed to it.'

'Well, that's ... lovely.'

'And you and Lynx, I hear you've finally done the fandango too.'

'Where did you hear that?'

'The ether,' Ness gestured to the air around her as if it had been whispering Iris's secrets to her. Iris wouldn't be surprised if it had, her nan seemed to know everything. 'Was it good?'

'It was incredible,' Iris said, softly.

Her nan grinned. 'Are we staying here?'

'Yeah, I think we might be.'

Ness nodded. 'I thought we might be.'

'Are you OK with that?'

'Surprisingly I am. And you and he will be very happy together, I can see that. Just don't waste too much time dilly-dallying, I'd like to meet my great-grandchildren before I go.'

'Nan! You're not going anywhere. You'll still be here when they get married.'

'Now wouldn't that be nice, but I'll settle for seeing you happily married. That would fill my heart right up.'

Iris smiled.

'We'll have to go back and get the rest of our things,' Ness said.

'We will, I promise, we just need to let things settle down for a few weeks first.'

Her nan nodded.

'I'm going to Lynx's house for dinner and then I have potions club tonight. I'll leave you to tell Morag the good news.'

'What good news?' Morag said, coming in from the kitchen.

'Ness has a fancy man,' Iris said.

Morag stared at her in horror. 'What?'

Ness dismissed it. 'It was just sex, nothing to get worked up about.'

'I told Iris to be careful with this man she's just met and now you're having some fling with some man you barely know.'

'I know, isn't it exciting,' Ness said. 'Me, having a fling. I've never been flung before, I rather liked it.'

'So you two are very happy here?' Morag said.

Iris bit her lip, feeling awful. 'Are you not?'

'It's nice enough, I suppose, it's just not Scotland. This place is too... full, there was a lot more empty space back home. It was peaceful, whereas this village is busy. And there's one cat too many in my opinion. And people see me walking round the streets and want to pet me like I'm a dog. I'm not a dog.'

'I could get you a collar that says, "Do not stroke, may bite",' Iris offered.

'I am *not* wearing a collar.'

'A little jumper then?'

'No.'

Iris sighed. 'I don't want to make you unhappy but I think my future is here. I know I've made mistakes in the past with the men I've been with but Lynx is different, he makes me feel different.'

Morag nodded. 'I like him and I want you to be happy, you deserve it. And I can grow to like it here. If need be.'

Iris smiled at the small concession. 'Thank you, I'll make it up to you somehow.'

'I'll think of something.'

'And we'll probably be visiting Scotland fairly often. Lynx has these things called key stones and they can get us there in seconds. The journey is a bit rough and you feel like you've been on a rollercoaster for a minute or so after you get there, but it means we can go as often as we want. Not to our farmhouse, not yet, but the surrounding hills, woods and lochs. If we go, I'll take you with us so you can have some peace for a while.'

'That would be nice.'

'I better go. I'll leave Ness to share all the sordid details of her fling.'

Iris waved and hurried out.

She knocked on Lynx's door and after a few moments he answered, immediately leaning down to give her a kiss.

'Hey,' he said.

She smiled and kissed him back.

He took her hand and led her inside the house. 'I'm making vegetarian lasagne, hope that's OK?'

'Yes, I love lasagne. It smells delicious.'

'It's nearly ready, can I get you a drink?'

'Just a water please.'

Lynx waved his hand and a glass floated out of one of the cupboards.

'Do you know a man called Charles?' Iris asked.

'Yes, grumpy old man, complains about everything. Why, has he been giving you hassle?' He sipped his own drink as the glass of water floated into Iris's hands.

'No, nothing like that. Apparently he and my nan had sex this afternoon in the waterfall at the back of the village.'

Lynx choked on his drink. 'I wasn't expecting that.'

'Neither was I.'

'I'd like to say the man's a teddy bear underneath, but I've never seen evidence of that. Eighteen months ago he cursed one of the women in the village after she threatened his dog. Every time she said something nasty the mole on her neck grew. The woman was vile so it didn't take long for the mole to be as big as a watermelon. I thought it was going to kill her and I think Charles was secretly hoping for that too, until Star persuaded him to explain how to stop the curse. The woman just had to be nice, which was no mean feat, let me tell you.'

'Oh no, I'm not sure I want my nan involved with someone like that.'

'He's dated quite a few of women in the village over the years. It never seems to last but he hasn't cursed any of the women when it came to an end, so I guess he can't be all bad. Just as long as your nan doesn't try to hurt his precious dog, I think she'll be fine.'

Iris took a swig of her water. 'I obviously want her to be happy here, and if Charles can give her that, then I'm all for it. It's just a little weird though, because she hasn't been with anyone since my grandad died. She always said there could never be anyone else for her but five seconds in a witch village and she's completely changed her tune. She doesn't even like witches.'

'Maybe it was the pleasure of witch sex, that can

change anyone's mind.' Lynx looked at her mean-ingfully.

'Ah, you had me way before that.'

'And I plan to have you again tonight when you get back from potions club.'

She laughed, but although the thought of making love to him again was very very tempting, she was bone tired from working in the shop all day. She had barely stopped with the steady stream of curious customers. Witch sex had exhausted her too.

He dipped his head to look into her eyes and smiled. 'Or we can just sleep together.'

She felt a rush of gratitude that he understood her so well. 'As much as I loved my prize this afternoon, just sleeping with you is infinitely more appealing right now.'

He laughed. 'That's totally fine.'

She watched his face. 'You really don't mind?'

He cupped her face and kissed her. 'You're undates-timating how much I really enjoyed just holding you in my arms last night. Why would I mind about doing that again?' He studied her face. 'What assholes have you dated that objected to you saying no to sex?'

She pulled a face. 'Christopher always used to sulk about it if I was too tired. I always stood my ground but he did make me feel guilty about it.'

'Dear Gods, Iris, that's a red flag if ever I heard one.

Never ever settle for a man that ranks his pleasure over your happiness.'

She smiled and slid her arms round his neck. 'Fortunately, I don't think I'll have to.'

He smiled and kissed her and she felt her heart fill a little bit more for him.

Lynx smiled as Iris tried to contain a yawn as she sat opposite him. They had talked a lot over dinner and the more time he spent with her, the more he knew he was falling for her. She was going to have to go soon for potions club so he wanted to spend as much time with her as possible, so he was a bit frustrated when there was a knock on the door.

'Let me see who this is and try to get rid of them,' Lynx said.

Iris laughed.

He went to the door and found Wolf there. He loved his brother but there was no way he was asking him in to interrupt his limited time with Iris.

'Hey, what's up?' Lynx asked, casually putting his arm up on the doorframe.

'Sorry, I won't keep you but we're going to need you there tomorrow when we open the locket. You're probably the strongest fire witch in the village and we need all four elements there to create a strong protective spell.'

'I was planning on coming anyway, to support Iris. Does Ashley still think it's something dark inside?'

'It's confounded her, which is worrying. There's something moving around inside so we know something is in there. She says either there is something dark in there or the person that put the thing in there is dark and dangerous. We already know that Christopher is dangerous, he brought a gun with him to the exhibition to stop Iris from stealing the locket back. So it could be his darkness she's sensing, you know how sensitive she is to people's energy, good and bad. But she says the locket is definitely giving off a weird energy too. I think we just have to take all precautions until we know what we're dealing with.'

Iris appeared behind Lynx and he looped an arm around her to bring her into the conversation.

'Ah sorry, I didn't realise Iris was here.'

'Wolf, I'm so sorry this locket is causing you so much trouble.'

'We brought it here, you have nothing to apologise for,' Wolf said.

'But I feel kind of responsible for it.'

'None of this is your fault,' Lynx said. 'This is all Christopher.'

'I just can't think what he could have possibly put inside that locket that would be dark or dangerous. He doesn't know about magic. I can't see how it could possibly be cursed.'

'Even Zofia has said that if we open it, something bad would happen,' Wolf said.

'And she can't give us any more information than that?' Lynx asked.

'She says it's fractured, she says she sees fire and water and darkness.'

'Helpful,' Lynx said dryly.

'Then let's not open it,' Iris said. 'I know my nan will be upset but at least she'll have the locket back.'

'If it is a curse, we can't leave it in there. And in good conscience I can't give it back to your nan either,' Wolf said.

'Then let's get it out of the village before it does any damage,' Iris said. Her nan would be devastated but not putting anyone in danger was more important.

'We can't do that either, we can't put mundanes in danger. The curse will come out at some point and we have no idea how many people it could hurt or what it will do when it does.'

'Can we destroy it?'

'If we do that the curse will come out anyway. It's better we do it this way, in a controlled environment where we can prevent it doing any harm. Ashley will know exactly what kind of magic it is as soon as she sees it and then we can deal with it then.'

'OK,' Iris said, quietly.

Wolf turned back to his brother. 'Ashley has suggested we use Storm for the earth element, do you think he'll be up for that?'

'He will,' Iris said. 'We've become friends and he's a good man.'

Lynx nodded. 'He seems a lot nicer than we originally thought. But actually I think Erin is probably our strongest earth witch.'

'I'll ask them both.' Wolf turned back to Iris. 'Try not to worry. I'll leave you to your night,' he said. 'Twelve noon at Ashley's house.'

Lynx nodded and Wolf left.

They went back inside and Lynx could tell Iris was sad.

'This isn't your fault,' he repeated. 'If I had stolen the locket before I'd even met you, we'd still be dealing with this without you. Christopher did this when he stole the locket and then did whatever the hell he did to it. You can't take the blame on your shoulders for this.'

Iris shook her head. 'I trusted him, I brought him into my life. Now I've had to uproot mine, my nan's and Morag's lives because of it, and I've brought danger to a village who have been nothing but welcoming. Midnight Village is a safe haven and I feel like I've ruined that.'

'You haven't ruined anything. We have no idea what we are dealing with here, it could be nothing.'

'A nothing that brings fire, water and darkness to the village?'

'Zofia always did like a touch of the dramatic with her predictions. Fire and water is us, our magic, it would make sense that whatever happens involves us. And darkness could mean anything, it doesn't mean literally. And whatever it is, we will handle it. Wolf has great power and I'm not short of a trick or two. I promise, we will deal with it before anyone gets hurt.'

Iris sighed.

He took her in his arms and kissed her forehead. 'It will be OK.'

She looked up at him and nodded. 'I trust you.' She looked at her watch. 'I better go.'

'You'll come back here after?'

'Yes, but I don't know what time it will be. Erin said it might be a late one.'

'That's OK. The door will be open, you can come and join me in bed.'

She smiled. 'OK.'

Lynx bent his head and kissed her and she pressed herself against him. He relished in the feel of her warm body against his, making his heart swell with love for her. This woman was everything and as she pulled away and gave him a little wave before leaving, he swore to himself that whatever was inside that locket he would fight to the death to protect her.

Iris knocked on Ashley's door and after a few moments she opened it.

'Come in, I'm glad you're here,' Ashley said. 'I wanted to talk to you before the others arrive. I'm so sorry about all this locket stuff.'

'You have nothing to apologise for.'

'I know, but I feel really bad. You trusted me with the locket and now I've made it into something much bigger and Wolf is talking about protection spells. I bet you're wishing you never came to me with it in the first place.'

'This isn't your fault. If you feel there is something bad in the locket then you did the right thing in telling Wolf. The last thing I want is for anyone to get hurt because of it. If we have to do protection spells or create a magical forcefield around it, then I'm all for it.'

'I don't even know what it is, which is the annoying thing.'

'I'm not sure if Lynx has told you, but my nan has been creating tiny memory crystals and attaching them to the inside of the locket on the rim. Her wedding day, her daughter's birth, things like that. Her memory isn't as good as it was and this is her way of keeping those memories close to her. Is there any chance it could be that that you're feeling?'

Ashley smiled. 'When I examined the locket, I could feel love more than anything else. It's so strong it's almost overpowering. And what you've described explains that, but no, there's something else there and I don't even know if it's magical. With spells or potions I can feel what kind of spell it is, I can see it. If you were to cast a spell and capture it somehow in a bottle, I could tell exactly what spell you were casting. Right now, I can't pick that up which makes me think it's not magical at all. But it's possible the huge amount of love that's been added in your nan's memories is blocking me from being able to see whatever else is in there. Or the locket has some kind of insulating properties. Do you know what metal the locket is made from?'

'I would presume gold. We've never had it valued or authenticated but Christopher apparently has and he says it's twenty-four carat gold.'

Ashley shook her head. 'It's not gold. I would guess copper, maybe mixed in with silver or steel. I'm not an expert but it's definitely not gold of any carat. We use gold dust or flakes in some of our potions and the locket has a very different quality to gold. But hundreds or thousands of years ago, people used to wear copper amulets as a form of protection, some believed that it would protect them from bad magic. We now know that copper is an electrical conductor so there may have been some truth in that. But that's probably why I can't get a sense of what it is – because the copper is insulating it and stopping the energy in there from coming out. But whatever it is I just get this bad feeling from it.'

'So we take all the precautions we need to,' Iris said. 'And if it's nothing and we've completely overreacted I'll feel only relief, not anger, that you got it wrong.'

Ashley nodded. 'Well, I should be able to start the spell to open it tonight at midnight and with any luck it should be ready to open at lunchtime tomorrow.'

There was a knock on the door and the sound of laughter outside.

'Time to meet everyone else. We're a bit light on the ground today as Darianna and Nithya are visiting family for the summer solstice, so there'll just be the six of us tonight.'

Ashley went to answer the door and soon the room was filled with laughing, chatting women, Star and Erin amongst them. It was clear they were all very good friends and Iris couldn't help feeling a bit jealous about that; she'd never really had friends.

Erin gave her a big hug as soon as she saw her, as did Star, which made Iris smile.

'I'm so glad you came,' Star said.

'I am too.'

Star turned and took one of the other women's hands, pulling her over to meet Iris too. 'This is Kianga, this is Iris.'

'Lovely to meet you,' Kianga gave her a hug.

'And this is Maxine,' Star indicated the other

woman who was so busy chatting at a hundred miles an hour with Ashley that she hadn't noticed there was someone new in their midst.

'Sorry, hello,' Maxine said, rushing over to give Iris a hug.

A few of them placed snacks on the food table and Iris felt a bit bad that she hadn't brought anything.

'Ladies, please take your seats,' Ashley said.

Everyone quickly sat down and Erin pulled Iris down to sit between her and Star.

'I was sorting through some of my old potion recipes the other day and I found this vintage one, which dates back to the seventeenth century. Our understanding of magic has moved on quite a bit since then, but I thought it might be fun to try. Especially as this one contains rum.'

'I'm definitely up for that,' Maxine said.

'Can we substitute rum for wine?' Erin said, gesturing to the wine bottles in the middle of the room. 'I hate rum, it always makes me sick.'

'Sadly not, it's the sugarcane in the rum that's the important part in this recipe. But you only need to add a few drops. The wine is for our second potion. But this potion allows you to see your true heart's desire, the thing you want most in the world. And when you drink the potion technically it should help you get it. But of course, as with all things, magic has its limitations – it can't bring back the dead, it can't make someone fall in

love with you, it can't give you mountains of gold, so
don't be disappointed if you're not suddenly a billion-
aire overnight.'

The women eyed each other, clearly excited at the
possibilities.

'You have a list of ingredients next to your cauldrons, so go over to the middle table and start selecting
what you need,' Ashley instructed.

Iris looked at her list, which contained things like
frankincense, myrrh, nutmeg, lupins, marigold, nettle,
rose and lavender, amongst many others. She moved
over to the table and very carefully started selecting the
ingredients, a pinch of this, a handful of that. It didn't
seem that accurate in terms of measuring. But the
smells were amazing and she loved touching each of
them, some soft leaves or petals, some hard crystals.
She carried her list of ingredients back to where she'd
been sitting.

'It's important to clear your mind for this one,'
Ashley said, when they were all sitting back down. 'The
potion will supposedly show you what you want most
in the world, without you willing it one way or another.
So I want you to concentrate on the smell of the sage
that is burning in the room, that will help to cleanse
your mind. I want you to concentrate on your breathing, deep breaths in, deep breaths out, as you add the
ingredients to the cauldron one by one.'

Flames under the cauldrons burst to life and a jug

floated between the cauldrons, adding water to each one.

Iris did as she was told, as did the others, very quietly adding the ingredients, breathing in the scent of the sage, focussing all of her attention on what she was doing.

'OK, the rum is the last ingredient. Once you add that, stir it three times clockwise. When the liquid settles, look inside the cauldron and you will see the one thing you want most in the world.'

Iris added a few drops but, judging from the giggles around the room, some of the women were adding a bit more than that.

She stirred it and saw Erin and Star doing the same thing, then peered into the liquid, waiting for the potion to settle and show her what her heart desired.

She smiled when she realised that staring back up at her from the depths of the cauldron, was Lynx carrying their daughter.

She quickly stirred it away before anyone else saw, but Erin letting out a bark of laughter next to her was a sure sign she'd spotted it.

'Someone's got it bad if he's the thing you want most in the world.'

Iris flushed, but she knew she was falling for him and there was a big part of her that wanted that future.

'What did you see in yours?' Iris asked, gesturing to

Erin's cauldron which she had quickly swiped away too.

'A puppy,' Erin said, blatantly lying.

Star laughed as she looked inside her own cauldron. 'Mine is a bed. I've been so tired lately because Blaze exists on two hours' sleep. The thing I clearly want more than anything is some sleep.'

'I can beat that, mine is a pizza,' Maxine said. 'I really wanted a pizza tonight but my husband wanted to cook something healthy and not remotely filling. So I'm starving and now even my cauldron is showing me a nice cheesy pizza.'

Everyone laughed.

'Well everyone, drink your potions. The magic is supposed to help you realise your heart's desire,' Ashley said. 'You should see in your mind a clear path to get what you want, although it may take an hour or two for that path to become clear. But you need to drink the whole thing.'

Iris tipped out the potion into a glass and took a sip. It tasted surprisingly good so she drank the rest.

Kianga and Maxine both downed theirs and were giggling about getting what they really wanted.

'I can't drink mine,' Star said, quietly, and Ashley's eyes widened slightly with understanding.

'Well, as with all potions, they need to be drunk by the potion-maker or given to someone else who will drink it. Once you've created magic it has to be used,' Ashley said.

Star passed Iris her potion.

'But is this going to help me get what I want or what Star wants?' Iris said. Although she wasn't opposed to the idea of getting a decent night's sleep, it had been a busy day.

'Generally with potions you have a clear purpose or the person you're making the potion for in your mind when you make it. If you make a happiness potion and give it to someone else, you're making them happy, even if you thought about what would make you happy when you were making it. This one was different because you had to focus on clearing your mind. But I would guess it would be the same, it will help you to find the path to *your* heart's desire.'

'You guess?' Iris laughed.

'A lot of potion work and magic is trial and error. And some of it doesn't work at all, especially some of the older recipes. But a potion like this can't do you any harm. It can't make you go after something you don't really want.'

Iris took the potion and drank it in one. Even if it did make her want a good night's sleep, there was no harm in that.

'You can drink mine too,' Erin passed her an over-flowing glass. 'Rum makes me sick.'

'What did the cauldron show you?' Iris said.

'Trust me, it will help you with yours too,' Erin said.

Iris sighed and downed it in one. And the smile Erin gave her after was one of pure mischief.

Ashley turned her attention to getting ready for the next potion and Star wandered over to talk to her.

'What was it you saw in your cauldron?' Iris asked Erin, who laughed and leaned in closer, although Maxine and Kianga were too busy chatting to hear.

'The thing I apparently want most in the world is really great sex.'

Iris felt her mouth fall open in shock. 'What? You made me drink a potion that makes me want great sex?'

'Surely everyone wants great sex, don't they? No one wants disappointing boring sex.'

Iris thought she probably had a point there. 'But what if it turns me into a horny sex maniac?'

'Again, probably not a bad thing.'

Iris rolled her eyes. 'So what exactly did you see?'

Erin sighed. 'Storm Quinn, or rather great sex with Storm Quinn. Remember I told you I keep having sex dreams about him? I can't help it, I go to sleep trying to think about nice beaches, or my holiday in Australia, and as soon as I fall asleep, it's like he's there waiting for me. And we don't talk, we just have the most amazing sex and then I wake up. Every single night. And the thing is I don't even like the man. Every time we've spoken he's been angry and rude. But the first time I saw him, I thought, I bet he's good in bed. It was a nothing thought, just a fleeting thing like when you see an amazing pair of heels in the shop window and think, oh I'd love them. And then you remember you can't wear heels and you definitely can't walk in them, and you move on. But my brain hasn't forgotten that initial thought. And the problem is, I haven't had great sex in a very, very long time so my mind keeps focussing on that.'

'Lynx said you were dating a witch from outside the village. Greg, was it?'

'Oh I was, he was nice, a bit dull, but a nice man. But the sex was unbearably boring and awful actually. It was kind of what I imagine sleeping with a squid would be like, all flailing limbs and rubbery and very wet with no idea what he was doing. Even when we connected on that witchy level, it was more of a damp firework than a big explosion. I figured that sex wasn't the be-all and end-all in a relationship and we got on well so I just endured it. But once I started having dreams about Storm I knew I had to end it. It wasn't fair, especially when I was lying in bed with Greg and wishing he was Storm instead.'

'Well no, I guess not. But what happens if I start having sex dreams about Storm now I've drunk that potion?'

'I don't think it works like that. You're not just going to want someone you never wanted before. But if all three of our potions work for you, you'll leave here wanting really great sex with Lynx in a bed so you can have a good night's sleep after.'

Iris laughed. 'I'm more likely to leave here very drunk. How much rum was in your potion?'

Erin showed her with her hands the equivalent of a large glass of wine.

Iris groaned. What had she done?

CHAPTER 16

Iris was drunk. There was no doubt about it. As someone who probably had two or three glasses of wine a year, if that, she had no tolerance for alcohol. She felt dizzy, her head was spinning and she felt bone tired. She'd never liked drinking because she never liked feeling like she wasn't in control. She had deliberately only added a few drops of rum to her potion because she didn't want to get drunk so why had she let herself get badgered into drinking Star's and Erin's potions too?

She wondered if the potions had worked. It wasn't exactly a surprise to see that Lynx was the thing she wanted most in the world. She knew she was falling in love with him. But while there was a part of her that was excited about that future she'd seen – marriage, children, the happy ever after – it still felt like a big scary step to go from dating to the whole caboodle. He was so calm and unfazed about it all. She wanted to wrap herself in his arms and let that laid-back attitude seep into her, fill her bones and her heart. He wasn't worried about any of this and she would love to share that 'what will be, will be' philosophy in life.

He'd told her to come round after potions club so she would do that, wrap herself in his arms and not worry about the future for a while. And then maybe she'd sleep in his bed for a hundred years. That sounded like the perfect plan. She smirked because maybe Star's potion was kicking in too.

Everyone was getting up to leave but she barely had the energy to do that.

Ashley turned round to look at her, slumped on the sofa.

'Iris, I'm really sorry,' Ashley said. 'I didn't realise how much rum Erin had put in her potion. And I didn't realise you don't normally drink, I should have given it to Kianga or Maxine to finish instead.'

'It's OK.'

'I promise, next week, there will be no alcohol in the potions. There rarely is actually, I just thought it would be fun to try this one.'

'The night has been fun, I'm just feeling a little worse for wear now.'

'Come on,' Erin said, hauling her to her feet. 'I'll walk you back.'

Iris wasn't going to argue, she wasn't even sure she would find her house on her own.

They waved goodbye to everyone and walked out onto the street, Erin guiding her back towards the village green with her arm through hers.

'I can't believe you made me drink your sex potion,' Iris said.

'Do you have any desire to go and find Lynx, climb him like a tree and have the greatest sex of your life?' Erin said.

Iris laughed. 'We've already done that. We made love today and it was magnificent. I definitely want more of that.'

She clamped her hand over her mouth. She wasn't sure Lynx would appreciate her sharing details of their sex life.

Erin let out a squeal of excitement which made the inside of Iris's head throb.

'Oh well, this is wonderful news and if you demand more hot sex next time you see Lynx, I don't think you can blame me for that.'

'Probably not.'

They turned into Iris's road.

'I'm going to Lynx's house,' Iris said.

'I'm not sure you turning up at his house in this state is a good idea,' Erin said.

'I'm in this state because of you. Besides, he's expecting me.'

'For a night of hot sex?'

'No. I don't want hot sex.'

Erin looked at her in confusion. 'You want crappy sex?'

'No.'

'You want damp squid sex?'

'Definitely not.' Iris was confused by the way this conversation was going. 'I want great, earth-moving kind of sex. The kind of sex that would be completely life-changing. But not now. Maybe after I've slept for a few hours first. Lynx said he just wants to hold me in his arms.'

'You two do have it bad for each other if you just want to cuddle. Oh look, there's Storm,' Erin giggled.

Iris quickly clamped a hand over her eyes.

'What are you doing?' Erin asked.

'What if I see him and, thanks to your potion, I want to climb *him* like a tree?' Iris said.

Erin burst out laughing. 'Well, most of the village women do, so you won't be alone. But I really don't think the potion works like that. Go on, have a peek, see for yourself.'

Iris looked over at Storm as he walked towards them but thankfully for her she still wasn't attracted to him. Erin, on the other hand, was blushing bright red, and as he approached she let out a little gasp.

He glanced at her before diverting his attention to Iris.

'Iris, are you OK?'

'I'm a bit drunk, Erin made me drink her rum potion and there was a lot of rum.'

Storm glowered at Erin. 'You got her drunk?'

'Yes, although not deliberately. But I'm taking care of her.'

'She's taking me to Lynx's house for hot sex,' Iris giggled.

Storm looked furious. 'You're taking a drunk woman to a man's house for sex?'

'It's not like that,' Erin said.

'What if he takes advantage of her?'

'This is Lynx we're talking about, he's a perfect gentleman. I would trust him with my life. You, on the other hand, I wouldn't trust you as far as I could throw you. Which let's face it, wouldn't be very far,' Erin said.

'What's that supposed to mean?'

'Look at the size of you, what are you, seven foot tall? Eight? I doubt I could even lift you, let alone throw you.'

'I meant, why wouldn't you trust me?'

'Because you're angry, grumpy, rude to everyone, including me. I wouldn't trust you to be kind and sympathetic to anyone.'

'I can be kind. To the right person.'

'He's been pretty kind to me,' Iris said.

'Oh, I see what this is,' Erin said, glaring at Storm. 'You don't want Iris to go and see Lynx because you fancy your chances with her. Well, let me tell you, she can do a lot better than you.'

Storm frowned. 'Iris and Lynx are fated to be together, there's nothing that can stand in the way of that. Nor would I want to.'

Iris sighed and, seeing Lynx's front door, decided to leave them to their argument.

She walked up to the door and opened it, letting herself in and leaving Storm and Erin still arguing in the middle of the street.

Lynx had just got into bed when he heard a bump downstairs. He sat up and, with a wave of his hand, turned the light back on. He could hear someone, probably Iris, coming up the stairs, but by the sounds of it she was really struggling.

He got out of bed and went out into the hall, leaning over the banister to look. He smiled to see Iris staggering up the last few steps.

'Hey,' Lynx said.

She turned to look at him. 'Oh, I was going to surprise you.'

She wobbled down the landing towards him and then gave him a big hug. He wrapped his arms around her to keep her steady.

'So you had a good night at potions club?'

'There was rum in the potion. Rum. I don't drink. Apart from a glass of wine on special occasions. But I never drink rum. And I only put a teeny-tiny bit of rum in mine but Star didn't want to drink hers because she's pregnant and Erin didn't want hers and they said I had to drink theirs to make my potion triply effective and there was a lot of rum in theirs and I didn't realise until I'd drunk it and then you can't undrink it.'

'What was the potion?'

'How to get what you really want. And here I am because you're the thing I want more than anything.'

He smirked and kissed her head. 'I see.'

'Erin said I should come round here, climb you like a tree and have hot sex.'

Lynx suppressed a snort of laughter. 'Is that what *you* want?'

'I definitely want more of the sex we had this afternoon. But probably not tonight.'

He bent down and scooped her up, carrying her into his bedroom.

He sat her on the edge of the bed and removed her shoes. To his surprise she stood up and pulled off her jeans so she was standing there in just a tiny t-shirt and her knickers. He quickly reached out and magically extended her t-shirt down to her knees.

'How did you do that?' Iris stared at her t-shirt in disbelief.

'It's magic, baby.'

She giggled. 'You called me baby.'

He shook his head with a smile. He really bloody liked this woman.

She scooted back into the bed, flashing those beautiful legs before he covered her with the duvet.

'Stay here, I'll be back in a second.'

Lynx went downstairs and, with a few waves of his hand, made a quick potion. When he took it back to her she was already snoozing.

'Hey, wake up for a second and drink this.'

She sat up sleepily and took it. 'What is it?'

'It's my special anti-hangover potion.'

She downed it in one and then lay back down. He got into bed next to her and wrapped his arms around her. She immediately snuggled into his chest and closed her eyes.

'I love you, you know,' Iris said, sleepily.

He smiled at that drunken declaration of love.

'I don't need a potion to tell me that I love you or to show me that I want a child with you because I do. Just not yet. It doesn't mean I don't love you.'

'OK,' Lynx said, kissing her head. 'We can talk about it tomorrow.'

Seconds later she was fast asleep. As he stroked her hair he wondered if she would remember any of this in the morning.

CHAPTER 17

Iris woke with a start the next day as she realised where she was, wrapped tightly in Lynx's arms.

She looked up at him and he smiled at her.

'We haven't had sex, nothing inappropriate happened and you didn't make a fool of yourself,' Lynx said.

She smiled, feeling herself relax. He made her feel so calm and right now she felt too happy to move out of his arms. 'I remember some of it. I don't remember coming here but I remember you made my t-shirt really big, did I imagine that?'

He laughed and she looked under the covers to see her cropped t-shirt was down to her knees. 'There are some things in this magical world I'm never going to get used to.'

She looked back up at Lynx and he stroked her hair. He was so lovely.

'Did you sleep OK?'

'Yes, blissfully so.'

'And do you remember anything else from last night?'

Iris tried to remember the night before. She remembered leaving Ashley's house with Erin, seeing Storm... and then like a flood it all came back. It was very kind of Lynx to say she hadn't made a fool of herself but the fact that she'd turned up at his house in the middle of the night, drunk, was enough to make her cringe. But telling him she was in love with him was probably a step too far. Even if it was true. He hadn't said it back and she couldn't expect him to, it had only been a few days. She was surprised he was still here after that declaration.

'No, I don't remember,' she lied, embarrassed. Hopefully, he'd just think it was the rum talking.

He stroked her face and kissed her. 'That's a shame, I was looking forward to talking to you about that.'

She frowned in confusion.

'Come on, I'll make us some breakfast before we go to work,' Lynx said.

'No, let's stay here and not face the world.'

'Are you worried about today?' he asked.

'A little. It's the not knowing what's in the locket

that's the worst, but I trust that Ashley will do every-thing she can to protect the village.'

'She will. She's very knowledgeable and we'll all be there to help too.'

Iris nodded.

He kissed her on the head and then climbed out of bed and left the room. Maybe, once this was all over, she could be brave enough to have a conversation with him about their future.

Iris had barely been able to concentrate all morning in the shop. There had been a lot of customers who had come in and bought things, or just popped in to chat to her, and she'd had to force a smile on her face and be polite, even though inside she was worried to death that she'd brought some great plague to the village.

Just before twelve, she went downstairs where Lynx was waiting for her. He didn't say anything, just took her in his arms and gave her a kiss on the head before they left the shop. He took her hand as they walked the short distance to Ashley's house. The door was open when they arrived and Wolf was already in there. The locket was on a table in the middle of the room, candles flickering from every surface.

Ashley looked up from lighting the last of the candles and smiled at Iris.

'I hope your head wasn't too sore this morning.'

'Thankfully Lynx made me an anti-hangover potion, so I felt fine.'

'That's good.' Ashley nodded towards the locket. 'Hopefully we can laugh about all this in a few minutes. I've probably gone completely over the top for nothing.'

'I hope so too.'

Just then Erin arrived and a few seconds later Storm came through the door. They scowled at each other; clearly the argument from the night before was still ongoing.

'Thank you both for coming,' Ashley said. 'So, there are a few protective spells around the locket at the moment to try to contain whatever it is, but the main one will come from us using the four elements. Lynx is a fire witch, Wolf is air, Iris is water and you two are earth. For this spell earth is the one that needs to be the strongest, which is why it's good you're both here. So if we all stand in a square around the locket I can put that protective spell in place too.'

They all positioned themselves around the locket, with Erin and Storm reluctantly standing together on one side of the square.

'Erin, can you and Storm hold hands to link your power together?'

They scowled at each other as if they couldn't think of anything worse but they did it anyway.

Ashley muttered a few words under her breath and waved her hand in the air. A beam of light suddenly came from each of them and joined above the locket, briefly creating a pyramid-shaped cage around it before fading away.

'Are we ready?' Ashley asked.

Everyone nodded.

Iris bit her lip as she watched.

Standing a few metres away, Ashley magically lifted the clasp and slowly opened the locket and... nothing happened. There was no black smoke or fire, nothing came out, no demons or evil entities swirled around the room.

They were all standing well back from the locket but, after a few moments of nothing, they shuffled forward to look.

There was something small and black, about the size of a five-pence piece, sitting inside. But other than that, there was nothing of interest in there whatsoever.

'What is it?' Iris whispered, wondering if the release of the darkness was delayed.

Lynx peered closer and after a moment he picked it up. 'Oh crap.'

'What is it?' Ashley asked.

'It's a tracking device. It works by picking up the

signal from mobile phone towers and uses other people's phones to get an exact location.'

'Oh no,' said Ashley. 'That's what I was feeling, I could feel it giving off this weird signal and it wasn't something I've felt before so I didn't know what it was. But now it's open I can feel the darkness I felt was from him. He's not a good person.'

Iris felt so much relief that the whole village wouldn't be cursed but then a new realisation hit her. 'The police will be tracking that, they'll know the locket is here.'

'Not for long,' Wolf said.

He took the tracker off Lynx, walked out the door and took off into the air.

'Whoa! I didn't know he could fly,' Iris said.

'He'll take it far away from here,' Lynx said.

'It may be already too late for that,' Storm said. 'That locket has been here for several days. Which begs the question, why haven't the police turned up already?'

'Maybe the copper of the locket blocked the signal, maybe the magical energy protected it too,' Ashley said.

'But not now we've opened it,' Iris said.

'It was only here for a few seconds, we might have got rid of it before they got a lock on it,' Lynx said.

What would happen if the police came here? All the magic that was constantly happening around the village, in people's gardens, their homes, the shops, the police would think they'd walked into some creepy paranormal dimension. Sure, Wolf could get everyone to not do any magic for a day. But what about the kids, children like Blaze who magic just sort of happened around – there was no controlling that. What if the police went into everyone's homes, looking for her and the locket? Iris couldn't let that happen. She'd worried about a curse and the damage it could cause but this suddenly felt so much worse.

She looked at the picture inside the locket, which was magically infused with the metal. It really wasn't very clear who the people were. The photo had that grainy quality that all old non-digital photos had. It could be anyone. Her nan would surely have the original wedding photo somewhere. If so, then coupled with the pressed flower book and the list of possessions from her dead ancestor, maybe she could go to the police and prove the locket was hers and that she had simply been stealing it back. But would it be enough?

'I wish I'd known what it was,' Ashley said. 'We could have done something about it.'

'It's not your fault,' Lynx said. 'At least you alerted us to it, and we've dealt with it as soon as we could, rather than having it here open for several hours or days. And it wasn't a curse, this is a good thing.'

'And at least you can give the locket back to Ness now,' Ashley said, handing Iris the locket.

But Iris couldn't even feel happy about that right now. She shoved it in her pocket.

Lynx glanced at her. 'What are you thinking?'

'We need to be prepared for the police to come here and I need to go back home and see if I can get together some proof that the locket is ours.'

'You can't go back there,' Lynx said. 'Christopher could be waiting for you.'

'Can't you do the finger clicking summoning spell?'

'No, I'd have to know what the documents or books look like, I'd need to be able to picture clearly where they were too, I've never been to your farmhouse so that wouldn't work.'

She sighed. 'This isn't going to go away and I don't want to bring trouble to the village.'

'The tracking device might not have got a signal here. The police might not have any idea about our existence. And even if they do show up, they won't be able to get in, the armed guards will make sure of that.'

'And they'll come back with guns of their own. They're not going to let this lie, this is one of the biggest jewellery heists they've ever seen, at least in terms of value.'

'Let's just wait and see, there's no need to rush into anything,' Lynx said.

'Lynx is right,' Erin said. 'It's not safe for you to go back home yet.'

Just then Wolf landed back outside the cottage and

walked back in. 'I flew it down the coast so hopefully it would have pinged off a few other mobile phone towers, then flew it out to sea and destroyed it.'

'What if the police come here?' Iris asked.

Wolf shrugged, unperturbed. 'They won't get in.'

'And they won't give up either.'

'They'd need more evidence than just a few seconds of location data to justify searching four hundred homes. Of course we'll deny that you and Ness are here but, if they do come in, you can disguise yourselves in plain sight. We'll do whatever it takes to protect you.'

Iris felt touched by that but she knew she had to protect them too.

It was probably only an hour later that Lynx got a call from Wolf to say the police had passed the outer gateposts and were on their way down the drive to the main gate.

Lynx called up to Iris, wanting to be honest with her and not hide anything from her.

She appeared at the top of the shop stairs looking worried and he wished he could take that worry away from her.

'The police are here.'

She let out a little gasp and then nodded as she

came down the stairs. 'I want to hear what they have to say.'

'OK, but you're not coming as you. And promise me, no matter what they say, you don't say anything to them. Let Wolf handle this.'

Iris nodded and changed to an exact copy of Storm again.

They walked out of the shop and started making their way to the main gate.

How had they got a lock on that tracking device so quickly? It could only have been from opening it today or they'd have been here way before this.

They met Wolf just as a police van arrived outside. Wolf eyed Iris with confusion and then realisation dawned on his face and he nodded. The gate opened fractionally, just enough to let them through, and then closed behind them.

A couple of policemen and a woman in a suit got out.

'Hello,' said the woman. 'I'm DI Kim Gibbs.'

'Hello, I'm Wolf Oakwood, the mayor of the village. How can I help you?' Wolf said, calmly.

'We're investigating the theft of a priceless locket, the Ocean Flower. I'm sure you must have seen it on the news.'

Wolf looked confused. 'Of course, but that was in London. I'm not sure how we can help you with that.'

'We're looking for a woman called Iris McKenzie.'

Lynx felt Iris stiffen fractionally next to him.

Wolf looked blank. 'There's no one here by that name.'

'What about Ness McKenzie?' DI Gibbs asked.

Wolf shook his head. 'No, no McKenzies here at all.'

'I don't understand why you're here. Are you going door-to-door at every house in the country?' Lynx said.

DI Gibbs shook her head. 'The owner of the locket had the foresight to put a tracking device inside the locket. An hour ago it switched back on and gave us a location which led us to here.'

'Here?' Wolf said in surprise. 'There must be some mistake.'

'No mistake.'

'And you're still getting a reading from in there now?' Wolf asked.

'No, it, umm...' DI Gibbs paused. 'It moved from here very quickly and went further down the coast. But the fact that its first location was here makes this village a place of interest.'

'But why aren't you checking where the locket is now?'

'We believe the locket and the tracking device have become separated after the locket was opened and that the tracking device was removed from here with the help of a drone as it was moving so quickly. If it became separated here, the locket is very likely still here.'

'That's a lot of assumptions,' Wolf said.

'It's fair to assume the locket was here or near here at some point,' she replied.

'You only know that the tracking device was briefly located near here,' Lynx said. 'That tracking device could have become separated from the locket at any point since the robbery.'

'We'd like to come into the village and have a look around, talk to the residents,' DI Gibbs said.

'I'm afraid that won't be possible. This is a privately owned village and the residents demand their privacy. And what you are telling me here is not enough evidence for me to disrupt hundreds of lives on what seems like a wild goose chase. The woman in question does not live here, and you say the tracking device was only here briefly, if at all, so maybe it was simply flying overhead in this drone you talked about. There is nothing to suggest the locket is here. If you come back with more evidence then I will consider your request,' Wolf said, and Lynx had to suppress a smirk at how calm and matter-of-fact his brother was.

'We'll come back with a warrant,' DI Gibbs said.

'Yes, please do. If you think the magistrate will issue a warrant to search three hundred and eighty-seven houses based on this evidence, please do come back. I'd love to see it.'

She narrowed her eyes at him and signalled for the other police officers to return to the van. 'We'll be back.'

Wolf nodded. 'I'll put the kettle on when you do.

You'll need it if you're going to search three hundred and eighty-seven houses. Have a safe journey back.'

The policewoman got back in the van and Wolf, Lynx and Iris waited for it to turn around and drive back down the road before they went back inside.

As soon as the gate closed behind them, Iris walked off at quite the pace.

'Nicely done,' Lynx said to Wolf.

'There's no way they'll get a warrant for that,' Wolf said.

'And if they do?'

'They won't. I've already spoken to a former member of this village who is an ex-police detective. I wanted to know my rights if the police did come here. He said they couldn't even get a warrant for a block of six flats when they knew the suspect was in one of them. They'd never get a warrant for nearly four hundred houses.'

'So we're good?'

'It won't stop them coming back but their evidence is flimsy at best. They'll give up eventually.'

Lynx made his way back to the shop, wondering how Iris was going to react about the police coming here. Even though Wolf wouldn't have told anyone yet and

Lynx knew Iris wouldn't have mentioned it, somehow the whole village already knew. Three people stopped him on the way to Stardust Street, worrying over the police coming here. The police had never had any reason to come to the village in all the years he'd lived here, or at any point in the past, so he understood why they were worried. He was too. It was important that their way of life was protected, they couldn't risk the police finding out Midnight was magical. And despite Wolf's bravado, Lynx was fairly sure the police would be back. The theft of the Ocean Flower was a huge news story and this was their only lead, despite the flimsiness of the evidence.

He finally reached their shop to find that it was still locked up.

He let himself in and checked inside and upstairs just in case Iris was there, but the place was completely empty. He quickly hurried back to his house but she wasn't there either. He crossed over the road and knocked on her door.

The door opened slowly and then Morag peered round it.

'She's in the garden,' Morag said.

'Is she OK?'

'Not really. She's talking about handing herself in.'

'That isn't going to happen,' Lynx said, grimly.

'It better not. You said you were going to protect her.'

'Morag, I will fight to the death for her if need be.'

'That's a bit overdramatic, but you have a good heart. Go and see her,' Morag pointed a paw in the direction of the back garden.

Lynx walked outside. The garden was quite long and dipped down at the end. There were lots of trees and bushes near the back but no sign of Iris. He walked a bit further and eventually saw her standing barefoot in the little stream that ran through her garden. Her eyes were closed, as if she was meditating.

He slipped off his shoes and socks and carefully stepped into the stream with her. She smiled slightly although she didn't open her eyes, she just stepped up and wrapped her arms around him, leaning her head against his chest. They stood like that for the longest time, Lynx holding her tight, but she didn't seem willing to move so he didn't either.

Eventually she looked up and kissed him, briefly on the lips.

'Thank you.'

'Of course, I'm always here for you. But we need to talk.'

She placed a finger on his lips. 'Can we not talk about it here, not yet. I need some time to think.'

'OK, whatever you need.'

'Come lie with me for a bit.'

He nodded and she took his hand. She stepped up onto the grass then lay down and he lay down next to her, wrapping his arms around her again as he held her against his chest.

'You're not alone Iris, we'll face this together.'

She didn't reply but he was determined to find a solution to this.

Iris felt so peaceful right now, wrapped in Lynx's arms as she tried not to think about what she had to do. The sun was setting above them, leaving scarlet and orange clouds across the sky, the moon was shining brightly and even a few stars were twinkling in the darkening sky. They were completely secluded here, the over-hanging trees blocking them from the view of any other houses. Right now, it felt like they were the only people in the world and her problems – Christopher, the locket, the police – they could all be easily pushed away.

She looked up at Lynx and he looked back at her and smiled, making her heart ache.

'Thank you for being here for me,' Iris said.

'Always.'

'Will you promise me something?'

'Anything, whatever you need.'

'If I go to prison, will you look after my nan for me?'

'Iris, you're not going to prison.'

'But if I do, will you look after her and Morag?'

'I promise you, that will never happen. Even if the police come back here, we can hide you in plain sight. The villagers will protect you, we won't let them take you.'

'Lynx, will you look after them?'

'Of course I will, but it won't come to that.'

She reached up to kiss him to stop him talking. Her nan would be OK, the villagers and Lynx would look after her. That was all she needed to hear. She could only hope that the police would believe her and if not, at least she would have protected the people of Midnight. She had been so worried that the locket was going to bring a great danger to the village, but it was her presence here that was the biggest threat. If she took that away, then the quiet, peaceful life that Midnight enjoyed could continue.

He moved his hand through her hair and she wanted to feel alive one more time. She unfastened the buttons on his shirt and stroked her hand over his chest, causing him to moan against her lips. She slid her hand lower towards the waistband of his jeans and undid the button and the zip. She moved her hand inside and had the pleasure of feeling him go instantly hard for her, just from a simple touch. She pushed his jeans and shorts down and he quickly shoved them off.

He rolled half on top of her, his mouth on hers as he slid a hand underneath her dress along her thigh. His touch was so gentle and soft it made her stomach clench with need and desire. His finger traced the edges of her knickers at the sides, at the top, and then touched where she needed him the most with the barest whisper. He hooked a finger through her knickers and slowly slid them down and she helped him by wriggling out of them. Then his hand was moving back up the inside of her thigh and he instantly found that spot that made her go weak. She arched against him, moaning against his lips. He was perfect for her, knowing instinctively how she liked to be touched. She felt a tingling in her stomach, building up with such force it was almost painful, and then she was crying out as he swallowed her moans on his lips.

She rolled on top of him and straddled him, sitting up, and he immediately sat up too so he could continue the kiss, cupping her head in his hands. She pushed his shirt off his strong shoulders. He slid his hands down her back and down her thighs before moving them back up, shifting her dress up to her waist and then pulling it over her head, casting it to one side. He made quick work of her bra too, then his mouth trailed over her chest, her breasts, driving her crazy.

'Lynx, I need you.'

'I'm here, always,' Lynx said. She knelt up and he guided her down on top of him, the feel of him inside her making her gasp. She kissed him, cupping his face. She pulled back slightly to look at him and he was gazing at her with such adoration it brought tears to her eyes. Her heart felt so full of him.

'Lynx, I am falling for you so fast and so hard. I don't want to hurt you.'

He frowned. 'Why do you think you'll hurt me?'

She shook her head.

'Did you see something?'

'No, I just...' she stroked his face. 'I'm kind of used to being alone and—'

'You're not alone, not anymore. And I will do everything I can to shield you from this.'

She smiled slightly. 'I feel the same, I will do whatever it takes to protect you.'

He frowned but she kissed him again to stop him from talking and started moving against him. He slid his hands down to her hips, holding her tight against him, moving perfectly in sync with her.

A glow built up inside of her, filling her with warmth and shining so brightly it surrounded them. She could feel him in every part of her, feel his magic connecting with hers in the most beautiful and intimate way. Then suddenly she was falling, holding onto him, moaning against his lips, taking him with her. And as she came down from her high, he stroked her and kissed so gently, her heart filled to the top for him. She knew she would do anything to protect him and the village she had fallen in love with too.

The night was lit up only by the moon and the stars above them and Lynx was fast asleep next to her, one arm loosely round her shoulders as she lay on his chest.

Iris sat up very carefully, lifting his arm gently so she could climb out of his embrace and placing it softly back on his chest. She stood up and looked at him, her chest aching. He'd pulled his jeans back on, but he was still topless, the moon painting his skin with a gorgeous silvery glow.

She quickly pulled her clothes back on and ran back into the house. She went upstairs and crept into her nan's room. She was fast asleep too, and she placed a soft kiss on her cheek and made her way back down-stairs. Morag was curled up asleep on the sofa. Iris gave her a stroke and Morag stirred slightly and looked at her with one beady eye, then raised her head to look at her.

'I have to go,' Iris said.

Morag looked at her in alarm. 'Go where?'

'I have to go home to get the evidence we need to prove the locket is ours.'

'You can't go back to Scotland alone. If he's there he'll hurt you. I'll come with you.'

'No, I'm not risking you. Besides, I'm going straight from our farmhouse to the police in London, I can't exactly turn up at the police station with a talking fox and I can't leave you in Scotland either. Look, when I show them the evidence they will have to believe me. I'll probably be back in time for dinner.'

'I don't like this.'

'I don't either but it's the middle of the night. Christopher's unlikely to be standing around outside waiting for me at two in the morning.'

'I don't want you to go to the police either, you're safe here.'

'I can't let the police come back here. I can't put a whole village at risk, just for me. This is the right thing to do. If I don't come back, look after Ness for me. And tell Lynx I'm sorry.'

Iris gave Morag a kiss on the head and, before she could protest anymore, she slipped out of the house and ran across the road to Lynx's house. Letting herself in, she switched on the lights and she found the key stones sitting in the bowl.

She picked one up to find it felt surprisingly warm in her hand. She needed to do this quickly before Lynx woke up and found her gone, or before she changed her mind. The locket was still in her pocket after they'd opened it earlier that day. She would go back to her home in Scotland, find the wedding photo that matched the one inside the locket, the list of items from her ancestor and the book of pressed flowers with the diagram in it, then take it all straight to the police, and hope it was enough. And if it wasn't, at least it would stop them ever coming back to Midnight. They would have their thief. The case would be closed. She felt sick at the thought.

She thought about Star and Blaze, Erin, Storm, Ashley, Kianga and Maxine, the people who'd come here to escape the judgement of the mundane world. Resolve settled in her gut and a grim determination. She couldn't let the police come back here and ruin their perfect little haven.

Iris closed her eyes, pictured the farmhouse she had grown up in, the place she had lived in almost all of her life. Suddenly she felt a pulling, wind rushing around her fierce and hard as if she was caught in a hurricane. She knew she was spinning, twisting and turning, and then she was spat out the other side.

CHAPTER 18

Morag leapt off the sofa. She had to do something. She had to stop Iris or find Lynx, he could stop her, or at least go to Scotland with her.

She ran out onto the dark street and looked around. There was no sign of Iris or anyone. The car was still there so she wasn't planning on driving to Scotland. Would she use the rivers and lakes in the same way they had to travel down here? She'd need water for that and the stream was in the back garden and Iris had gone out the front. Where had she gone?

Movement caught her eye and she saw Viktor prowling down the road.

'Viktor, have you seen Iris?'

'No, I don't keep a tab on all the witches. If you've

lost your *owner* that is your problem.' Viktor carried on walking past her.

'Viktor, this is serious. She's gone back to Scotland to get the evidence she needs to prove the locket is hers and to stop the police coming back here. If her ex is there, he'll kill her.'

Viktor stopped. 'Where is Lynx?'

'I don't know.'

'Have you checked Iris's bedroom?' Viktor said.

'No, I'll do that.'

'I'll check his bedroom,' Viktor said, taking off at a run.

Morag ran back into the house and up the stairs but the bed hadn't even been slept in. She ran back down again and across the street just as Viktor was running out of Lynx's house.

'The house is empty, but the front door was open and the lights are on.'

Morag looked around, trying to think. Iris had talked about Lynx's key stones and how she could travel to Scotland in seconds using one of them. That must be how she planned to go.

'The key stones. Lynx has stones that help him to travel to places. Do you know where he keeps them?'

Viktor gestured for her to follow him back inside the house and then jumped up onto the side. Morag did too. Viktor gestured to a bowl with two dark stones inside.

'He has three key stones. One is missing, so I guess Iris took one.'

'How do they work?'

'You just hold them and think of the place you want to go and it takes you there.'

Morag reached out a paw to touch one of the stones but Viktor batted it away.

'No, it's too dangerous. You have to hold the stone really tight in your hand and you don't have one of those. Touching it is not the same. If you drop the stone mid-travel, you'll be lost in the fabric of space forever.'

'I could hold it in my mouth.'

'No, it's too risky. I won't allow it.'

Morag felt the anger rise in her. 'You won't allow it? I can't leave her there alone.'

'We need to find Lynx and if we can't, we'll go and tell Wolf. He'll know what to do.'

Iris staggered a bit as she landed, caught her balance and opened her eyes. It was hard to tell where she was, it was dark, the only light coming from the moon above her. Her head was spinning, she felt sick. She closed her eyes again, taking deep breaths through her nose, and that's when the smell hit her: the smell of burning, the scent of smoke and fire. It overwhelmed her.

She opened her eyes again and looked around. She still couldn't see anything, the key stone must have made a mistake. There was no sign of any building, let alone the farmhouse. Sky spread out above her with no buildings at all blocking her view.

She conjured a light in her hands and floated it above her head so she could see where she was. There was a large pile of smouldering rubble in front of her, which was obviously where the burned smell was coming from. She looked around her in confusion, recognising the courtyard with the little pineapple-shaped birdbath that had always sat in front of her farmhouse, the pale pink paving slabs she had tripped on when playing on her roller-skates as a kid, the old willow tree she had spent many an hour lying under. She looked around again, not understanding what she was seeing. Her head was still spinning, she was still dizzy, none of this made sense.

The full horrific realisation hit her like a bus. The smouldering rubble was her home. She conjured a few more lights and they floated over the remains of her home. There was nothing left. The house that had sat there for hundreds of years was gone, her home was completely destroyed.

Acute, agonising pain sliced through her and she quickly let the lights wink out so she wouldn't have to look at the devastation anymore. She curled up in a ball and sobbed.

Lynx woke up with a start, feeling pain in his chest so severe he thought for a second he was having a heart attack. He leapt up and realised that Iris was gone and the pain he was feeling was coming from her. He didn't know how he knew that, he just did.

'Iris!' he yelled.

There was no answer. Where was she and what had happened that was causing her so much pain?

He ran into the house and out onto the street just as Morag and Viktor were coming out of his house, looking very worried.

'Where is she?' he demanded.

'She's gone to Scotland,' said Morag. 'She said she has to get the evidence to prove the locket is hers so the police don't come back here. She's taken one of your key stones.'

Lynx tore through the door. The pain still throbbed in his chest. He needed to get to her. He had never used the key stones to connect to a person before, just a place, but it had to be worth a try, despite the danger involved.

He quickly moved over to the bowl and grabbed one. He closed his eyes, thinking of her, her smile, her scent, her hair, and suddenly he was moving through the fabric of space, wind roaring past him, so hard he could barely breathe, spinning, falling, twisting, turning, until he landed with a thud on the other side. He opened his eyes. His head was still spinning but he had no idea where he was. The darkness around him was complete and it took him a second to get his eyes accustomed to the lack of light. He conjured a few balls of light that floated above him and frantically looked around. She had to be here.

He spotted the charred remains of a house, but this wasn't a recent fire, he could tell it had been put out a few days before.

Suddenly he heard sobbing and looked around to see Iris, curled up in a ball, her shoulders heaving as she cried.

He rushed over to her, putting his arm round her. 'Iris, are you hurt?'

She jolted with shock and looked at him through tear-filled eyes. 'Lynx, what are you doing here?'

'Are you hurt?' he said, urgently.

She shook her head and relief coursed through him.

'Is this...' he gestured to the pile of bricks and wood but he had already guessed the answer.

'My home,' Iris said, fresh tears filling her eyes once more.

Anger raged in him. Christopher had done this and that meant he could still be here, waiting for her.

'We need to go.' Lynx scooped her up in his arms

before she could argue and, holding her close, gripped the stone tightly. 'Hold on and don't let go.'

She quickly wrapped her arms around his neck as he closed his eyes and thought of home. This connection was always so much easier than to anywhere else and within seconds he felt that rush of roaring wind, the spinning and twisting. Through it all, he held onto Iris like his life depended on it.

He stumbled out the other side and opened his eyes to see his lounge and Iris still in his arms. He sat down on the sofa with her on his lap as he tried to catch his breath. She cried against his shoulder and he stroked her hair.

Movement caught his eye at the door and he saw Viktor poking his head around.

'Is she OK?'

How could Lynx even answer that question? He couldn't tell him what had happened because he was sure Iris would want to tell Morag herself. It shouldn't come from Viktor.

'She's not hurt. Can you tell Morag she's safe and we'll talk to her tomorrow?'

Viktor nodded and disappeared.

Lynx was so angry right now, angry at Iris for putting herself at risk and for going home alone. But mostly he was angry at Christopher for doing this, for stealing the locket, for bringing the police into their lives, and now burning down Iris's home, either in some act of revenge or to stop her getting the proof of ownership for the locket. He was furious and he knew he had to get his revenge in some way, preferably one that would cause Christopher the most pain.

'I can't believe my home is gone,' Iris said. 'And everything I own. My photos of my parents, my nan's wedding album, my mum's jewellery, every memory I had there, completely destroyed.'

'He can't take your memories, Iris.'

She lifted her head to look at him. 'You think Christopher did this?'

'I do.'

She let out a gasp. 'Dear Gods, I slept with this man, he told me he loved me... How could he do this to me? Stealing the locket was bad enough, but this is... horrific.'

'We're going to get him back for this,' Lynx said grimly. 'And we're going to put a stop to this once and for all.'

'What are you going to do?'

'I don't know, but I'm sure I can find a couple of very painful curses.'

'We can't hurt mundanes.'

'Oh, I think we could make an exception.'

She shook her head and he could see the moment her sadness turned to anger. 'Do you think he did this for revenge?'

'Probably. I think he came up there to get the locket

back from you, found you gone and no sign of the locket and he did that. Or he wanted to destroy the evidence of any connection between you and the locket.'

'That's what I went up there for. I was going to go to the police and hope the evidence was enough.'

Lynx shook his head. 'You should never have gone there alone, he could have been waiting for you, it was a huge risk. And going to the police, why the hell would you do that?'

'I couldn't risk them coming back here. What you've created here, your ancestors and Wolf, is a safe haven for witches. Somewhere for them to create magic without fear or judgement. And what about Blaze and the other children? We might be able to warn all the villagers not to do their magic, but we can't stop the children from doing it.'

He sighed. 'I understand why you did it but you should have told me. We're a team or at least we're supposed to be. You're not alone anymore, we'll face whatever troubles come our way together.'

'Would you have let me go if I'd told you?'

'That's not the point, we're supposed to talk to each other. And while I wouldn't have been happy about going back to your house, I would have come with you to protect you. We could have taken Wolf and Storm too if need be. But going to the police would have been unnecessary, which you'd have known if you'd talked to me. They can't get in here without a warrant and they can't get a warrant for four hundred houses.'

'But they can keep coming back and harassing Wolf, causing worry and stress in the village. And with us being the only lead, no matter how flimsy it is, they aren't going to give up on us that easily.'

He sighed, knowing she was right about that. 'You still need to talk to me, we don't have any hope of a future together unless we can communicate. There are two people in this relationship, that means we can't run around and do whatever the hell we want without discussing it with the other person. And with us being fated, our connection is deeper than I think you realise. I felt your pain tonight, this heartbreaking, agonising pain in my chest.'

Iris stared at him with wide eyes. 'You felt that?'

'It was that pain that woke me up. Your actions have consequences for me and for our future. We have to work together, in all things, or that beautiful future you've seen will never happen.'

She bit her lip and nodded. 'OK, I'm sorry, you're right. I was trying to protect you and the village but I should have spoken to you about my plans. But what are we going to do now? There's no evidence to tie us to the locket. And I really want to see Christopher rot in jail for all of this.'

He looked at his watch. 'It's gone half two in the

morning. What we're going to do now is sleep. Tomor-row, we'll come up with a plan.'

She nodded. 'OK.'

He stood up with her in his arms and carried her upstairs to bed.

CHAPTER 19

Iris opened the door to her house just as Ness and Morag were finishing breakfast. Ness turned round and saw her. She looked furious, and rightly so. Although Iris didn't want this argument now, she needed to tell her nan about their home.

'What the hell were you playing at last night?' Ness said, getting up from the table and putting her hands on her hips.

'I know, I'm sorry, it was a mistake.'

'You're damned right it was a mistake. You make all this noise about coming down here to protect us from Christopher and you go back there, on your own. Have you lost your marbles?'

'I was trying to protect the village. I'm sure you heard yesterday that the police came here looking for me, demanding to be let in. I thought going back to get the evidence to prove the locket was ours would make the police leave the village alone. It's something we should have done from the beginning as soon as Christopher stole it. If we'd gone to them straight away with our proof then none of this would have happened.'

'I didn't want the police to see my memories,' Ness said. 'If they got the locket back and touched those memory crystals and saw everything I've put in there, they would know that the locket was magical and I couldn't let that happen.'

Iris sighed. 'I understand now. And I'm sorry but I thought going back to get the evidence was my only option to protect everyone in the village. I didn't mean to hurt anyone or make anyone worry,' she addressed that to Morag. She swallowed down the pain of what she was about to say. 'I have some bad news.'

'What?'

'Maybe you should sit down,' Iris said.

Ness sat down at the breakfast table and Iris sat opposite her, taking her hand. Tears filled her eyes as she took a deep breath. 'Our home is gone.'

Ness frowned. 'What do you mean, gone?'

'There was a fire. There's nothing left.'

Ness gasped, her hands going to her mouth, tears filling her eyes and pouring down her cheeks.

'I'm so sorry,' Iris said softly.

'Everything is gone?'

Iris nodded and Ness put her head on her arms and sobbed.

Iris quickly got up and hugged her nan. She looked at Morag over her nan's shoulder and even she looked broken-hearted too. She held out an arm for her and Morag jumped up on Ness's lap, leaning her head against her chest. Iris embraced them both. She stood like that for the longest time before her nan's sobs finally subsided.

'What happened?'

Iris went and sat back down, but Morag stayed cuddled up on Ness's lap.

'We think it might have been Christopher, although we have no proof. It's likely he came back up to the farmhouse after I stole the locket and either burned it down as revenge or to destroy any evidence we had to claim the locket as ours.'

'That little shitbag,' Ness said.

'I know. We're going to get him back for this, for all of it. We're going to find a way to turn the tables on him, to make the police see the truth, that he's the thief here, not us.'

'You make him pay for this, you hear me. I want to see him rot in jail for a very very long time.'

'I will.'

'And if you can't make a criminal conviction stick, then you need to come up with something very painful.

Eternal fleas or maybe a spell that makes his willy fall off.'

Iris let out a bark of laughter. 'I will, I promise.'

She fished in her pocket and pulled out the locket. 'This is yours now. It's open, your memory crystals are all intact, as far as I can see. There doesn't appear to be any damage.'

She slid it across the table and her nan took it eagerly. She opened it and smiled at the picture of her and Pops on their wedding day. Then she slid her fingers over each crystal, smiling at the memories they showed her.

'Hopefully some of those memories will be of inside the farmhouse so not everything is lost.'

Ness nodded. 'They are. Some of my best memories are in that house and most of them are in here.'

'That's good. We can rebuild. I know it won't be the same but we can still have a home there.'

Ness nodded sadly. 'I think I'm going to go out to the stream.'

'And I'm going to talk to Lynx about what we're going to do next.'

Iris watched her nan get up and walk out into the back garden. It broke her heart to see how small she suddenly looked. They had lost everything, nothing of any monetary value, just sentimental things that were irreplaceable. If Iris had given Ness more time to pack when they left in such a hurry, they could have taken

MEET ME AT MIDNIGHT

more of the important things, not just clothes. But Iris had assumed they were going back, it was never supposed to be a one-way trip.

Iris stood up and went out the front.

Lynx was waiting for her outside, sitting on her front lawn. He'd wanted to come with her to tell her nan but Iris thought it was probably better to do that alone. Ness didn't know Lynx well enough to be comfortable crying in front of him.

He hopped up as soon as he saw her and took her in his arms. 'How did it go?'

'As you would expect, tears, anger and a determination for revenge.'

'And while I agree with that sentiment, I think our biggest priority has to be to find a way to get the police off our backs for good and somehow put the blame for all this on Christopher. All of this is his fault. And even if the police don't pursue us anymore, he won't ever give up, that locket is his golden ticket.'

'Which is why cursing him is a brilliant plan,' Iris said, though she knew they couldn't really do that. 'I have been thinking about it actually. We have to discredit him somehow, turn the tables on him. I was looking into the exhibit information this morning while we had breakfast. I had no idea the locket had so many precious gemstones on it until Christopher announced it on the exhibition leaflet and gave a detailed description of it. And it all seemed a bit too convenient that

329

there were rare and expensive stones like jadeite on it, which hadn't even been heard of fifty years ago. The locket has been in the family for hundreds of years so that just doesn't ring true. Even Ashley said the locket wasn't twenty-four carat gold as he claimed and was more likely to be copper than anything else. I wouldn't be at all surprised if the stones were simply crystals or something that was created magically, nothing rare or precious at all.'

Iris pulled her mobile phone from her pocket, swiped the screen a few times and passed it to Lynx.

'The locket was supposedly verified by leading gemologist Professor Wolfgang Augustin,' she said, pointing to the photo. 'There is a video online of this supposed professor and Christopher discussing the rare stones. I can't find anything online to say this man exists. Not saying he doesn't, he might have better things to do with his time than have an online presence, but I did a search for his image on Google and found someone who looks identical called Steve Abernoth, who's an actor. Now maybe I'm barking up the wrong tree here but I think Christopher faked the verification. How could anyone with any knowledge of jewellery identify the locket as twenty-four carat gold when it's not even gold, it's copper? And if that part of the verification is fake, I think the rest of it is too. And Christopher has done it before. I looked him up. Six years ago he sold a diamond ring at auction that turned out to not be a diamond at all. He got into a lot of trouble but he offered to give all the money back. He said he'd been duped as well and he had no idea it wasn't real, so it never got as far as the police being involved, or at least he was never charged. But if he's done it before, then he could have done it again, either because he's trying to sell it for a much higher value than it's worth or as part of some big fraud scam.'

'What are you thinking?'

'I could be Professor Wolfgang Augustin. I could do a video which I post online saying I was paid to confirm the authenticity of the locket and that really I'm an actor with no knowledge of gems at all.'

'That could work. Although what if the real actor comes forward and says the person in the video isn't him?'

'If you were an actor whose video was now at the heart of a major jewellery heist or fraud scam, would you be sticking your head above the parapet and saying, "I made that fraudulent video not the person on the video."? Or would you keep your head down, grateful someone else is taking the blame for it?'

'Good point. Oh, I know a cloning spell, I could make an exact copy of the locket, appearance-wise anyway. It won't be diamonds or opals or anything like that, if they are indeed real, but it will look exactly the same.'

'A cloning spell? What is that used for?'

'I have no idea. While on my travels around the world, I've found tons of worthless spells that I can't see what use they would have. One that makes grass grow five times as quick, and it literally only works on grass, not plants or crops. I know another that helps to find lost socks, another that helps to tie your shoelaces. None of them will change the world. I came across the cloning one in Finland. It's like a photocopy of something – it looks the same but when you pick it up and touch it, it's not the same. My point is that while you're discrediting him online we can send the fake back to the police to prove your video is the truth. If they get a real jewellery expert to analyse it, they'll soon see that it's not real gold and that none of the jewels are real. We'll make out that Christopher never had any intention of selling it, that it was one big insurance scam. He'll go to prison for that.'

'Oh, I like that. I can do another video of me as the blonde woman who stole the locket, saying I'm a magician that normally works on cruises or in clubs and that I was paid to steal it and that there is definitely nothing real about it.'

'I like it. But my only worry is discrediting Christopher will make him angry and I don't want him coming here.'

'Why not? We have armed guards on the gates and a whole village of firepower. We can handle him.'

He smiled and nodded. 'You may be a water witch but I love your fire.'

'He's not going to get away with this.'

'No, he won't. Let's go and talk to Wolf and make sure he's OK with all of this.'

Iris nodded. She knew that doing anything that could bring danger to the village had to be approved by Wolf but she just hoped he'd be on the same page.

'I am Professor Wolfgang Augustin, leading gemologist at Smithfield University,' Iris said, in her best male voice. 'Well, that's what Christopher Matthews would like you to think. In reality I'm an actor, you might have seen me on TV commercials selling floor cleaner, beer and erectile dysfunction medicine.'

On screen, Iris adjusted her glasses. 'I was asked by Christopher to take the part of learned gemologist and authenticate the gemstones. I was told it was for a joke video that would go on TikTok or some other form of social media. I was paid eighty-five pounds for an hour's work. I was given a script before and in the video, which is widely available online, we chat about the rarity of the gemstones on the locket. But I'm not an expert, I know nothing about precious jewels. However, I can say that in my opinion the locket was made out of copper and the stones looked like they were made from glass. After I did the job, I didn't think any more of it. With most acting jobs you never see the end result for months afterwards. I had no idea Christopher was going to use it to try and pass off that lump of cheap metal as something real. I don't know whether the intention was to try and sell it, although I can't see that anyone would be fooled that the locket was genuine. It might look good but as soon as they touched it they would know straightaway it was a fake. After talking to the woman seen stealing the locket at the exhibition, who you'll hear from in a moment, I now worry it was part of a big insurance scam. But I have been horrified by the events of the last few days and my unwitting part in it. It was never my intention to deceive anyone and I hope now the police will look closer to home in their investigations.'

The video Iris was watching cut to her next alter ego, the blonde woman who stole the locket. Of course, she knew what the video was going to say, she'd practised both parts enough times, but she wanted to see the comments from the public too now it was live in the world. Lynx had gone down to London, heavily disguised, and posted the video from an internet café so it couldn't be traced back to Midnight. So now it was out there and there was no taking it back. Not that she would. Christopher needed to pay for this.

'I, too, have been taken in by Christopher

Matthews,' blonde Iris said, on screen. 'I'm a magician, I do performances in clubs mainly and a few cruise ships. Christopher asked me to do a magic trick where I stole the locket for a video on TikTok. It was all set up with smoke machines and darkened rooms and a special kind of glass that would melt as soon as I touched it. We practised it several times before I actually did it and he was there for the whole thing. I just thought it was some big joke. I was paid a hundred pounds to do it. When I saw the locket during my practice runs, I could tell it wasn't real so I didn't think anything of it. And now my face is on the cover of every newspaper, plastered over every TV news story as if I'm some kind of Great Train Robber. It was a magic trick and Christopher was fully aware of it, it was his idea. I can only assume it was part of some insurance fraud. I have the locket and it's being couriered to the police as we speak. They will see for themselves the whole thing is fake and I'm hoping I can finally come out of hiding. I urge the police to look at the real criminal here. I haven't done anything wrong.'

'That felt very genuine,' Lynx said as he sat next to her. 'Very heartfelt.'

The video changed to Iris as herself. She was definitely pushing her acting capabilities to the max with this one.

'My name is Iris McKenzie. You may have seen my name in the news associated with the theft of the

Ocean Flower locket but that is simply not true. The locket belongs to my nan, it was a wedding gift from my grandad over sixty years ago and she has worn it every day since. And while it looks genuine – the person who made it is obviously very skilled – it has no value. The stones are glass, the locket itself is made from copper. But it has huge sentimental value.'

On the screen, Iris took a drink of water before she continued. 'I dated Christopher for a few months and then one day he drugged my nan and stole the locket she was wearing. I don't know why, maybe he believed it was worth more than it was, or maybe he thought he could convince people of its worth. My nan was heart-broken but at that time we decided not to tell the police and that was a mistake. We believed that because it was completely worthless the police wouldn't care or be willing to do anything about it. We also had no proof the locket belonged to us, other than the wedding photo from my nan's wedding day that was engraved inside.'

The video cut to a shot of the fake cloned locket, complete with the photo inside.

'But the photo is so grainy that it could be anyone. We no longer have the original photo this was taken from and so we felt like it would be our word against Christopher's. I knew nothing of the exhibition until I heard the locket had been stolen for a second time and it was all over the news, along with my name as the person who had stolen it. I can't believe, after the time we spent together, Christopher would steal from me, let alone try to use my name in whatever fraud scam he's trying to pull off. And it would seem this is not the first time he's done this. Six years ago, he got into a lot of trouble for selling a supposed diamond ring which turned out not to be a diamond at all. Maybe this was another attempt at deceiving people. Hopefully, now the police have the locket, this can be put to bed once and for all.'

The video came to an end and Iris sat back and looked at Lynx.

'Do you think it's enough?'

'I don't know,' he said, wrapping his arm around her and sinking back on the sofa. She snuggled into his chest. 'They have the locket now, which they'll be able to tell is fake. But if the police can't speak to Professor Wolfgang, the blonde lady who stole the locket or you, then there may not be enough evidence to take this any further. At the moment all they have is three people claiming one thing and Christopher saying something else. But it may be enough to look twice at him, maybe do some digging into his past, ask some questions they hadn't thought to ask before. As you've mentioned that he's done this kind of thing in the past, and you found the details online easily enough, I'm sure they will too. That will definitely send alarm bells ringing.'

'I hope so. Do you think he'll come here?'

'I think this place is the only lead he and the police have. I think once the police show him the fake locket, he'll know we have the real one. A man who is desperate enough to burn down your house is a man that will act outside of the law. I give it a day max before he's at the gates.'

'Good, then we can carry out the rest of our plan.'

'We'll be ready for him.'

CHAPTER 20

It had been two days since the videos had gone live and shortly after it had gone viral. The theft of the Ocean Flower locket had attracted so much attention because of the way Iris had stolen it. So the videos explaining the truth of it, or rather the truth that Iris had claimed, had obviously piqued the public's interest too. There were thousands of comments on the video, some people saying that they'd known it was taken via some kind of orchestrated illusion, others saying they'd seen the locket in the exhibition and known it was fake. Some people were unconvinced, but the majority of the public now believed Christopher was some kind of con artist or criminal mastermind.

Although it didn't matter what the public thought, it mattered what the police thought and whether they had enough evidence to convict him. They had announced they were aware of the video and had simply said they were continuing their investigations and would like to speak to the three people in the video to help them with their enquiries. Iris had no intention of going to the police under any guise, at least not yet. If their plan was to work, they needed Christopher to come here and now she wasn't sure if he would.

She supposed he was having to talk to the police about her revelations, which of course he would deny, but hopefully they wouldn't make things easy for him.

It had been a worrying few days but at least being with Lynx made her feel safe and calm. It was weird how easily they just fitted together.

'Iris!' Lynx's voice came from downstairs in the shop and she knew straightaway from the tone of his voice that something was wrong.

She quickly ran downstairs to find Wolf and Lynx standing there, looking very serious.

Her heart leapt. 'He's here, isn't he?'

Wolf nodded. 'Outside the gates. You don't have to see him. We can do this next part without you.'

'I think I have to be there.'

'No, you don't,' Lynx said. 'Me and Wolf can handle it.'

'I want to see him, I want to see what he has to say and I really want to be there when he gets his comeuppance. Besides, we need to talk to him before you two knock him out. We need to know where the police stand and he's more likely to talk to me than two people he's never met.'

'We're not knocking him out, just sending him into a deep sleep,' Wolf said. 'There won't be any violence involved.'

'Unless we have to,' Lynx said, menacingly.

Iris smirked.

'I think there's a greater chance of violence if you're there,' Wolf said to Iris. 'Seeing you is going to make him very angry, especially if he thinks you have the real locket.'

'He knows I'm here, or at least assumes I am, that's why he's come. I presume he's asking for me?'

Wolf nodded.

'Not seeing me and getting fobbed off by you two will also make him angry. This is what we planned. We talk to him, see what information we can get from him and then act accordingly.'

'But what if he has a gun?' Lynx said. 'We know he's dangerous, we know he's angry, we've seen what he's done to your house. The likeliness of him bringing a weapon is very high.'

'This is why Star isn't here. As she's pregnant, I didn't want her anywhere near him,' Wolf said.

'I don't want you anywhere near him either,' Lynx said to Iris.

She smiled with love for him. 'We know what he's capable of and we have enough magic between us to be able to stop him. Let's finish this once and for all or it will always be hanging over our heads.'

Lynx sighed and nodded reluctantly.

They walked out of the shop and headed towards the entrance of the village. Iris couldn't deny how nervous she was to see Christopher again, but she was also filled with anger. He had ruined her life and now she wanted her revenge.

As they passed by one of the houses, Lynx ran up and banged on the door. A few seconds later Storm answered. He looked at them in confusion and then in concern, clearly picking up on the atmosphere between them.

'What's wrong?'

'I'm about to meet with my mundane psycho ex-boyfriend who is probably here to try and kill me,' Iris explained.

Storm blinked in surprise.

'We could kind of do with a man of your size to intimidate him,' Lynx said.

Storm stepped out onto the street and closed the door behind him, then joined them.

Lynx came back and took Iris's hand, offering her comfort.

The four of them approached the gate and she saw Christopher standing on the other side. It was the first time she'd seen him since he'd stolen her nan's locket. The last time they'd been together, she'd been lying in bed with him at the farmhouse on the morning he ruined everything. She'd gone out to do some shopping and he'd given her a loving kiss goodbye, and when she'd come back her nan was unconscious and the locket was gone. She'd wanted to track him down and cut off his balls but her nan had persuaded her not to. Now, seeing him again after all this time, she felt none of the feelings she'd had for him, only anger and hatred. It ended here today.

The gate opened a fraction and they all walked out. Iris could see the hate she had for him mirrored in Christopher's own eyes. Had it all really been fake, purely to get the locket? That thought made her sick.

'I knew you were here, I knew you were behind all of this,' Christopher spat.

Storm took a threatening step forward and Christopher's eyes widened with fear and he took a few steps back. Storm moved forward again and Christopher moved back even further. It made Iris feel a bit happier, not having him right there in her space.

'What do you want?' Iris said. Already she could feel magic humming through Lynx and Wolf, they were ready.

'You've ruined everything with that video and your lies. The police have been asking me so many questions, trying to put the blame on me. Before they were bending over backwards to try to help me retrieve the locket, now they think I'm the guilty one.'

'You are the guilty one,' Iris pointed out. 'You drugged my nan and stole her locket. She adored you, she trusted you and you betrayed her and me. And then when the locket was stolen a second time you drag my name into it and burn down my house as revenge.'

A smug smile of satisfaction crossed Christopher's face and anger boiled up in he. She could feel it bubbling in Lynx too.

'I want the locket,' Christopher demanded.

'The police have it,' Iris said in confusion. They didn't know at this stage whether he had come of his own volition or whether he was here working with the police, trying to get her to say something that would incriminate her. He could be bugged or wearing a camera for all they knew.

'Don't give me that crap, you and I both know the locket the police have is a fake. The fact that you haven't had the balls to go to them to give your statement in person shows you don't want to get involved in this and you don't want to press charges. Give me the locket and I'll make sure all this goes away. I'll spin them some lie completely clearing your name. They never have to know I have it. And you never have to see me again.'

'What an overinflated sense of entitlement you have. I don't owe you anything. How dare you come here and act like the injured party after everything you've done. As I've already said, the police have the locket.'

'You don't understand, I need that locket. I've already been paid for it and the new owner is getting very angry that I can't give it to him.'

'The police have it. Give him it once you get out of prison and everyone will see you for the fraud you are.'

Christopher screamed in anger and whipped out a gun, firing it blindly in Iris's direction. Everything happened very quickly after that. Lynx let out a wall of white-hot fire that melted the bullets before they got anywhere near the four of them. The ground shook and cracked as Storm's earth magic ripped the ground around Christopher like paper, causing him to drop the gun. Iris hit Christopher with a force of water that knocked him off his feet while Wolf's wind struck him a second later and sent him flying through the air. He landed with a thud and didn't move after that.

'Are you OK?' Lynx asked Iris.

She nodded. 'He didn't touch me.'

They all looked at Christopher, lying on the road.

'Is he dead?' Iris said. That hadn't been part of the plan.

'Unfortunately not,' Wolf said. 'I can see him breathing.'

'He'll hopefully have a few bruises to show for it though,' Lynx said.

They all moved closer and Wolf checked him over.

'He's breathing OK, no broken bones that I can tell. Come on, let's do this before he wakes up.'

Wolf lifted Christopher's limp body off the ground with his magic and carried him into the gatehouse where he let his body slump back down on the floor.

'Modifying memories isn't easy, so it might take a while. Are we sticking to the memories we discussed?'

Iris nodded. 'But could we also add in a knowledge that he is really crap in bed? I want him to really believe how inadequate and pathetic he is in the bedroom department.'

Lynx laughed.

Wolf nodded. 'I can do that.'

'And I want him thinking for the rest of his life that he smells really bad.'

Wolf shook his head with a smile. 'I'll try. You lot might as well wait outside for a bit. I'll give you a shout when I'm done.'

They headed out of the gatehouse.

'Thanks for your help, Storm,' Iris said.

He nodded. 'Any time.'

He walked off back into the village.

'Let's sit down over here,' Lynx gestured to a shaded area under a tree.

Iris sat down and Lynx settled next to her. After a while she lay down, staring up at the sun filtering through the leaves of the tree, and Lynx lay down too. She cuddled up to his chest and he kissed her forehead.

'Are you OK?'

She nodded. 'I am now. If Wolf can do what we discussed then it will all be over and we can start the rest of our lives together without having to keep looking over our shoulders the whole time.'

'So no more fighting it? You're accepting the future you've been shown?'

'Why would I fight it when you make me so damn happy?'

His face lit up in a big smile. 'So you're planning on staying?'

She stroked his face. 'Of course I am. I'm in love with you. I tried to tell you the other night when I came to your house drunk, but I also offered to climb you like a tree and have hot drunken sex with you when I could barely stand so I'm not surprised you didn't take me seriously. But I do love you. I've fallen for you so fast and so hard over the last few days and I'm excited about our future. And it's OK if you don't feel that way yet. I know we were just taking it slow and no sensible person would fall in love this quickly but—'

He smiled and kissed her, stalling the words she'd been trying to say. He pulled back and stroked her face. 'I love you too. So much. I tried to tell you the night of our date. Well, then I wanted to tell you I was falling for you but now I've definitely fallen. Head over heels in fact.'

'Wait, you didn't talk about this on our date.'

'You were asleep, obviously bored by my scintillating conversation.'

She laughed.

'I love you, Iris McKenzie, and I can't wait to take that path with you, wherever and *whenever* it may lead us.'

Wolf came out of the gatehouse a while later. 'It's done. Come and see.'

'He's awake?' Iris asked.

'Yes but don't worry, he's very compliant.'

Lynx and Iris got up and followed Wolf back into the gatehouse. As soon as Christopher saw her he threw himself to his knees in front of her.

'Iris, I'm so so sorry for all of this, I'm such a shit-bag. I can't believe what I've done to you, and to Ness of course. Stealing the locket, dragging your name into all of this and your beautiful house... I burned it to the ground and I can't say sorry enough for that.'

Iris knew that none of this was real or heartfelt but it still felt good to hear his apology.

'And I'm sorry for being so crap in bed too,' Christopher went on. 'I know I have a small penis and that I could never satisfy you, or any woman for that matter. I know sleeping with me was like sleeping with a wet fish. And I'm sorry I smell so badly too, I'll be taking lots of showers from now on.'

Iris suppressed a bubble of laughter. This was too good.

Lynx snorted behind her and Christopher glanced over at him. 'Who are you?'

'The man that can make her scream in bed.'

'Oh good, I'm glad you've found someone nice, you deserve great sex,' Christopher said.

'What are you going to do now?' Iris asked.

'I'm going to go home and film a confession which I'll put out on social media. And then I'm going straight to the police. I'll tell them everything. Hopefully they'll put me away for a very long time.'

'Let's hope so,' Iris said.

'Will you ever forgive me?' Christopher asked tearfully.

'No, I won't and you'll have to live with that for the rest of your life.'

'I understand and I don't deserve your forgiveness after everything I've done.' He looked around. 'Can I go now?'

Wolf nodded. 'You're free to leave.'

Christopher walked out of the gatehouse and started walking down the road, his shoulders slumped as if he was carrying the weight of the world on them. Iris watched him go without feeling an ounce of guilt.

'You did a great job,' she said to Wolf.

'It wasn't that hard. Most of his memories are the truth, I just layered in that he realised the locket was fake and it was all part of an insurance claim, and then I added in a whole ton of guilt on top.'

'And it won't wear off?'

'No, those memories and thoughts are as real to him as everything else that's ever happened to him. He won't remember what happened with the gun and our magic, only that he came here to apologise to you.'

'Let's hope it's enough for the police,' Lynx said.

'I do think it might help if they have a full statement from you and that you tell them you want to press charges,' Wolf said. 'But we can let things die down first with his confession and see if it's necessary.'

'I'll do whatever it takes,' Iris said.

Iris and Lynx walked back towards their road, hand in hand. She felt such relief that it was all over, or it would be once Christopher had confessed to the police – and she had no reason to think that he wouldn't.

She saw Zofia coming out of one of the houses in front of them. Her eyes lit up at seeing them together and she hurried over to talk to them.

'Iris, I'm so sorry to hear what happened to your home. I know Lynx always talks about me being omniscient, but I don't see it all. If I'd seen that happening I would have told you and we could have done something to stop it.'

'Thank you, I know you would have.'

'We can help you rebuild. There's enough magic in this village to make it happen very quickly.'

'Thanks. Wolf has already offered to help with that, using the same magic he used to create Stardust Street.'

Zofia nodded and her eyes cast down to where Iris and Lynx's hands were still linked. She was clearly bursting to ask if they were together, but trying to stick to her promise not to interfere.

'And I know that the plan was always to return to Scotland but maybe you might be happy here, at least for a while longer?' Zofia said.

'I'm going to be happy here for a very long time,' Iris said, deciding to put her out of her misery.

Zofia looked like she'd won the lottery. 'You mean... you're together?'

Lynx looped an arm around Iris's shoulders. 'We're in love.'

'I knew it! I was starting to think my gift was on the fritz when I kept seeing your future together and you two were saying you didn't even like each other.'

'We've been together since before the poker game,' Iris confessed. 'We just didn't want any interference when we were still trying to figure it all out on our own.'

'Oh, you sods. I was so confused. But fair point. You don't want someone interfering when everything is still so new. So have you thought about when you're going to get married?'

Lynx sighed. 'Zofia.'

'I'm just saying, traditionally couples got married at the summer solstice and those that did always had a happy marriage.'

'That's tomorrow,' Iris protested.

'Well it doesn't need to be a big deal. You just need a pretty dress, some flowers and some rings, and Lynx can make those.'

'We're not getting married tomorrow,' Lynx said, firmly.

'OK, OK, it was just an idea. Maybe the winter solstice then. Much prettier flowers in my opinion. Oh yes, I can see it now.'

'You can see it?' Iris said.

Zofia gave her a mischievous smile. 'Maybe.'

Iris smiled and shook her head in despair. Zofia was clearly going to be relentless.

'Anyway must dash,' Zofia said, giving them a wave. 'Think about it.' She hurried away.

'I am so sorry about her,' Lynx said.

'It's fine. Living somewhere as small as Midnight, people are bound to be interested in us, especially as we got together so quickly. And her meddling comes from a good place, she wants to see you happy.'

'I am happy, that should be enough.'

'Ah, happiness can only come from marriage and babies apparently.'

He smiled and rolled his eyes.

Iris opened the door to her home to find Ness sitting on the sofa, reading her favourite spy story.

'Oh, I'm reading that one,' Lynx said. 'Have you got to chapter fourteen yet?'

'Yes, what a shock,' Ness said.

Iris sat next to her and took a deep breath. 'Christopher came here this morning.'

'And?'

'And he was angry. Which I loved. His plan has failed spectacularly and the police have already been asking him a ton of questions. But we were able to carry out our plan perfectly. Wolf modified his memory and he's now going to the police to give them a full confession. As he's likely to be charged with insurance fraud, I think he'll be going away for a long time.'

'Good, it's what that little bawbag deserves.' Ness paused, shaking her head. 'It doesn't bring back my home though.'

'No, it doesn't. But Wolf has said he'd help us to rebuild it, exactly as it was. I know it won't be the same but we can fill every room with your memory crystals so you'll still have the memories of each room, whenever we visit.'

Ness nodded. 'I'd like that.'

'And Lynx has suggested we go back to Loch Fyne tomorrow, for the summer solstice sunrise. We can have a swim as the sun rises above the hills.'

A big smile stretched on her face. 'I'd really like that.'

'Maybe not naked though, we should probably save Lynx's blushes.'

'I can keep my clothes on for once.'

'A bit of nudity doesn't bother me,' Lynx said. 'Besides, if there's nudity involved, my eyes will be firmly on this one,' he gestured towards Iris.

She laughed. 'Pervert.'

'Oh you know it. My future wife parading around naked, I'm never going to get enough of that.'

'Your grandfather was the same,' Ness said. 'He loved seeing me naked. When we honeymooned in a little holiday cottage on Skye, I spent the whole time butt-naked. We never left the house.'

'Now that's the kind of honeymoon I could get on board with,' Lynx said.

Iris laughed and shook her head. 'What have I got myself involved with?'

Ness took her hand. 'He makes you happy, blissfully so.'

Iris looked at him and smiled. 'I know.'

CHAPTER 21

The sun was setting over Midnight and Morag was watching the summer solstice festivities that would probably go on for many more hours yet. There was dancing around the fire, music and singing, and there was the promise of fireworks later once it got dark. Morag loved fireworks.

She'd always loved the solitude of walking around the hills and fields in Scotland but this place with its happy little community was growing on her.

She saw Viktor prowling towards her and smiled. He sat down next to her looking out over the village. Pre-empting any more sarcasm, she slid the purple cupcake towards him.

'I got you this.'

He stared at it. 'You got me a cake?'

'Lavender-flavoured.'

Viktor licked his lips and bent his head to eat it then stopped. 'Is this poisoned?'

Morag laughed. 'I promise it's not.'

Viktor thought about it for a moment and shrugged. 'There are worse ways to go than death by cake.'

He almost faceplanted himself into the cake as he ate greedily and noisily. Finally he finished and licked himself clean.

'Thank you,' Viktor said.

'Well thank you for not letting me kill myself trying to get to Scotland to help Iris.'

'It would have been... unfortunate if you had died.'

'Really? Surely that would have solved your problem of me being here.'

'I'd have missed winding you up.'

Morag smiled. 'Well, it looks like we'll be staying. Look at them.' She gestured to Lynx and Iris cuddled up together under the branches of the tree. 'They look ridiculously happy.'

'Disgustingly so.'

'So I guess there'll be more sarcasm, more grumpiness, more insults between us – unless you want to call a truce.'

'Never. I'm quite looking forward to it.'

He gave her a wink and stalked off and she smiled because she was too.

Iris was blissfully happy, cuddled up against Lynx's chest as the sun started its descent across the sky. Their sun-catchers glittered beautifully above them, catching the pinks, reds and golds of the setting sun. The summer solstice celebrations had been wonderful, starting with a sunrise swim in the waters of Loch Fyne with Ness, followed by a lot of singing, dancing and eating back in the village. The bonfire on the village green was roaring away quite happily and they were looking forward to the fireworks that would start as soon as it got dark enough.

The confession had gone live on social media the evening before, where Christopher explained to the world how he stole the locket because he thought it was real and when he realised it wasn't he set up a fake insurance scam, claiming the locket was worth millions and had been stolen. He said he felt awful for what he'd done and didn't like the person he'd become. A few hours later the police released a statement that confirmed Christopher had turned himself in and had been formally charged. They said they weren't looking for anyone else in relation to the crime but would still like to speak to Iris so they could press charges for the theft as well as the fraud. She was going to go down to

London in a few days to speak to them once everything had calmed down.

She looked up at Lynx and smiled. It was the weirdest feeling, looking at someone and knowing without doubt they were your forever. It made her feel so content.

He realised she was looking at him and smiled at her, kissing her head.

'You know, I suppose in some weird way, I should be thanking Christopher,' Iris said. 'If it wasn't for him, we would never have met and I wouldn't be here now.'

'We would have met eventually, we were supposed to be together. I'm actually going to Bute in September, I have a friend's wedding to go to, and then I was going to stay in Argyll for a week or so and enjoy west Scotland as I've not been to that part of the country before. Well, I hadn't been before our date.'

'Bute is right around the corner from me. I can actually see it from my farmhouse on a good day.'

'So maybe we would have met then even if you'd never met Christopher. When two people are supposed to be together, fate always finds a way.'

Iris smiled. 'I like that.'

'And that way we don't owe Christopher anything.'

She nodded.

People started gathering around the fire, throwing little bits of paper into the flames.

'What are they doing?'

'They're writing their wishes or intentions for the year ahead. Burning them sets them free so they'll come true. Do you want to write a wish for the coming year?'

She nodded, although she had no idea what she could wish for. She had everything she needed right here.

He got up and held out a hand to help her to her feet. They wandered over to the fire where Ashley was handing out bits of paper and pens to write their wishes on.

Lynx was already writing his but Iris took a few moments to think about hers. And then she thought of something. They both folded their bits of paper up and tossed them into the fire. The flames caught them and within seconds they were gone, leaving behind two thin plumes of smoke that danced up into the air, taking their wishes with them.

'What did you wish for?' she asked Lynx.

'I'd like to be married by the next summer solstice.'

She smiled at that. 'I think that can be arranged.'

'What did you wish for?'

'The whole caboodle, our happy ever after.'

A Letter from Holly

Thank you so much for reading *Meet Me at Midnight,* I had so much fun writing this story, revisiting the wonderful Midnight Village and including all the magical ingredients. I hope you enjoyed reading it as much as I enjoyed writing it.

One of the best parts of writing comes from seeing the reaction from readers. Did it make you smile or laugh, did it make you cry, hopefully happy tears? Did you fall in love with Lynx, Iris, Viktor and Morag as much as I did? Did you like the magical village of Midnight. I would absolutely love it if you could leave a short review on Amazon. Getting feedback from readers is amazing and it also helps to persuade other readers to pick up one of my books for the first time.

Thank you for reading.

Love Holly x

Also by Holly Martin

Midnight Village Series

The Midnight Village

Meet Me at Midnight

Apple Hill Bay Series

Sunshine and Secrets at Blackberry Beach

The Cottage on Strawberry Sands

Christmas Wishes at Cranberry Cove

Wishing Wood Series

The Blossom Tree Cottage

The Wisteria Tree Cottage

The Christmas Tree Cottage

Jewel Island Series

Sunrise over Sapphire Bay

Autumn Skies over Ruby Falls

Ice Creams at Emerald Cove

Sunlight over Crystal Sands

Mistletoe at Moonstone Lake

The Happiness Series

The Little Village of Happiness

The Gift of Happiness

The Summer of Chasing Dreams

Sandcastle Bay Series

The Holiday Cottage by the Sea

The Cottage on Sunshine Beach

Coming Home to Maple Cottage

Hope Island Series

Spring at Blueberry Bay

Summer at Buttercup Beach

Christmas at Mistletoe Cove

Juniper Island Series

Christmas Under a Cranberry Sky

A Town Called Christmas

White Cliff Bay Series

Christmas at Lilac Cottage

Snowflakes on Silver Cove

Summer at Rose Island

Standalone Stories

The Secrets of Clover Castle (Previously published as Fairytale Beginnings)

The Guestbook at Willow Cottage

One Hundred Proposals

One Hundred Christmas Proposals

Tied Up With Love

A Home on Bramble Hill (Previously published as Beneath the Moon and Stars

For Young Adults

The Sentinel Series

The Sentinel (Book 1 of the Sentinel Series)

The Prophecies (Book 2 of the Sentinel Series)

The Revenge (Book 3 of the Sentinel Series)

The Reckoning (Book 4 of the Sentinel Series)

STAY IN TOUCH...

To keep up to date with the latest news on my releases, just go to the link below to sign up for a newsletter. You'll also get two FREE short stories, get sneak peeks, booky news and be able to take part in exclusive giveaways. Your email will never be shared with anyone else and you can unsubscribe at any time
https://www.subscribepage.com/hollymartinsignup

Website: https://hollymartin-author.com/
Email: holly@hollymartin-author.com
Facebook: facebook.com/hollymartinauthor
Instagram: instagram.com/hollymartin_author
Twitter/X: x.com/HollyMAuthor

Acknowledgements

To my parents, my mom, my biggest fan, who reads every word I've written a hundred times over and loves it every single time, and for my dad, for cooking celebratory steak every publication day

For my twinnie, the gorgeous Aven Ellis for just being my wonderful friend, for your endless support, for cheering me on, for reading my stories and telling me what works and what doesn't and for keeping me entertained with wonderful stories. I love you dearly.

To my lovely friends Julie, Natalie, Jac, Verity and Jodie, thanks for all the support.

To the Devon contingent, Paw and Order, Belinda, Lisa, Phil, Bodie, Kodi and Skipper. Thanks for keeping me entertained and always being there.

Thanks to my fabulous editors, Celine Kelly and Rhian McKay.

ACKNOWLEDGEMENTS

To my lovely agent and the team at Lorella Belli, thanks for all your hard work taking my books to different countries.

To all the wonderful bloggers for your tweets, retweets, facebook posts, tireless promotions, support, encouragement and endless enthusiasm. You guys are amazing and I couldn't do this journey without you.

To anyone who has read my book and taken the time to tell me you've enjoyed it or wrote a review, thank you so much.

Thank you, I love you all.

978-1-913616-56-4 paperback
978-1-913616-57-1 Large Print
978-1-913616-58-8 hardback
978-1-913616-59-5 audio

Cover design by Dee Dee Book Covers

Printed in Great Britain
by Amazon